THE
ULTIMATE THRESHOLD

A Collection of the Finest in Soviet Science Fiction

Edited and Translated by
MIRRA GINSBURG

PENGUIN BOOKS

Penguin Books Ltd, Harmondsworth,
Middlesex, England
Penguin Books, 625 Madison Avenue,
New York, New York 10022, U.S.A.
Penguin Books Australia Ltd, Ringwood,
Victoria, Australia
Penguin Books Canada Limited, 2801 John Street,
Markham, Ontario, Canada L3R 1B4
Penguin Books (N.Z.) Ltd, 182–190 Wairau Road,
Auckland 10, New Zealand

First published in the United States of America by
Holt, Rinehart and Winston 1970
First published in Canada by
Holt, Rinehart and Winston of Canada, Limited, 1970
Published in Penguin Books 1978

LIBRARY OF CONGRESS CATALOGING IN PUBLICATION DATA
Ginsburg, Mirra, comp.
The ultimate threshold.
Reprint of the 1970 ed. published by
Holt, Rinehart, and Winston, New York.
CONTENTS: Altov, H. Icarus and Daedalus.
—Anfilov, G. Erem.
—Dneprov, A. Formula of immortality. [etc.]
1. Science fiction, Russian—Translations into
English. 2. Science fiction, English—Translations from
Russian. I. Title.
[PZ1.G388U1] 1978] [PG3276] 891.7'3'0876 78-2250
ISBN 0 14 00.4873 1

Printed in the United States of America by
Offset Paperback Mfrs., Inc., Dallas, Pennsylvania
Set in Electra

"The Horn of Plenty" by Vladimir Grigoriev
previously appeared in *Galaxy*.

CONTENTS

PREFACE

The freest and liveliest published writing in Soviet Russia today is in the field of fantasy and science fiction. On its present scale, Soviet science fiction is a fairly recent phenomenon. There were individual practitioners in the first ten or fifteen years after the revolution. But like all frivolity and play—and science fiction is, essentially, a literature of play, no matter how serious its preoccupations—and, indeed, like all art that did not serve the purposes of the dictatorship, the genre all but went out of existence during the gray, grim Stalin years. It was not until the 1960s that a number of writers turned to this field. And within a single decade they created a distinct, vital, and flourishing literature, which aroused a tremendous response among the Russian readers. The demand for it is so great that editions running to 100,000 or 150,000 sell out within days of publication.

A recent questionnaire disclosed some interesting facts. Science fiction is read in Russia by people of all ages, from twelve to seventy, and up. About half of the readers are from fifteen to twenty-five. About half have primary and secondary schooling; the other half consists of people with higher education. Thus, the readers of science fiction include school children, students, workers of every variety, teachers, the military, engineers, physicians, economists, journalists, writers, and scientists in various fields. Curiously, the bulk of the readers is drawn from urban, rather than rural, areas and is predominantly male.

Science fiction and fantasy in Soviet Russia is not generally mass-produced by hacks manufacturing an endless stream of tales of horror and gadgetry merely to amaze or shock or thrill. While a good deal of it repeats old clichés in new settings, much of it is fresh, bold, and original. Many of the authors are distinguished scientists who happily combine scientific and technical knowledge with literary talent, a literary, as well as scientific, imagination, and often a marvelous sense of play. The best of the stories are both entertaining and intelligent, and are written with style and skill.

Perhaps because the authors are scientists, and thus are accustomed to greater freedom in their work, or because the science fiction form has not received as much attention from the political censorship as the rest of Soviet literature, the writers in this field can often say much more than those working in more realistic and conventional areas. Whatever the cause, the best of Soviet science fiction is far removed from the dreary mainstream of the standardized, made-to-order, didactic writing that still dominates the Soviet literary scene.

We are essentially self-oriented. What delights us in animal tales is the humanity of the nonhuman, or the human relationship between man and a nonhuman being. What charms or horrifies us in tales of ghosts and the supernatural is, again, the humanity of the inhuman or once-human, the grotesque juxtaposition of familiar motives and weird creatures or non-creatures whose actions are prompted by these motives. The imagination does not invent anything totally unknown. It combines aspects of the known and extends them beyond experience, past and present, producing new, sometimes startling, sometimes delightful patterns. This is equally true of science fiction, both in the West and in Soviet Russia.

Like all literature of fantasy, Soviet science fiction projects from the known to the unknown, from the present to the possible, and, often, the impossible. In theme and approach, it ranges far and wide—time and space, man and machines, the structure of matter, antimatter, gravity, death and immortality, the creation of artificial intelligence, artificial biological processes, the creation of life, and even of man, cybernetics, the existence of sentient life on other planets and in other galaxies, and so on. But above all, there is the concern with man in relation to the world, natural and man-made, and man in relation to himself and to others.

An interesting aspect of many of these stories is the insistence on the value of the individual—both as a person and as a scientific innovator. The latter is often something of an eccentric who works on his own and does not fit into the "establishment," and as a rule he is treated sympathetically—quite a departure in a totalitarian bureaucracy. This unorthodox attitude is especially evident in stories like "The Horn of Plenty," "When Questions Are Asked," and "One Less."

Again and again, as in "Formula of Immortality," we hear the warning: Don't meddle! Consider carefully before experimenting with man's life. Even "Erem," the touching, animistic robot who commits suicide in the service of his master, is a reminder of the value of the individual, carelessly sacrificed to the needs of "production" or "society."

The humanist element is also prominent in "The Ultimate Threshold," which poses a basic moral (and political) question, and in the lovely fantasy on a classic theme, "The Useless Planet," which brings Great Logitania, where everything is controlled by reason and logic, into confrontation with the strange, imperfect, and frustrating planet Gea, whose creatures live in disorder and filth and are moved by such outlandish and unnecessary things as love and beauty.

Another question that occupies an important place in Soviet science fiction concerns the potentialities of man and the extension of these potentialities, either through external devices or through the restructuring of the human organism. This theme is dealt with in "He Who Leaves No Trace" and "When You Return," the former a witty play on the limitations and possibilities of the man-made machine, the latter a moving reassertion of the primacy of feeling, of the purely human experience.

"Invasion" and "Preliminary Research" are, perhaps, closer to pure play than the other stories in this volume—jests on the themes of time travel and automation.

"Icarus and Daedalus," on the other hand, is an affirmation of the greatness of the questing human spirit and, again, of the value of man. At the moment of ultimate crisis, the cool and purely rational Daedalus learns that "there is something higher than formulas—Life, and something higher than Life—the proud name of Man." Quite an assertion to make in a society dominated by formula!

Unexpectedly, we also come across the element of mysticism, as in the tender story, "We Played Under Your Window," in which sentient celestial powers (the Lord's fiery ministers?) intervene beneficently in the destiny of individual man. What could be further from "socialist realism"?

The reader must not infer, however, that Soviet science fiction has entirely escaped the vigilant eye of those who hold that art and literature must serve. There has been of late a great number of articles, both in periodicals and in science-fiction collections, setting forth the desirable goals and stressing the need to show "Communist man," "Communist achievements," and the "Communist future," as contrasted with the wretched destinies of the non-Communist world. And these themes and lessons permeate a good deal of Soviet science fiction. Nevertheless, much of the writing in the field ignores the pressures and continues to create free and valid works of the imagination.

The material in the present collection was selected, first

and foremost, for its literary excellence. I chose stories written with skill and wit, interesting in their ideas, free of clichés, and, above all, free of the political dogma and "lessons" which the "larger" Soviet literature is still compelled to promulgate. Who knows, perhaps the best of the current Soviet science fiction may point the way for the rest of Soviet literature?

New York   MIRRA GINSBURG

ICARUS AND DAEDALUS

by

HENRIK ALTOV

HENRIK ALTOV was born in 1926. An engineer, inventor, and author of several theoretical works on the methodology of invention, he first entered the field of science fiction in 1957. He has published several collections of science-fiction stories, studies of the "technology" of science fiction, and interesting analyses of prophecies of Jules Verne, H. G. Wells, and A. Belyayev in the light of subsequent scientific progress.

> I warn you, Icarus,
> To fly in a middle course.
> For, if you go too low,
> The water may weight your wings;
> And if you go too high,
> The fire may burn them.
>
> Ovid—Metamorphoses

It was a long time ago. Time has erased from the memory of succeeding generations the true names of those who had flown

to the Sun, and people have come to call them by the names
of their ships—Icarus and Daedalus. Indeed, it is also said that
the ships had other names, and that the names of Icarus and
Daedalus were taken from the ancient myth. But this is probably wrong. For the first to say to men, "We shall fly through
the Sun!" was not Daedalus, but he who is now called Icarus.

It was a long time ago. People were still timid about
leaving the Earth. But they already knew the heady, intoxi-
cating beauty of the Stellar World, and a restless, irresistible
spirit of discovery led them to the stars. And if one ship perished, two others would fly into the Stellar World. They returned after many years, scorched by the heat of distant suns,
chilled by the cold of infinite space. And they left again for
the Stellar World.

He who is now called Icarus was born on a ship. He
had a long life, but he seldom saw the Earth. He flew to
Procyon and Lacaillé's star. He was the first to reach Van
Mahaen's star. In the planetary system of Leiten he fought
the oroho—the most terrible of the creatures known at that
time.

Nature had given Icarus much, and he spent her gifts as
generously as the Sun. He was recklessly brave, but his luck
never abandoned him. He aged, but he did not grow old.
And he knew no weariness, or fear, or despair.

His beloved flew with him most of his life. They say
she perished during the landing on a planet in the Eridanus
system. And he went on, discovering new worlds and giving them her name.

Among those who flew to the stars, there was no man
equal to Icarus in courage. And yet people were amazed and
startled when he said, "Let us fly through the Sun!" Even his
friends—and he had many—were silent. How was it possible to fly through the fiery Sun? Would it not reduce the madman to ashes? But Icarus said, "Look at this gaslight tube.
The temperature within it is hundreds of thousands of degrees. But I pick it up without fear of getting burned, be-

cause the gas in the tube is in a state of extreme rarefaction." They said to him, "Don't you know that the substance at the center of the Sun is not plasma but something twelve times more dense than lead?"

That was what many people said. But Icarus laughed. "This will not prevent us from flying to the Sun. We shall make the ship's casing of neutrite. Even at the center of the Sun the density will be negligibly small compared with the density of neutrite. And, like the glass of the fluorescent light tube, the neutrite will remain cool."

People did not believe him at first. And then he was helped by the man who is now called Daedalus. Daedalus was young, but people esteemed him for his knowledge. He had never flown into the Stellar World, and science alone opened to him the mysteries of matter. Cool, calm, and rational, he was the opposite of Icarus. But where people were not convinced by the fiery words of Icarus, the dry and exact formulas of Daedalus said to everyone, "The flight is possible."

In those times scientists already knew a good deal about the fifth state of matter. It was first discovered in the stars known as the white dwarfs. Small though they are, these stars possess enormous density, for they consist almost entirely, save for the gaseous envelope, of densely compressed neutrons. After the first flight to the satellite of Sirius, the white dwarf nearest the Earth, man learned to produce neutrite—a substance consisting only of neutrons. The density of neutrite is one hundred and twenty thousand times the density of steel, and one million times that of water.

The ships in which Icarus and Daedalus were to fly to the Sun were assembled on an extraterrestrial station. Here people could easily lift the neutrite sheets, and the work proceeded rapidly, although, as we have said, neutrite was the fifth, superdense state of matter.

As for the ships themselves, they are said to have been the best ever to fly into the Stellar World. Their powerful engines could withstand the fiery cyclones of the Sun, and their vast speed permitted them to hurtle through it. It is also said that it was then that Daedalus invented the gravilocator, for inside the Sun, in the chaos of electronic gas, radio is powerless. Gravity, however, remains gravity. The locator caught the gravitational waves, and the ships could see.

And then came the day of departure. From the Earth came the last warning: "Don't bring the ships too close, or gravitation will pull them together. But do not separate too much either, or the careless one will be caught up in a fiery cyclone and carried into the depths of the Sun."

Icarus laughed when he heard these words. Daedalus listened calmly. And both replied, "We are ready." Icarus impatiently put his hand on the control lever. Daedalus attentively looked over the instruments. And from the Earth came the words, "Good luck, and great discoveries!" This was the Earth's parting wish to its ships leaving for the Stellar World.

And so the flight began.

The engines furiously ejected white flame, and the ships shuddered, gathering speed. And from the Earth it seemed as if two comets were flying toward the Sun.

For the first time Icarus flew without companions, for he was not permitted to take anyone into the ship. But Icarus laughed at danger, and watching the silvery screen of the locator, he sang the song of the old captains of the Stellar World.

And Daedalus never noticed his solitude. This was the first time he had left the Earth, but the beauty of the Stellar World did not move him. And his thoughts, exact and dry like formulas, were occupied with the secrets of matter.

Sometimes Daedalus' calculations said, "Attention! Danger ahead." But Icarus, who flew first, knew it without calculations. For among those who piloted ships into the Stellar World there was no captain more experienced than Icarus.

And so they flew toward the blazing Sun, and people of the Earth followed their flight with beating hearts.

Every hour the speed of the ships increased, for the powerful attraction of the Sun spread its invisible arms toward them.

By terrestrial time, the fifth day of the flight was drawing to a close when the ships disappeared in the blinding rays of the Sun. The last, distorted, radio waves brought back to Earth a fragment of the song of the old captains and the dry report of Daedalus: "Entering the chromosphere. Coordinates . . ."

The Sun met the ships with the fiery torches of its protuberances. As though indignant at the effrontery of man, the raging star threw up giant tongues of flame, compared to which the ships were as a grain of sand against a mountain. In silent fury the flames rushed up and greedily licked the neutrite. But the density of the flame was very small, and the neutrite armor remained cold.

More terrible than the tongues of flame was the gravity. Invisible, all-permeating, enormous, it pressed Icarus and Daedalus down. They felt as though lead had filled their bodies, and every inhalation demanded desperate effort, and every exhalation seemed to be the last. But the strong hand of Icarus was firmly on the controls. And the impassive eyes of Daedalus were fixed on the bright disks of the instruments.

The gravity increased relentlessly.

The Sun wanted to crush the uninvited guests. The hearts of Icarus and Daedalus, flooded with mercury-heavy blood, beat feverishly, using up their last reserves of strength. A film seemed to cloud their eyes.

Then Icarus smiled (he could no longer laugh) and cut off the engine, letting the ship fall freely toward the center of the Sun. And the weight vanished at once.

On the locator screen—no longer silvery, but blood red—Daedalus saw the maneuver. And almost losing consciousness, he just had time enough to repeat it. But the moment gravity disappeared, consciousness returned, and Daedalus' eyes, calm as ever, were again on the instruments.

Every second increased the velocity of their fall. Through the fiery storm the ships hurtled toward the center of the Sun. Fire, fire, endless fire rushed to meet them. Fiery clouds billowed around them, fiery winds raged, and everywhere —above, below—were flames.

Three times the silvery screen before Icarus dimmed. It was a signal from Daedalus: "Time to turn back." But Icarus answered with a smile, "Forward!"

The ships continued their flight through fire. And the bright disks of the instruments were reflected in Daedalus' eyes. There was no gravity, but the instruments warned of a new danger. Pressure was rising, upsetting all calculations and hypotheses. The fiery whirlwind was growing in density and violence. The ships shook under the blows of heavy waves of flame. And the waves struck with ever greater fury. And now they turned into solid walls of fire, crashing against the thin neutrite armor.

Again the silvery screen dimmed, warning, "Time to turn back!" But Icarus answered, "Forward!"

And he was right. The dense wall of fire itself reduced their speed. A moment came when the ships hung almost motionless amid the raging fiery storms. Pressure barred forward movement, gravity prevented retreat.

Daedalus' eyes were on the instruments, for they spoke of the most secret mysteries of matter. And Icarus sang the song of the old captains and remembered those who had traveled with him along the paths of the Stellar World.

But the Sun refused to acknowledge defeat and was preparing its final and most terrible onslaught. Somewhere in its depths arose a giant cyclone. It was like a waterspout, but magnified a million times and there were no bounds to its fury. It caught up the ships and tossed and whirled them like splinters. Then it flung Daedalus' ship back.

And on the silver screen Daedalus saw the swirling pillar of fire carrying Icarus into the depths of the Sun. The engines of the ship were silent, and Icarus did not answer his calls.

Daedalus knew this was the end. Nothing could save Icarus. Dry and exact data measured the giant force of the fiery spout and told Daedalus, "You are powerless. Go!"

And now a fire flashed for the first time in Daedalus' eyes. It was only an instant, but, like an explosion, it transformed him. For at this instant he knew that there was something higher than formulas—Life, and something higher than Life—the proud name of Man.

And, with a strong pull on the control stick, he plunged his ship into the flaming cyclone.

The engines threw out spurts of flame, and the fire that was obedient to man clashed with the savage fire of the Sun. The tight coils of the spout closed around the ship, but Daedalus thrust forward, forward, catching up with Icarus.

And the fury of the spout increased, strangling the ship in its coils. The neutrite armor quivered under the strain, and the needles of the instruments swung far beyond the warning red lines. But Daedalus was oblivious of danger. His eyes were on the locator screen. And he could see that every moment brought him nearer to Icarus.

The fiery spout still raged, but the attraction of the ships had already caught them up and softly drew them toward each other. The jolt was scarcely noticeable, and Daedalus saw on the screen: The ships had joined. Now even the vicious force of the cyclone could not divide them. For a moment the silvery screen dimmed, and Daedalus knew: Icarus was alive.

The engines howled agonizingly under the double load. The frenzied spout thundered, weaving its coils around the ships. The needles of the instruments danced wildly. And the neutrite shell began to turn hot. But Daedalus directed the ships, and his heart, which for the first time had learned to know happiness, was jubilant.

Breaking the tight coils of the spout, the ships were moving outward. Their flight was ever faster. But with speed, gravity returned. And again their bodies were filled with lead, and again their hearts seemed choked with mercury-heavy blood.

The ships sped through the fiery whirlwinds.

The flames still raged, but the edge of the Sun was near. And the bright disks of the instruments called: "Into the sky, into the sky!"

The engines roared madly, throwing the ships into a final leap. But the gravity wrung the control stick from Daedalus' hands. And he had no strength left to raise them, no strength to reach out to the panel on which the instrument disks glimmered dimly.

The ships stopped in midflight, suspended over the fiery abyss. And Daedalus' heart went numb with fear. But someone's will had once again commanded the ships: "Forward!"

And then, forgetting fear, Daedalus knew: The strong hand of Icarus was on the controls.

Day came, and people on Earth saw two ships, closely joined together, moving away from the Sun. Anxiously, breaking in on one another, antennas spoke: "Are you coming to Earth with good news?" This was already then the greeting sent out to ships returning from the Stellar World.

Anxiously, the Earth waited for an answer. And the answer came. Two voices were singing the song of the old captains of the Stellar World.

EREM

by

GLEB ANFILOV

Gleb Anfilov *is a young writer. "Erem," published in 1963, is one of his first science-fiction stories.*

At the sound of the siren. Spassky snatched up the telephone receiver. With his left hand, he dialed the number of the industrial cybernetics expert, and with his right he hurriedly turned the safety switches.

"Nothing I can do here! There's a breach in the wall!" he shouted into the receiver.

"What, what?" They did not understand him at the other end.

"There's been an accident! The wall is breached, the silicon is gushing out!"

"Failure of the blocking system?"

"I tell you, there's a breach in the wall!"

"It must be repaired at once."

"I know that myself. Can I use Erem?"

"Erem?" There was a pause. "I guess it can't be helped . . ."

9

Spassky put down the receiver and pressed the button for the repair machine. A few seconds later the door opened and Erem rolled into the room. Four quartz lenses stared questioningly at Spassky.

"There's a bad leakage of the molten silicon in the southern sector," said Spassky. "I don't know the exact place: the television cable burnt out. Will you remember?"

"Yes," creaked Erem. "What is the temperature inside?"

"A thousand degrees. And it's rising rapidly."

"How much liquid in the crystallizer?" asked Erem.

"A million tons. . . . The heatproofing material is on the left as you enter. Go on, Erem," Spassky said warmly. "Hurry up!"

Erem turned and disappeared. Spassky threw himself back in his chair, sighed, and stretched his hand for a cigarette.

While Spassky was taking the first puff, Erem rolled headlong to the southern sector of the crystallizer, unlocked the door, and burst into the vestibule. Even here it was hot —about five hundred degrees. Erem checked the rhythms of his logical center. This took a second. To make sure the memory crystals did not crack, he waited another second, then threw open the inner door and found himself in the interior, facing the red-hot ceramic wall. Directly over him, some eight meters from the top, a wide, uneven gap gleamed like white flame. Streams of molten silicon ran down from the gap, bubbling and shooting sparks.

"The breach is found," said Erem over the radiotelephone.

"Large?" asked Spassky.

"About three meters long."

"Make it fast," said Spassky.

Drippings of the thickening liquid formed a ribbed pattern running down the wall. It would be difficult to reach the gap. Erem thought for a few milliseconds. Then he threw out a horizontal manipulator and seized a large wad of fire-proof cotton from the pile near the door. Now he had to climb up. "It's very high," he thought. He thrust out his bottom hoist and two side-pieces. The temperature was twelve hundred degrees. The oil in his chamber became liquid like water. Erem knew that it could stand another hundred degrees, and connected the hoist.

A shiny, jointed leg thrust itself out of the white asbestos jacket. The oil was drying, coagulating into a wrinkled crust.

"What are you doing?" Erem heard Spassky's impatient voice.

"Climbing to the breach."

"Faster!" cried Spassky.

Erem knew himself that he must hurry, but there was nothing he could do. The speed of ascent was three meters per minute.

Bracing himself against the wall with his side-pieces, Erem climbed up and up. The stream of molten silicon became wider. The gap spread. Beneath it, a round bulge had formed, and the molten fluid fell from it in large, heavy splashes. One of them struck Erem's side-piece. It bent and slipped off the wall. Erem swayed on the long leg of the hoist. His massive body nearly lost its balance. But he instantly thrust out a reserve piece, pressed it into the overflow, and stopped his fall.

"How is it going?" asked Spassky. "Why are you silent?"

"I am climbing to the breach," answered Erem.

He could not extend the leg of the hoist any farther. The oil was boiling. Erem opened the valves and poured it out. Then he disconnected the inner attachment of the hoist. The leg separated itself and toppled slowly. It was easier now. Some two meters remained between him and the gap, and Erem managed to scale them with the aid of the side-pieces which held him between the walls.

The temperature was already over fifteen hundred degrees.

Despite his internal cooling mechanism and the thick layer of heatproof jackets, his logical scheme began to deviate from normal. There was confusion of visual images. Against the dark crimson background of the wall with its streaming liquid there suddenly appeared Spassky's face with silently moving lips. This interfered with concentration. By an effort of will, Erem banished the image from the wall and turned on the spare sections of his electronic brain.

It was getting still hotter. It would not take long before his logical scheme disintegrated. To delay disintegration, Erem switched on the pain center. And then he felt the incinerating heat directly, with his own indicators. His side-pieces were aching, his asbestos casing was fiery hot, the lenses of his eyes were burning, but his mind began to work clearly and fast. Erem realized that no more than a minute remained before total failure of function unless . . . unless the temperature was reduced. He needed cold, he needed it badly. Just a little of it. And it was so easy to achieve: merely switch on the fans. But cooling was bad for the molten silicon; it was strictly forbidden. Nevertheless, Erem asked uncertainly:

"Is it possible to turn on the cooling for twenty seconds?"

"No," Spassky answered at once. "Under no circumstances! The silicon will be ruined. What are you doing?"

"Starting the repair."

Erem had been almost certain that Spassky would not permit the cooling. And he accepted the refusal as a matter of course. But to him it meant a death sentence. This repair job would destroy him. Evidently, the crystallization of a million tons of silicon was more important than the life of a repair machine. Erem accepted the order and went to work.

He moderated the pain of the burns with his psychocorrector. He brought out his second horizontal manipulator and seized a strip of the heat-resistant cotton with it. He stretched it and aimed it at the uneven, fire-breathing gap, framed in gleaming lips. With a precise movement, he thrust the strip into the fiery ooze. Both manipulators bent, cracked, and fell away.

Erem brought out a second pair of manipulators, separated a second strip of cotton, drove it in. Again the tungsten arms broke with a dry, crackling sound and dropped off. Confusion returned to the logical scheme. The memory of his first day came to Erem with sharp clarity. Desperately manipulating his psychocorrector, Erem vainly tried to eliminate from consciousness the uninvited picture of the assembly shop where he was born, the smiling human faces, the glints of sunlight on machines. . . . Light! It was his first light! . . . The noise of the plant, human speech, someone's merry voice: "I congratulate you with existence, new intelligence!" The gap . . . He must coordinate the movements of his last pair of manipulators. The casing of an essential block of mechanisms was slipping off. Aim it right! Push it in! The third strip of fireproof cotton closed the gap. He leaned back sharply . . .

Someone chattering on the telephone . . . Spassky. Erem no longer understood what he was saying, but he forced out the answer:

"Repair accomplished. That is all . . ."

Then came delirium. The school for training repair machines. The teacher Kallistov, shouting during the efficiency test: "Up! Touch the ceiling, touch the left wall! . . ." His first job, repair of a bridge piling on the Black Sea . . . Stones dropping easily and slowly through the water. And fish . . . A lesson in fearlessness . . . A lesson in mechanics . . . "It's called the Coriolis force . . ." People, machines, fragments of thoughts flashed before him. . . . "It was a difficult job, it was the last job, but an important one . . ."

Erem did not notice when the entire lower block of his

mechanisms dropped off. No more pain. The pulley of the central motor whirled senselessly, irregularly. Stopped. Like a broken phonograph record, two empty signal words, over and over again: "Scheme disintegrated, scheme disintegrated, scheme disintegrated . . ."

Spassky took a last puff and stubbed out the cigarette butt. He picked up the telephone and dialed the number of the industrial cybernetics expert.

"Everything in order," he said. "The crystallizer is O.K."

"What about Erem?" asked the expert.

"The signal is 'Scheme disintegrated.' "

"A pity," said the expert. "A pity . . . I don't know if we can restore him. When the crystallization is finished, call me. I'll come and take a look."

"I will," said Spassky, and put down the receiver.

FORMULA OF IMMORTALITY

by

ANATOLY DNEPROV.

ANATOLY DNEPROV *is the penname of A. P. Mitskevich, a distinguished mathematical physicist, who was born in 1919. Employed at a research institute of the Soviet Academy of Sciences and the author of numerous scientific works, he began to publish science fiction in 1958. He is especially concerned with the perspectives of scientific development, chiefly in cybernetics, physics, and biology.*

1

It all began on the day when Albert returned from his European trip. He drove up to his father's villa and was paying the taxi driver when a huge varicolored ball flew out from behind the fence and bounced down the asphalt road.

"Please get my ball," he heard a female voice say.

He turned and saw a girl's blonde head. She looked out from behind the fence, a pearl necklace gleaming like silver around her slender neck.

"Hello! Who are you?" asked Albert, holding out the ball to her.

"And you? Why do you ask?"

"Because this is my house, and you are playing in my garden."

The girl glanced at him in wonder, jumped down, and ran away into the garden without answering.

He found his father in the study. It seemed to Albert that he was not too glad of his arrival. Or, perhaps, he was simply tired. After several questions about life abroad and the work of some of the largest European laboratories, he suddenly said:

"You know, Albert, I am tired of everything. I've decided to leave the institute and to continue only as a consultant."

Albert was astonished. He had been gone only a month, and his father had never mentioned retirement before.

"You are not so old, Father," he objected.

"It's not the age, Alb. I've spent forty years in the laboratory, and that tells. And, you know, those were stormy and difficult years, when science went from revolution to revolution. They had to be absorbed, assimilated, checked by experimentation. . ."

His father's words seemed unconvincing, but Albert did not press him. Perhaps he was right. As far back as he remembered, his father had always worked hard, without regard for time, without sparing himself. People said that a kind of frenzy seemed to have taken possession of him after his wife's death. He stayed at his laboratory for days on end and literally brought both himself and his colleagues to the point of exhaustion. At that time, when Alb was still a child, his father's group was working on the structural analysis of nucleic acids and the deciphering of the genetic code. He had developed an interesting methodology of controlling the sequence of nucleotides in the desoxyribonucleic acid chain through the action of mutagenic substances on the primary material. This discovery had been widely discussed. Newspapers published articles with sensational headlines: "Key Found to the Genetic Code," "The Riddle of Life—in Four Symbols," and so on.

"I hope that Professor Birkhoff will appoint you to my post after a trial period."

"Oh, Father, that's too much. I haven't accomplished even a thousandth of what you have."

"You know everything I've done. The important thing is not to repeat it. I am sure you will be able to avoid that."

Glancing out of the window, Albert asked, "Who is that charming girl?"

"Oh, I forgot to tell you. She is the daughter of an old friend of mine, Elvin Shauli. She is an orphan now," the Professor said quietly. "But she must not know it."

"What happened?"

"Elvin Shauli and his wife died in an air crash over the Atlantic. I was so shocked by the news that . . . that I invited the girl to come and live with us. I told her that her parents had gone for several years on an expedition in Australia."

"But she'll find out sooner or later!"

"Of course. But the longer she is unaware of it, the better. The girl is called Midgeia. She is sixteen."

"A strange name."

"Yes, it is somewhat strange," the Professor said pensively. "Ah, but here she is."

Midgeia ran into the room and stopped for a moment at the door. Then, with a shy smile and a graceful curtsy, she said, "Good evening, Professor. Good evening, Mr. Albert."

"Good evening, my dear," said the Professor. He walked up to her and kissed her on the forehead. "I hope you and Albert will be friends."

"We're friends already. And where's your ball, Midgeia?"

"Oh, I don't play ball very often. I prefer to read. But this is such a lovely day."

"You should be out in the open more," Albert said in the tone of an elder. "Will you accept my company? I am also fond of playing ball."

The girl flushed with embarrassment.

"Of course, Mr. Albert."

"Well, then, if it is 'of course,' let's drop the Mr. Simply call me Alb, and I'll call you Midgeia. Agreed?"

She nodded, took the Professor by the arm, and they went down to the dining room.

At dinner they hardly spoke. Alb observed that his father looked long and with deep anxiety at Midgeia. He was probably worried over the girl's future.

2

When Albert returned to the laboratory, Professor Birkhoff suggested that he turn his attention to analysis of the structures of X and Y chromosomes, which determine female or male sex. The problem was quite complex, but some things were already known about it. As before, the principal tools of research were artificial mutations, brought about in the genetic material with the aid of chemical mutagenic substances of the acridine class. The mutants were then controlled in an artificial "biological cradle," where, after ten to twenty divisions of a cell, it was already possible to determine the sex of the future organism.

He would have to produce vast numbers of mutations. When he began the work, Albert tried to estimate the time he would have to spend in the search for an answer, and was appalled. Even at the very best, a whole lifetime would not suffice!

"Talk it over with your father," said Birkhoff. "He may have some suggestions."

In the evening Albert entered his father's study. Midgeia was there too. The Professor sat in a rocking chair with closed eyes, and Midgeia read Byron's poems to him in a low voice:

> "Oh, that the Desert were my dwelling
>   place,
> With one fair Spirit for my minister . . ."

"What a lovely idyll! With whom would you like to escape into the desert, and why?" Albert asked gaily.

His father raised his sad, reflective eyes to him.

"Ah, it's you, Alb! Midgeia reads very well. When I listen to her, I recall my youth."

"I envy you, you probably have much to remember. But you've told me so little about your youth."

The girl closed the book and quietly left the room. Albert sat down near his father and said, "It's too bad you left the institute. Alone I'm like a blind kitten. I'm afraid I'll have to trouble you for help. For instance . . ."

And he told his father about the problems he had encountered during the very first days on his new assignment. As he spoke, his father's face assumed an increasingly harsh, even hostile expression. Finally, he rose abruptly and said, "Enough. I know, it is a completely hopeless task, and there is simply no sense in spending time and energy on it."

"But all the other human chromosomes have been deciphered," argued Albert.

"That's something else. They are built along a single pattern. It's enough to get the formula of the initiator, and everything else falls in line. In the X and Y chromosomes there is no such formula. Here the uniform sequence of the nucleotides . . ."

He was suddenly silent, and the room was still. The window was wide open onto the park, from which came the slight rustle of chestnut leaves, the scarcely audible buzzing of nocturnal insects, and . . . a song. The song was very simple, melodious, and familiar. For some reason it reminded Albert of a scene from his childhood: a flower bed, thickly overgrown with tall azaleas, and himself, a tiny, tiny boy, and someone singing that song on the other side of the flowers. He runs around them, intent on seeing the singer, and she walks away from him, interrupting her song from time to time to say in a warm, tender voice:

"Come, catch me, Alb!"

And he runs and runs, and bright flowers flash past his eyes, and he cannot catch up with the beautiful, elusive, loved voice. Then he throws himself on the flower bed, crawls through the jungle of flowers, and cries . . .

"Who is that singing?" he asked his father, scarcely moving his lips.

"That? Don't you guess?" He sank heavily into his rocking chair.

"No."

"It's Midgeia."

For a few moments they said nothing. Why was his father breathing so painfully? His pale hands nervously clenched the edge of the table. Noticing his son's attentive look, he suddenly said with feigned indifference, "The girl has a charming voice, hasn't she? As for the X and Y chromosomes of man, tell Professor Birkhoff that, in my opinion, it is a hopeless task. I see no sense in working on it."

"No sense in working on it?" Alb repeated like an echo. "Strange. You spent your whole life studying every detail of the molecular structure of the genetical substance. And now . . ."

His father interrupted him with a sharp movement of his hand.

"There are researches which are utterly unjustified . . . from the ethical and moral point of view. And, generally, Albert, I am very tired. I want to go to sleep."

As he was leaving the study, Albert saw his father take a small bottle of medicine from the pocket of his robe and bring it to his lips. He was probably very ill but did not want to show it. It was also clear to Albert that, for some incomprehensible reason, his father simply did not want him to study the chemical nature of the X and Y chromosomes.

Alb went out into the park and slowly walked along the paths, already dark, and wet with the evening dew, toward the place from which he heard Midgeia's song. She sat on a stone bench before a small fountain.

"Oh!" she cried when Alb suddenly appeared before her. "God, how you frightened me! How could you, Mr. Albert. I hate things to happen unexpectedly."

He sat down near her, and for a long time they were silent. There was a murmuring of flowing water. Now and then a car rushed down the street outside the fence.

"Do you like living with us, Midgeia?" asked Albert.

"Oh, yes. You know, I feel so much at home. In fact, this is better than home."

"Where is your home?"

"In Cable. About a hundred kilometers north of here. But I don't like Cable. When Father and Mother went to Australia, I felt so lonely. I'm very grateful to your father for bringing me here."

"Cable, Cable . . ." Alb vaguely remembered the name of the village. Perhaps it had been mentioned in his home.

"Do you love your mother and father very much?" he asked, unaccountably to himself.

For a while she did not answer. She seemed to be troubled by the question.

"Is it possible not to love one's parents?" There was a note of bitterness in Midgeia's voice. Suddenly she laughed. "How strange. I've never wondered whether I love them. But now I realize. I stopped really loving them after Mr. Horsh began to come to our house all the time."

"Who is Horsh?"

"A most unpleasant man. He looks like a doctor. He probably is a doctor, because every time he came he examined me, and several times he took my blood for analysis, although I was quite well. I was very hurt that Mother and Father allowed him to do it. As though what he did was none of their concern. They used to leave me with him and go away. He is a terribly unpleasant doctor, especially when he smiles."

Albert suddenly felt sorry for the girl. He gently put his arm around her shoulders. She pressed herself to him trustingly and murmured like a child, "It's very chilly, Alb, isn't it?"

"Yes, dear."

Midgeia threw her slender arms around his neck, hid her face against his chest, and was still, breathing deeply and evenly. It seemed that, nestled against him, she had found extraordinary peace, complete release from all earthly trials and suffering. She sighed deeply, stretched, and her arms wound themselves more tightly around his neck. Albert rose and carried her, sleeping, across the park toward the dark house, feeling her warm breath on his cheek.

3

Albert did not tell Professor Birkhoff about his talk with his father. The difficulties presented by the study of the X and Y chromosomes, he felt, provided an opportunity for discoveries which would prove that he was not a bad research biophysicist himself.

He reorganized and reequipped his father's laboratory. He had a proton gun constructed that would enable him to bombard any nucleotide in the molecules of DNA and RNA with protons. He gave particular attention to setting up the "biological cradle," a miniature quartz cuvette in which proteins were synthesized in synthetic cytoplasm and artificial ribosomes.

When the equipment was ready, work in the lab went into full swing. As the research base broadened, Professor Birkhoff gradually assigned to Albert all the scientists who had formerly worked with his father.

They were charming and energetic men. Some of them, especially the physicist Klemper and the mathematician Gust, were part philosophers, part cynics, who worked on the theory of the continuous transition of matter from inanimate to animate. They regarded living organisms as giant molecules, all of whose functions could be described in terms of transitions of energy between different states. Klemper called their work "the search for a needle in a haystack." Their very first experiments convinced them that the sex of future individuals is coded not on the nucleotide level but somewhere deeper, perhaps in the sequences of atoms in the sugar and phosphate chains. Several times they succeeded by mutation in transforming an X chromosome into a Y chromosome, that is, in altering the sex, but no one knew why or how it happened.

The work soon settled into the usual channels: experiments were made, data collected, and nothing interesting seemed to happen. Albert felt that new ideas were needed, but neither he nor his colleagues had any. He did not turn to his father anymore. It was quite obvious that the old man was offering a strange sort of passive resistance to the research in progress. He not only ignored his son's activities, but whenever Albert wished to ask him anything, he seemed to sense his intention and either turned the conversation to another subject or dismissed him.

It was indeed a passive resistance, especially since his father willingly received individuals or entire delegations from antiwar organizations.

Alb had never suspected that his father was so interested in political questions. He had always been a typical university professor, who stood aside from all ideological struggles. And now, despite his fatigue and illness, his father would become totally transformed when people came and spoke about political affairs, which scientists usually ignored.

"You are a scientist, not a politician," Albert said to him bitterly one day, applying a compress to his chest.

"I am a man first. It has long been time to tear off the mask of supposed neutrality behind which our scientists try to hide. They look at you naïvely when it suddenly turns out that the results of their studies are being used for the destruction of millions of human beings. They pretend to be fools who cannot foresee a simple thing—the consequences of their studies and discoveries. They shift all the blame to politicians. If I give a weapon to a madman, then I am answerable for the consequences, not the madman. . ."

After this tirade, Albert decided that his father saw some unexplained danger to mankind in research on decoding the X and Y chromosomes in man.

One dull autumn day Albert came home earlier than usual. The air was damp and chilly. A fine drizzle was falling.

As he approached the door, he suddenly saw it swing wide open. Midgeia, wearing only her dress, burst out of it and ran headlong into the park.

"Midgeia, Midgeia!" he called.

But the girl did not hear. Albert caught up with her at the very end of the garden, where she huddled like a hunted little animal.

"Midgeia, darling, what's wrong?" he asked, panting.

"Oh, it's you, Alb! I'm so glad you've come!"

"What happened?" Albert threw his raincoat over her trembling shoulders.

"He wants to take me away."

"Who?"

"Mr. Horsh. He's there now, talking to your father."

"But why?"

"I don't know . . . He says, for medical study."

"Come home. I won't let anyone take you away."

She followed him obediently.

"Sit down here," said Alb, bringing Midgeia into his study on the first floor. "I'll go upstairs and clear everything up."

From behind the slightly open door of his father's study, he could hear the Professor's voice and another one, sharp and grating. Albert stopped for a moment.

"But you must realize, my friend, this is insane!" the Professor argued. "I've told you many times that making a great scientific discovery is a heroic feat, but not making it is ten times more heroic!"

"I can't do anything else," the stranger's creaky voice answered. "I don't see how you can throw the results of a lifetime's work into the wastebasket. We imagined everything quite differently!"

"We were stupid and naïve. That's not the way . . ."

"No, it is the only right way! You're simply a coward! A naïve pacifist! If not Solveig . . ."

Albert threw the door open and entered. His father, deathly pale, sat in his rocking chair, and next to him stood a tall gaunt man, sallow-faced, with high cheekbones and a shock of thick brown hair. He had evidently been gesticulating wildly as he spoke, and at Albert's appearance he froze in an absurd pose.

"Alb, how many times have I told you to knock before . . ." his father began.

At that moment Horsh made a wide leap and seized Albert's arm.

There was suddenly a mirror on his forehead, a phonendoscope and a magnifying glass in his hand, and he turned into a man possessed.

"And now just a drop of blood, only a drop," he muttered, pulling out of his pocket an instrument for piercing the skin on the finger.

Alb recovered from astonishment and forcefully pushed the ranting doctor away. The doctor was taller, but his muscular system was nothing to envy. He flew across the entire study, and if it were not for the desk, he would have gone on beyond it. Bending over, he grasped the edge of the desk and looked at Albert with a revolting smile and . . . with curiosity. Yes, precisely, with the strange curiosity of a maniac.

"So that's what you're like, Alb," he whispered at last, straightening to his full height.

"What is going on here? Who is this gentleman?" asked Albert, approaching his father. The older man was utterly pale, his eyes closed.

"Oh, Alb . . . This is Mr. Horsh, my old pupil and friend. Don't be offended at him."

"Your friend has rotten manners, Father."

Horsh wearily sank into a chair and laughed. He did not take his fiendishly curious eyes from Albert for a moment. It seemed that everything that was happening in the room was of intense interest to him.

"Oh, how much I would give for a single drop of our Alb's blood," he said finally, playing with the automatic needle in his hand.

"Be quiet, Horsh . . . You'll kill me," moaned Alb's father.

The words "our Alb" threw Albert into a blind rage. He ran up to the chair where Horsh was sitting, seized him by the lapels of his coat, raised him to his feet, and dragged him out of the study. At the door, Horsh suddenly straightened up and shouted in his hoarse, revolting voice:

"But the girl is mine! Give me back the girl!"

Then he disappeared.

Recovering his breath, Albert went back to his father's

room. The Professor reclined in an uncomfortable position, with closed eyes.

Albert caught his hands. They were completely cold.

4

A month after his father's death, Albert delivered a report at a session of the learned council on the results of his work. They were not too promising.

"What are your plans?" Dr. Birkhoff asked after he had finished.

Albert shrugged his shoulders. He could offer nothing new beyond the methodology he had inherited from his father. The council obviously concluded that he showed no unusual talents in research, for Dr. Seatt, a dry, bent little old man, lisped, "The group needs a good consultant."

"Whom would you suggest, Doctor?"

"One of Professor Alfrey's old students . . . I remember, there was a talented young man . . . What was his name? . . . Something like Hirsh, Hursh . . ."

"Horsh!" cried Albert.

"Yes, yes! Exactly! He was a very gifted man. If we could find him . . ."

Albert became taut as a spring. And Dr. Seatt continued:

"I remember, when the deciphering of the genetic code was just beginning, he made several brilliant discoveries. As, for example, this . . . The reciprocal action between the RNA concentration in the cell nucleus and the concentration of amino acids in the cytoplasm . . . And . . . A very talented scientist. But no one knows where he is now."

Without waiting for the end of the meeting, Albert hurried home. He decided to visit Horsh and find out what connection the man had with him and Midgeia, what his differences were with his father, and, generally, what sort of man he was. He was even prepared, if need be, to apologize to that repulsive character for his outburst.

Albert entered the dining room.

"Where is Midgeia?" he asked the housekeeper.

"She must be in the park. She went there in the morning."

He walked along the paths, hoping to find the girl in some quiet corner with a book in her hands. But Midgeia was nowhere. He called her by name several times. Suddenly he saw something white on the bench near a break in the stone fence. Coming nearer, he discovered that it was a little volume of Byron's poems. Then his glance fell on the shrubs near the gap in the fence. They were bent and broken, as if something heavy had been dragged over them. He ran to the opening, and there he found the blue ribbon with which Midgeia tied her hair.

His first thought was of reporting to the police. But he remembered Horsh, and a terrible suspicion stirred in his mind.

It took less than a minute to bring the car out of the garage, and he sped toward Cable. Why Cable? Well, Midgeia had lived there before, and Horsh visited her there. . .

The hour and a half flew by unnoticed. Alb thought of his first meeting with Midgeia, then their talk about Horsh, and the meeting with him. Odd that his father had never told him anything about his most talented student and collaborator.

It was only now that Albert realized how much his father had kept from him. In fact, he stubbornly concealed from his son something central in his life and his scientific work. And this central thing had some mysterious connection with Horsh and the vanished Midgeia. What did Horsh want with Midgeia? What "only right way" was he urging that day when his father died?

Albert drove into the small town or village which, as

the road sign indicated, was called Cable. The streets were totally deserted, as if everyone had died, and for a long time Albert could not find anyone to direct him to the house of Midgeia's parents.

He finally drove up to the gate of a small Catholic church built of red brick and entered the tiny courtyard. It was already growing dark, and a quivering orange light came from the windows. Albert was met by an elderly, heavyset priest, who had evidently been occupied in housecleaning, for the skirts of his soutane were tucked into his belt.

"What can I do for you, young man?"

"I would like to know where the Shauli house can be found. They have a daughter, called Midgeia."

"Midgeia?" the priest repeated with a note of astonishment.

"Yes."

After a moment's pause, he said, "Won't you come in?"

They passed through the dark gallery, walked around the altar, and came to a tiny room, lit by a kerosene lamp.

"So you are interested in the girl called Midgeia?" asked the priest.

"Yes, and in her parents."

"Hm, that's strange. And would you mind telling me who you are?"

"A distant relative."

"Altogether strange."

"Why?"

"Well, the point is that the girl has no parents. I mean, naturally, she has parents, but they are unknown. She is a foundling."

"What?" cried Albert. "But she told me herself that she has a mother and a father, and that they had recently gone to Australia, and . . ."

"Alas," said the priest, "this is not so. The girl, of course, thinks that Madame Shauli and Monsieur Shauli are her

mother and father. In reality, she was brought here as a
newborn infant by two young gentlemen and left with the
Shaulis, who brought her up. If I am not mistaken, this was
about sixteen years ago. I remember the day very well, for
the entire village was talking about the new baby in the
Shauli home. I hastened there to baptize the infant, but . . ."

"But what?"

"A gentleman who was there said that the girl did not
need to be baptized. I was quite shocked. I asked him, 'Why?'
And he answered . . . Yes, I remember it. He said, 'Baptism
is for those who come from God. And she comes from man.'
I still don't know what he meant."

"We all come from man," Albert said hoarsely.

"Exactly. And man comes from God. But the girl was
never baptized."

"How long did Midgeia live with the Shaulis?"

"Six months ago an important-looking gentleman came
for her and took her away . . ."

"And she was never seen here again?"

"No."

"Does the Shauli family live here?"

"No, they left for Australia—people say, with the
money they received for bringing up the girl."

"A dead end," thought Albert. There was only one more
question.

"Tell me, do you know a Mr. Horsh?"

"May he be damned!"

"So you know him?"

"Of course! It was he who didn't permit me to baptize
the child."

"Tell me, where does he live?"

"Not far from here, in Sandic. He has a house in the
woods."

A few moments later Albert's car rattled along a pitted
road in Sandic. It was beginning to drizzle and getting very
dark.

5

Horsh's house was a huge, gloomy two-story brick building in antique style. It was surrounded by a half-ruined metal fence.

The car stopped among the trees, not far from the gates. Albert entered the courtyard, walked down the stone-paved path, and approached the door of the house. Dead silence reigned all around. Not a single window was lit.

He pressed the bell button. No one answered. He pressed again and again and then kept his finger on the button.

Obviously, no one was in. The door was locked, and Albert walked slowly around the house, looking up at the high windows. Over the back door, the roof projected, forming a small terrace, and an oval window could be seen above it. Albert returned to the car, took out a flashlight and a screwdriver, and then climbed easily up to the roof of the terrace. The window was closed. He pried it up with the screwdriver, breaking the latch, and entered.

He found himself in the library. The room smelled of book bindings, old paper, and formalin. Then he noticed that the smell of formalin permeated the entire building.

Frankly speaking, he was not too clear about the reasons why he had broken into Horsh's house. No one was home, and Albert was open to all sorts of accusations. He had prepared a number of explanations, one lamer than the other, in the event of Horsh's appearance.

The library was enormous. Book-filled shelves rose to the ceiling. Piles of books lay in disorder here and there. Evidently, there was not enough room for them on the shelves. He turned his flashlight at random at one of the shelves and found a set of several years' issues of *Biophysics*. On another shelf were books on the mathematical theory of information, beneath them—volumes on cybernetics.

On the floor were scattered old textbooks, monographs, collections of articles on physics, chemistry, the theory of numbers, topology. It seemed that the owner of the library was interested in literally every subject under the sun.

From the library, a door led to a short corridor. Albert went down a creaky staircase to a tiny foyer on the first floor. The foyer was furnished with a narrow leather sofa and a mirror in the corner. There were three doors, two on the right, and one on the left. One of the doors on the right led to the kitchen, which was directly opposite the dining room. The second door on the right was locked. Albert stepped back a few paces, took a running start, and struck the door with his shoulder. It swung open with a sharp creak, and he flew into a large room. The flashlight ran over the objects filling it, and he realized that he was in a laboratory. But what a laboratory! Its equipment—supercentrifuges, electronic microscope, measuring devices—was better than anything at the institute. He wandered around the room, dreaming of the fascinating projects that could be carried on in such a laboratory. On the table near the window he found a miniature proton gun, similar to the one he had ordered for his genetic work. But compared to this one, his apparatus seemed like the skeleton of some antediluvian animal.

And then he came to a large desk, with two sets of drawers and a transparent plastic cover. Under the plastic sheet were papers covered with notes, formulas, and tables. In the corner Albert saw a small photograph. He turned the light on it, and cried out with astonishment.

It was a photograph of his mother. With trembling hands he took it out from under the plastic and began to study it.

No, it was not a mistake. . . A beautiful young woman with somewhat slanting eyes and thick fair hair looked out at him with a kind, slightly mocking smile. He

for it was also made of stainless steel, but when he raised the lid he found that it was a simple box for storing papers. Albert mechanically glanced inside, at the thick book in green binding, and was on the point of closing the box, when his eye suddenly caught the small white label in its upper right hand corner, which read, in large black letters: "SOLVEIG, variation 5."

Solveig? What was that? Why Solveig?

With trembling hands he took the book from the box. He opened the first page and stared at the writing. Then he began to turn page after page and found the same thing everywhere—rows of figures. The figures were written out in sets of two lines. The upper line repeated only two—o and 1—in various combinations; in the lower line, four figures—2, 3, 4, and 5—flashed in endless fantastic relationships:

$$1 \quad 0 \quad 1 \quad 00 \quad 111 \quad 01 \quad 0001 \quad 0 \quad 11 \quad 10$$
$$4 \quad 4 \quad 2 \quad 34 \quad 224 \quad 52 \quad 5433 \quad 4 \quad 22 \quad 43$$

A code, a genetic code! 1 and 0 are the sugar and phosphate chain. 2, 3, 4, and 5 . . . Nitrous bases! Guanine, adenine, cytosine, and thymine.

Fifty pages of the book were filled with figures. In one place he discovered a small group of figures circled in red ink. Over them was the word *Lethality?*

The question mark was repeated several times and underscored with a thick line. *Lethality*—death . . . What could those figures mean? Whose code was recorded in the book?

Finding no answer in the mysterious rows of figures, Albert put aside the book and opened the box again. In addition to papers covered with similar rows of figures, he found a small plastic box which he struggled to open for a long time. He was seized with a strange excitement, a feeling that he was on the threshold of discovering a terrible secret.

The box was filled with photographs.

The first was a microphotograph of a single cell. Then the cell divided into two. Then more. Then came differentiation. The cells formed a small lump. The lump grew. Now there was a large foetus. . . . He did not stop to examine any one photograph in detail. His hands trembled, and he feverishly ran through the pictures, sometimes skipping one or two, until he finally saw a photograph of a child, at first tiny, then bigger . . . and now the child was smiling, then staring wide-eyed, and here it was quite grown.

Albert stopped suddenly, feeling that he was no longer capable of looking at the pictures in sequence. He clenched his teeth, his hand went down to the very bottom of the box, and took out the last photograph. It showed a coffin. The coffin was piled with flowers, and the face was that of a dead woman. . . . Albert seized the photograph preceding that and screamed in a voice he did not recognize as his own. No, it was incredible, it was monstrous!

He had a photograph of his mother in his hands.

He had no recollection of how he left Horsh's house, how he left Cable, how he raced home. He forgot everything—himself, Horsh, Midgeia. He saw only one face—kind, smiling, infinitely tender.

He came home and threw himself on the bed. Everything was scrambled in his head. Faces, figures, flasks, photographs whirled before him. At times he lost consciousness, and when he came to, he found himself in bed, with people bending over him—now his housekeeper, now Professor Birkhoff, now his colleagues, now doctors in white coats.

He vaguely remembered breaking away from someone in a frenzy, running somewhere—upstairs, it seemed to him, to his father's study, and there tearing papers, then photographs, into tiny pieces, until he was forcibly taken away and put to bed.

This fit of insanity lasted several days. After that he fell into a state of total apathy, total indifference, and lay for hours staring at the ceiling. Everything became gray, colorless. Albert felt totally devastated and crushed.

7

Soon after these events he had a visit from his colleagues, Victor Klemper and Antoine Gust. They entered the bedroom noisily, with the feigned gaiety and artificial optimism with which people usually come to a seriously ill person.

"You gave us quite a fright, Alb!" cried Klemper, shaking his hand. "We thought you'd never recover and we'd have to give you to Professor Cusano for experiments."

Professor Cusano was the director of the laboratory investigating the biochemistry of higher nervous activity. Of late, he had been studying the physiochemical processes in the brain of persons suffering from psychic disturbances.

"When he observed you, he said that a whole mescaline factory must have broken out of control somewhere in the depths of your organism. You had a real schizophrenic intoxication of the violent variety."

"Listen, my friends," Albert began, "has it ever occurred to you that it's a vile trick to turn a man inside out, as you're doing, together with Dr. Cusano, or any other biochemist or biophysicist?"

They exchanged puzzled glances. Without waiting for their answer, Albert went on:

"While a man is young, healthy, and full of energy, he sometimes allows himself the luxury of flirting with death, of joking about its inevitability. But it's only in exceptional cases that a man's actual encounter with the last stage of his earthly existence presents an esthetically pleasing spectacle."

"Alb, you are not entirely well as yet . . ." began Antoine.

"No, my good friends, I am quite well, and what I am saying to you now is a conclusion reached after a good deal of thought."

"In that case, won't you explain what you have in

mind? Not your own case, I hope? I must tell you that you
are out of danger. You've had an ordinary emotional breakdown, a complete suppression of the inhibiting mechanism,
something that psychiatrists call a reactive psychosis. Dr. Cusano demonstrated the chemical morphology of your blood at
his university lecture, and he showed that such cases are accompanied by a sharp increase in the concentration of adren-
alin and its derivatives. That's why we spoke about mescaline. You know . . ."

Because Alb knew, and they knew, and several dozen
university students knew, he felt the revulsion of a man
who had been brought out naked for demonstration before a
vast audience of curiosity seekers. He made an impatient gesture, and his friends fell silent. They said nothing for several
seconds, searching for another topic of conversation. Finally,
Victor, with his usual crude cynicism, said:

"While you were lying around here, we've decoded the
molecular structure of the X and Y chromosomes."

"Oh? And now what?"

"Now parents can have a balanced family, and govern-
ments can in every situation, even in case of war, achieve a
balanced population structure. Isn't that something?"

Albert shrugged. After all, this wasn't much of a discovery in comparison with the one he had learned about. He felt
that, behind the seeming casualness of their announcement,
his friends concealed the pride and vanity of scientists who
had made a new step on the way to the unknown.

That's how complicity in crime begins, thought Alb.
When should my friends and I be tried for crime against humanity—before or after the decoding of the X and Y chromosomes? Or when the government will be able to produce a
balanced population in wartime? Or when the war breaks
out and it's too late to change anything?

"What is the use of all this, Victor? Antoine? It seems to
me that researches into molecular genetics, all this probing

into the secret mechanisms of man's once mysterious nature, will bring about a situation when—with all knowledge available in school textbooks—life will lose all its beauty, all its marvelous enchantment. People will appear before one another and before themselves stripped of their layer of skin, like anatomical figures. Even worse, like vessels made of clusters of protein molecules of known composition, in which known biochemical reactions and biophysical processes take place."

Albert felt that he was not saying what he should. Of course, the results achieved by his father and Horsh would sooner or later be repeated in laboratories throughout the world. But what would follow? Sensible people would not start setting up chemical plants for the production of men to meet given specification. No, this would never happen. And nevertheless, such plants might be set up, secretly, underground, with the same bloodthirsty purpose. He suddenly imagined an energetic man in uniform, reporting crisply to his minister on how well the plant was functioning. And he wanted to shout to his friends at the top of his voice: "Stop! Stop! Open your eyes wider and imagine what will happen if . . ."

"Not making a discovery is ten times more heroic." He recalled the phrase spoken by his father before he died. He bit his lip to blood.

"But what do you suggest? To stop? To close up science? Return to primitive ignorance? Thus far we've heard only your negative views. Where are the positive ones? What about the achievements of medicine, of agriculture, what about the improvements in man's adaptation to his environment? What about the genetic aspect of the solution of the cancer problem?"

"All this is so . . . But I am afraid that soon there will be an end to the anxious hopes of parents waiting for their child, because children will be grown in flasks in accordance with previously set programs . . ."

"That's not impossible. Not impossible at all, Alb. For my part, I see nothing wrong with it. And the experiments in this direction are very promising . . . What's the matter, Alb? You look so pale. Are we tiring you?"

Klemper and Gust got up. Albert had a strong desire to tell them everything. . . . But he did not, because he was certain that they would immediately reproduce Horsh's apparatus and start, like men possessed, like medieval Fausts, to manufacture men by artificial means in the institute laboratories. It seemed to him that he had only now begun to understand how right his father had been when he spoke of the scientist's responsibility for the destinies of his discoveries.

8

Albert recovered completely and sat for days on end in his father's study, reading books on philosophy. He had never given much attention to the large number of philosophic works in his father's library. Now he realized how much his father had read about the problems of death and immortality. Reading book after book, he seemed to be following in his father's footsteps.

It was at this time that Horsh appeared. He entered one day, looking much older, stooped over. For a fleeting moment, Alb felt sorry for him. Horsh stood before him with his arms hanging, in an old faded cloak, with a colorless face which expressed infinite weariness and even greater guilt.

"Sit down," said Albert.

Horsh nodded and sat down. For a while they were silent.

"Yes, Horsh?"

He raised his head. "Why did you do it, Alb?" he asked at last.

"Do what?"

"You destroyed a lifetime's work, mine, and your father's."

Albert gave a twisted smile. He felt the stirrings of a sense of revenge. "What right did you have to make such inhuman experiments? What right did you have to give life to human beings in such a manner?"

Horsh smiled ironically. "What right, what right . . . What right did people have to invent gunpowder? What right did they have to create atom and hydrogen bombs? Tell me that, Alb! And planes? And rockets? And deadly viruses? All this is death, Alb, death. . . . What right! If you wish to know, our right—and I am speaking not only of myself, but also of your father—our right was based on the irresistible wish to neutralize the insane rush of science toward creating means for the destruction of everything that lives."

Albert raised astonished eyes at his guest. This was something he did not expect.

"Yes, yes, Alb, don't be astonished. If you are interested in the moral motives of our investigations, this is what they were. Many years ago your father and I swore that we would make man immortal, despite all the efforts of misanthropes and madmen."

"How?"

"You know, I'm sure, the history of the Dead Sea scrolls. A certain Jordanian shepherd found parchments that had lain in a cave more than two thousand years. The scrolls contained records of ancient tales, legends, laws. Contemporary scholars deciphered them, and now we have the opportunity of looking at our distant past with the eyes of people alive at the time. The earth had known wars, natural catastrophes, disasters of every kind, civilization followed civilization, and the scrolls bided their time. And take the Mayan inscriptions, and the clay tablets of Sumer . . ."

"What relation does all that have to your work?"

"Oh, Alb, a very direct relation. I and your father, when he was younger, decided to leave after us priceless records, the most sacred historic inscriptions ever made by man. We swore to create a golden book and record in it the results of our labors."

"And what did you intend to write in this book?"

"What? Of course, the Formula of Man."

"The Formula of Man?"

"Yes. The one you saw in my laboratory. And a description of the apparatus in which this formula could be synthesized. Isn't this the solution of the problem of immortality? The book was to contain a detailed account of the process of synthesis. It was to contain all the instructions—where and how the process should be started, when it should be completed, what should be done with the newborn infant after that. In the end, after we arrived at the exact chemical formula of the genetic substance of man, we even began to think about automating the synthesis from beginning to end, entrusting it to a cybernetic machine. Such a machine can easily be developed. We wanted to do this, and also enter it in the golden book. Do you imagine what this means? It means immortality in the full sense of the word. The book could be placed in a cosmic rocket and sent out into the universe. It could travel millions of years and come into the hands of reasoning beings different from us. And they could easily reconstruct man! And here, on earth? You, myself, anyone can be immortalized, so that he would reappear on earth again and again, and observe the eternal evolution of our planet."

Horsh's tired and indifferent face came to life. He began to speak with an ecstasy that disregarded Albert's presence. He spoke of fantastic possibilities which the Formula of Man opened before humanity, and Alb suddenly felt that the man before him was completely insane.

"It's a beautiful, but absolutely senseless idea," he said, trying to halt the delirious outpourings.

"After your father married Solveig and you were born, your father said exactly the same words . . ."

Albert started at the mention of his mother.

Horsh, in the meantime, went on.

"Nature is much simpler than we think. The whole crux of the matter lies in a small group of substances which initiate cyclic reactions. They are substances which begin a closed sequence of chemical reactions, the end stage of which is the new synthesis of the initiating molecule. You know what these substances are, Alb. To begin with, it is the genetic material: desoxyribonucleic acid, DNA. . . . That's all."

"And then?"

"And then we analyzed and synthesized the genetic material of man."

"And?"

"We succeeded in growing several children according to the same formula. . . . Solveig was the fifth."

"And the others?"

"The others died either in the embryonic stage, or soon after . . . birth."

"Why?"

"Well, this 'why' is something we had not solved entirely. The point is that a certain group of DNA molecules determines the life span of the individual. We discovered this group and tried to rearrange their nitrous bases in every possible way. . . . We succeeded in getting Solveig to live twenty-one years. But that is so little . . . We had hoped to enter in the golden book the formula of an extremely long-lived man."

"And what happened later?"

"Solveig grew up a very beautiful girl. She was brought up by the Shauli family . . ."

"Like Midgeia?"

Horsh nodded.

"Your father fell in love with her. I was categorically against their marriage. But he could not be swayed. Solveig loved him too. And so . . ."

"God!" Albert cried out, unable to control himself any longer.

Horsh winced. In a broken voice, he said: "It is unusual,

and therefore it seems unnatural. But people will become accustomed to it very quickly."

"When the synthesis of man is described in school-books?"

"Yes. Sooner or later, this will be so."

"Very well, continue. What happened then?"

"After his marriage, your father abandoned all work in this area. He transferred to the institute of genetics and cytology. He said there was no need for any golden book and that we should fight for man's immortality by other means. You know which. He was a member of every committee on earth working to save mankind from nuclear war. I don't think that was very intelligent . . ."

Alb walked up to Horsh.

"Look, Horsh, I won't have you talk to me like that about my father! You were only his pupil. It isn't for you to judge whether his choices were intelligent or not. I think that he was absolutely right to abandon this idiotic idea. And, anyway, why did you come here?"

Horsh looked at Albert with pleading eyes.

"Alb, for God's sake, don't be angry. . . . Give me your word you will be sensible."

"What do you want?"

"Two things . . . Try to find at least some fragments of the book you took from my laboratory. And then . . . one drop of your blood for analysis."

Alb held out his hand to him and watched with revulsion as Horsh's trembling hands hastily fumbled in his pockets, drew out a tampon of cotton, a bottle of ether, and a surgical instrument. A slight prick, and a red drop of blood appeared on Alb's finger.

Horsh applied to it a snakelike tube and began to draw the blood into a small bulb.

"What do you need it for?"

"Now I'll know whether you will live longer than

your mother. It will be interesting to see what happened in the structure of the DNA that determines lethality. . . . And now the book."

Alb rang, and the housekeeper entered. The woman nodded, and the men remained alone. A terrible question troubled Albert's mind, but he did not dare ask it. There was just one more mystery that demanded an answer, but the more he realized its nature, the more he feared to ask. Horsh was also silent, as if guessing what tormented Albert.

A few moments later the housekeeper returned with a large carton containing a mass of papers.

"Here is all that's left, Mr. Albert. . . ."

Horsh tore the box from her hands and hurriedly began to smooth the pieces of crumpled paper, covered with rows of figures.

"Yes. Some of it's here. . . . The main thing remains, and the rest can be restored. Here, here is the most important thing. Lethality . . . Now we'll try something else . . ."

As he became more and more absorbed in restoring the notes, his face increasingly assumed the expression Albert had seen at their first meeting. . . . At last he tore away his eyes from the paper and gave Alb a glowing look.

"Did you see the photographs? Isn't it an astonishing example of human history? From cell to death itself."

Albert was silent. Green and violet circles swam before his eyes. They shut out Horsh's face.

"Have you noticed the resemblance between Midgeia and Solveig?" Horsh continued.

Alb could endure it no longer and asked: "Is Midgeia my sister?"

"Oh, no, Alb, of course not! She is version Number 6."

And then . . . That heart-rending, hysterical shriek was still in his ears. And before his eyes—Horsh's pale face. Then pain, pain in his head, chest, feet. He was evidently beaten, pulled away from that crumpled body. He cried like a child, and tears flowed down his cheeks and fell on the unshaven chin of the lifeless Horsh. Then he was bound. Then a cold straitjacket. And, finally, a prison cell . . .

"The death sentence for murder may be reduced to a life sentence at hard labor if you offer sufficiently convincing motives for your crime," a man was saying to him calmly. He thought it might be his father's old lawyer.

"Death sentence? Lethality? Did Horsh have time to analyze my blood?" Albert asked, as after a hypnotic trance.

"Albert, collect yourself, think about it. The trial is tomorrow."

"Tell me, are there laws under which a man may be prosecuted for creating human beings doomed in advance?"

"What are you saying, Albert?"

"The time of your death, you know, is recorded in your DNA . . ."

"For God's sake, stop pretending madness. The doctors have established that you acted under extreme emotional stress. But nothing more. In every other respect you are entirely well."

"Well. Normal. How absurd it all sounds now. As if you knew my formula. But no one knows it. And never shall. And it will never be entered in the golden book of immortality. Don't you see—I am not viable enough!"

WHEN QUESTIONS ARE ASKED

by

ANATOLY DNEPROV

We hold annual reunions in memory of those distant, shadowy times when we were students. There is a new university building on Lenin Hills, and the five-story home of the physics department has long been occupied by new generations of budding Lomonosovs and Einsteins. But we cannot forget the vaulted basement rooms under the old club of the Moscow State University on Hertzen Street. And we meet there every year, and look at one another, and count those who are still here and those who are gone. We speak about life and about science. As we did then, in those long-gone years.

And so it was this time, but for some reason the conversation was lame and listless. No one brought up any stimulating ideas, no one argued against things said, and all of us suddenly felt that the previous year's reunion had probably been the last interesting one.

"We have reached that fine age when ideas and opinions have finally crystallized into a finished form and finished content," was the bitterly ironic comment of Fedya Yegoriev, doctor of science and corresponding member of the academy.

"A jolly thought," said Vovka Migay, director of one of the "clever" institutes. "And what do you call 'finished content'?"

"That's when you can add nothing more to what is," Fedya explained gloomily. "After that comes natural erosion but no growth. A man's intellectual life has a sharply defined maximum point. Somewhere around the age of forty-five."

"You don't need to explain, we know it without your lectures. But generally, my friends, I simply cannot believe that I'm no longer capable of responding to anything new. No new theory, no new science? How awful!"

Leonid Samozvantsev, a rotund little physicist with an odd manner of hurrying through his phrases and swallowing word endings and often entire words, did not look like a man of forty-five. And the rest of us took every opportunity to remind him of it.

"You were damned lucky, Lyalya. You were a sickly child, with a protracted infancy. You are still capable not only of inventing a new theory of space but even of learning the old one."

Everyone laughed, recalling that as a student, he had taken the examination in relativity four times before passing.

Samozvantsev took a quick drink from his glass.

"Don't worry, there won't be any new theories."

"Why?" asked Migay.

"The time is wrong, and so is the training."

"Not too clear."

"Perhaps I didn't put it very well," Lyalya began to explain. "Of course there will be new theories, but only refining and elaborating on the old. Something along the line of computing still another decimal place of "pi" or adding another term to the sum of an infinite series. But creating something entirely new—forget it!" Samozvantsev stressed the word *entirely*.

Seeing that a discussion was about to begin, people drifted over to us from other corners of the large, low-ceilinged room.

"In that case, define what you call an 'entirely new theory.'"

"Well, for example, the electromagnetic theory of light in relation to the ether theory."

"Ha-ha!" Georgy Sychev broke in with a thunderous laugh, as though awakening from a doze. He raised his aluminum crutch—a sad souvenir of the war years—and, poking Lyalya in the side with it, spoke to all of us at once: "This physicist wants to tell us that Maxwell is not the next term of the infinite series, after Young. Ha-ha, my dear friend! Give us a better example, or I'll fall asleep."

"All right, let's take Faraday. He discovered electromagnetic induction . . ."

"And so?"

"Well, this discovery was revolutionary; it immediately brought together electricity and magnetism, and electrotechnology developed on the basis of it."

"And what's the point of that?" Sychev insisted. Like most legless men, he tended to corpulence. Now he was simply fat, with a flabby, aging face.

"The point is that Faraday hadn't the slightest notion of your Young or his elastic ether. Or of Maxwell, either. It was Maxwell who dragged Faraday into his own equations."

Sychev threw his head back with a forced laugh.

"Stop braying, Zhorka!" Migay turned on him. "There is something to Lyalya's idea. Go on, Lyalya, pay no attention to him."

"I am sure that if Faraday had been intelligent—at least, like us . . ."

The group around him broke into laughter.

"Don't laugh. If he had been as intelligent and rational as we are, he wouldn't have made a single discovery . . ."

Everyone was quiet and stared at Samozvantsev. He looked at them with some confusion, holding his glass to his lips.

"There is something to the poke method. We have a whole group of able fellows and girls working at our institute. They never go to books or journals to find clues to the solution of their problems. They simply try. They do one thing, and another—whatever comes to mind. Like Faraday."

"You see! And do they get anywhere?"

"Imagine, they do! And I must say, they are the ones who find the most original solutions."

This was too much for our academician.

"Now you're going too far. In another moment you'll be saying that it's best to do scientific work without knowing anything. Physicists always like to play with paradoxes. But we're no longer at that age . . ."

"Oh, I'm sick of you, with your age. Let Lyalya speak. So Faraday, you're saying, worked by the poke method?"

"Of course. He was simply a curious fellow. What would happen if you struck a magnet with a hammer? What would happen if you got it red hot? Would a cat's eyes gleam in the dark if you kept it hungry for a while? And so on. The most absurd and improbable 'and what if?' And he tried to find his answers by experimenting. This is why he discovered such a mass of phenomena and effects, which were later shaped into new theories. But we, the clever ones, think that there are no more 'and what if's.' To us, the most important thing is theory."

"Mm-m," the academician commented uncertainly and walked away. He was followed by several others.

"We'll have to support and encourage the 'pokers,'" Vovka Migay said with a wry grin. "Who knows, perhaps we'll find a new Faraday . . ."

"There is a very simple method of discovering a Faraday," broke in Nikolay Zavoysky, our most eminent theoretician, also a doctor and also a corresponding member of the academy. We were always somewhat annoyed with him for his excessively aristocratic manners.

"Come on, let's hear your method."

"Declare a country-wide competition for the best 'and what if . . .' The participants should ask their own questions and find their own answers. Of course, with the aid of experiments. And the truly 'Faradayan' question will be the one that contemporary theory is unable to answer."

Everyone liked the idea, and soon the hitherto silent physicists animatedly began to "play Faraday." "And what will happen if . . . ?" came from all ends of the room. After a while we all gathered together and the game became active and gay. We set ourselves the most preposterous questions, and answered them ourselves.

"And what if we put glasses on a sperm-whale's eyes?"

"And what if we boil a meteor in cow's milk?"

"And what if we send an electric current of one million amps through a man for one millionth of a second?"

"And what if . . ."

There was a steady stream of questions, and now everyone answered them in chorus. This led to computations, equations, references to sources—the whole arsenal of physical knowledge, and before long it became clear that a "Faradayan" question was very difficult to find but nevertheless possible. And, the devil take it, this was almost always precisely the question that modern physics was struggling with at the moment. Lyalya Samozvantsev, the cause of all this excitement, sighed with disappointment.

"And I thought we'd appeal to the academy to set up a Scientific Research Institute of Faradayan Studies."

"Do you remember Alyoshka Monin? That's what we used to call him at school, Faraday!"

Everyone was silent. All eyes turned to Shura Korneva, the principal organizer of the reunion. Redhaired and freckled, she never tried to seem pretty.

"Shurka, why isn't Alik here today?"

"He couldn't come."

"Why?"

"He's on duty tonight, at the hospital. . . . Besides, he said . . ."

"What?"

"He said he felt awkward coming to our meetings. There were academicians here, he said, or, at the very least, candidates, and he . . . You understand . . ."

We understood. We all felt that Monin had been badly out of luck, and mostly through his own fault. It was enough to watch him at his laboratory work to realize he'd never amount to anything. Instead of doing the assignment and taking the generator's frequency characteristic, he'd sit for hours at the oscillograph, admiring the fantastic figures traced by the electronic beam. "Alik, you must shield the leads, or you won't get anything." "Oh, every fool knows that. But what will happen if they aren't shielded?" "Silly, ordinary induction. The grid current, the X-ray apparatus in the next lab . . ." Alik would smile mysteriously and shield the leads. The figures on the screen changed but remained fantastic. "You didn't shield it properly. Close the lid." He would close it, but the situation remained without improvement. "Ground the body." He would ground it, but the picture would become still worse. No one else got such results. Instead of finding the generator's characteristic, he would fill a thick copybook with notes. His report on the work done read like a science-fiction story about a generator's strange behavior—when it was shielded, when it was not shielded, when the amplifier tube was cooled by air from a fan, and when a wet cloth was placed on it. In the end, everything would become totally confused, and he would get his usual "Failed."

In our dormitory we always faced the problem of how to get washed quickly in the morning. The students liked to sleep as late as possible, and at seven every morning there was a rush to the sinks and total bedlam.

One day Monin became the cause of collective lateness in class. There was a long line for the sink, but he stood quietly over it, absorbed in some mysterious activity.

"Hey, Faraday, are you asleep?"

"No, but take a look."

The sink was clogged and filled almost to the rim with muddy water. Alik threw a pinch of toothpowder into the water, and the little lumps ran out in all directions.

"So what? Surface tension . . . Get out of the way."

But Alik had no intention of getting out of the way.

"Look now . . ."

He threw another pinch of powder, but this time the particles all ran together. We were astounded.

"Do it again."

He repeated the experiment. It turned out that, if the powder was thrown from a certain height, it dispersed; if it was thrown from another, it ran together.

All of us, from first to fifth year students, stuffed the sink drains and began to pour toothpowder into the water. The future corresponding member of the academy, Fedya Yegoriev, experimented with tobacco, shaken out of a cigarette. The elegant theoretician Zavoysky brought four kinds of powder, including foot powder. Others brought granulated sugar, salt, headache powders, and whatnot. A tense atmosphere of concentrated research prevailed in the washroom. The powders behaved in the most grotesque ways. They gathered in lumps on the surface of the water, ran to the edges of the sink, sank, then rose again, circled in one spot, formed nebulae and planetary systems, ran along a straight line, and even jumped up and down. And everything depended on the distance from which they were dropped, on how they were dropped, on the level of water in the sink, on whether there was any soap in the water, on whether any other powders had been dropped before. Everything the budding physicists knew about surface tension from their second year collapsed like a house of cards in that washroom, and the person responsible for all that was Al-yoshka Monin.

"A pity he isn't here. An interesting fellow," said Fedya Yegoriev with a sigh. "A real Faraday. But an unsuccessful one."

"I guess he didn't ask himself the right questions."

"Comrades, and what will happen if I don't come home in time?"

It was one o'clock in the morning. We burst out laughing. The speaker was Abram Chaiter, an amateur atomic scientist, as we called him for his passion for publishing popular articles on atomic physics. His own field was something else altogether. And everybody knew that Abram had a very jealous wife.

"The children will lose a favorite writer about the war," said Lyalya.

We all began to put on our coats.

It was drizzling outside. There was little traffic now. People said their good-byes and hurried off to the taxi stands. Four of us lingered at the club entrance—Fedya Yegoriev, Vovka Migay, Lyalya Samozvantsev, and I. For a few moments we smoked silently.

"There used to be a streetcar here in our time," said Fedya. "One day I found Alik standing right here with his head raised. Do you know what he was observing, for more than two hours?"

We did not know.

"The color of the spark along the wire. He said that he had been watching it for a week, and that there was a connection between the color of the spark and the weather. Just recently I read about it, as a new discovery . . ."

"Why don't we drop in on him now?" I suggested. "It's rather awkward. We all get together, and he's left out . . ."

"An excellent idea. Let's go," said Fedya.

We had always admired Fedya for his decisiveness. And

now, years later, he was still the same. Tall, lean, he started quickly down the avenue toward Gorky Street. We halted at the National Hotel. The corresponding member of the academy said, "Wait, I'll step in and buy a bottle of wine in the restaurant."

Fedya knew how to get in through the kitchen. He disappeared in the dark gateway, and a few minutes later we heard someone, probably the janitor or the cook, shout after him:

"Miserable drunks! The day isn't enough for them! Barging in through the back!"

But the purchase was safely with him. Soon we were speeding in a taxi to the other end of the city, where Alik was working.

The hospital was surrounded by a large park. We paid the driver at the gate and walked toward the building along the wet asphalt path, between tall shrubs and trees. There was a fine spring rain, and the young leaves fluttered like fireflies in the light of the street lamps. Migay was telling us excitedly how he had succeeded in seeing K-meson tracks and the formation of resonance particles in a bubble chamber. Samozvantsev boasted about his quantum generator, for which all the supplies could be bought at any drugstore, and Fedya called them "small fry," because their toys could not compare with his universal machine, which had beaten him in chess the day before. We stopped for a moment. Two attendants crossed the path with a stretcher covered with a sheet.

"That one couldn't care less about all our generators and resonance particles," sighed Migay. "This must be the morgue."

We glanced at the low, columned building. Along its gray pediment ran a depiction in high relief of a battle between Roman warriors and Gauls.

"It's damned humiliating, after all, to have to join this organization when all is said and done," remarked Lyalya.

"Unprofitable, but they're not about to close it . . ."

We walked the rest of the way to the neurosurgical department building in silence.

Alik Monin met us with an embarrassed smile. He wore an unbuttoned hospital coat, and his hands were fiddling with a fountain pen, which got in the way of our handshakes.

"Well, well, you look just like a doctor!" Migay barked out.

The term was most unfortunate. On the borderline between the two sciences—medicine and physics—the title of "doctor" has an ambiguous sound. Alik shrank altogether. We followed him along a darkish corridor. He merely whispered:

"Now, this way. This way. Upstairs. To the right . . ."

"You're not supposed to talk loudly," Fedya admonished Migay, the possessor of a resonant basso.

In a small office, illuminated only by a table lamp, we sat down around the desk. Fedya pulled two bottles of wine from his pocket and solemnly placed them before Alik.

"Oh, you old devils!" he exclaimed in a low voice. "Straight from the reunion?"

"That's right. We were talking about Faraday and thought of you. Why are you hiding out?"

"No, no, what do you mean . . . Just a moment . . ."

Alik disappeared into the corridor, and we examined the office. Nothing unusual. Bookcases filled with papers, probably case histories, along the walls. An apparatus of some kind on one side. A table with glass jars near the sink. And the desk.

Fedya picked up a book from the table and read in a whisper: "*Electrosleep*. Physics here too."

I wouldn't like to work here," muttered Samozvántsev. "Physics next to the morgue. Doesn't go together, somehow."

"Perhaps someday physics will help to close down that unprofitable institution."

Alik entered silently, bringing an armful of chemical measuring glasses of various sizes.

"One instance when the size of the container makes no difference," said the academician. "Everything with exact markings."

The wine was poured.

"To twenty-five years . . ."

"To twenty-five years . . ."

After that we drank one another's health. This toast had now become almost a necessity.

"Tell us what you are doing here."

Alik shrugged. "All sorts of things. I work with patients . . ."

"So you've really learned medicine? You treat patients?"

"Oh, no! Of course not. I am at the diagnostic end."

"And what does that mean?"

"I'm helping neurosurgeons."

"They do brain operations here?"

"Sometimes. But most often operations involving traumatized nerve tracks."

"Is it interesting?"

"Sometimes."

"Can you do research too?"

"Every patient here means a new research project."

"I'm crazy about interesting case histories. Tell us something, Alik. Some extraordinary case."

Migay drank another glass and moved his chair nearer the desk. Alik adjusted his metal-rimmed glasses with a nervous movement of the hand.

"I am most interested in cases of amnesia in connection with various diseases."

"Loss of memory?"

"Yes. Some have total loss, others partial."

"I've recently read McCulloch's *Robot Without a Memory*," said Fedya.

"I read it too. Nonsense. McCulloch's conclusions, based on mathematical logic, don't apply to human beings who've lost their memory. Their behavior is much more complex."

"I've always wondered where the memory center is situated," said Fedya.

Alik became animated: "Exactly, where? We can say with considerable certainty that the brain has no special memory center."

"Perhaps in some molecules . . ."

"Not likely," said Alik. "Continual metabolism means a constant regeneration of molecules. No, memory is too stable to be recorded on the molecular level."

We all thought about it. When you speak to Monin, things that are seemingly simple suddenly become enormously complex and tangled.

"What's this machine?" asked Migay, raising the edge of the cover on the small table.

"An old model of an electroencephalograph."

"Oh, brain waves?"

"Yes. An eight-channel machine. There are better ones now."

Alik opened a desk drawer and pulled out a pile of papers.

"These are encephalograms of people with amnesia. . . ."

We looked at the curves, which had an almost strict sinusoidal form.

"And here are the brain currents of normal people."

"A great device! So you can determine immediately with this toy whether a man has a memory or not?"

"Yes, although . . ."

"What?"

"Well, frankly speaking, I don't consider the term *brain waves* accurate."

"Why?"

"Well, after all, we don't take the electric potentials from the brain itself. The brain is shielded by the skull, then a layer of tissue rich in blood vessels, then the skin . . ."

"But the frequencies are so low . . ."

"It makes no difference. I made calculations. If we take into account the conductivity of the shielding, we have to conclude that enormous electropotentials are at work in the brain. But this was not confirmed in experiments with animals."

We had another drink.

"Then what are these?"

"These are the biocurrents of the tissues to which we apply the electrodes."

"Hm . . . But it was proven that these curves are connected with brain function. Take memory . . ."

"And what of that? Does the brain work by itself only?"

"You mean to say that memory . . ."

Alik smiled and got up. "How would you like me to take your encephalograms?"

Fedya Yegoriev scratched his head and looked at us. "Shall we chance it?"

We did, but for some reason we felt very awkward. As though we were being examined by a doctor, from whom nothing can be concealed.

Migay sat down in the armchair first. Alik adjusted eight electrodes on his head and switched on the encephalograph. The paper ribbon crept out slowly. The pens remained motionless.

"No mental activity," commented Samozvantsev.

"The apparatus hasn't warmed up."

Suddenly we started. The silence was pierced by the loud scraping of sharp metal on paper. We stared at the ribbon. Eight pens were racing over it, swinging widely, and leaving a fantastic design.

"*Cogito ergo sum,*" Migay declaimed with relief. "Now check the academician's brain. This is most important for the learned council of our institute. He is the chairman."

We were astonished to find that the academician's brain waves were exactly like Migay's, Samozvantsev's, and mine. If there was any difference, we didn't see it. We stared questioningly at Alik. He smiled mysteriously.

"Your electroencephalograms are the same because you are all in the same stage of intoxication. It's always so with drunken people. . . . Just as with schizophrenics or with epileptics before a seizure."

We felt embarrassed and took another drink. Monin stopped the ribbon and, after rummaging some more in his papers, showed us several other encephalograms.

"Here is a record of the brain waves of a sleeping man. And here is a typical curve in the waking state. Teta and Gamma are superimposed on the alpha-rhythm."

"Interesting," Fedya said pensively. "So where, according to you, is the memory center?"

Alik was nervously stuffing the papers back into the drawer. Then he sat down and looked at each of us in turn.

"Stop mystifying us, Faraday. We can see you know something. Tell us where it is . . ."

Migay rose and jestingly took Alik by the flaps of his coat. The coat was unbuttoned, and under it he wore an old, threadbare jacket.

"Well, if you insist . . ."

"That's a fine thing—'insist'! We demand! We must know, after all, where it is that we store our precious erudition for which the government pays us so handsomely!"

Migay was never distinguished for tact. His thinking was idiotically logical and disgustingly direct. When he said that, it seemed to me that a bitter, resentful spark flashed in Monin's eyes for a second. Firmly compressing his lips, he rose from the table and went to one of the cases. He returned with a human skull, such as may be seen in the biology laboratory of any school. Without a word, he placed it on the table next to the encephalograph and began to adjust the electrodes on it. We watched him, petrified with astonishment.

When the electrodes were in place, Alik gave us an intent look from the darkness, then turned the switch.

Eight pens shrieked in chorus and began to dance on the paper. Hypnotized, we stared at the mocking, empty eye-sockets. And the apparatus continued hastily and with great agitation to record the feverish curve of the biocurrents of a man in the waking state.

"There . . ." Monin said instructively.

We rose and hurriedly said our good-byes, afraid to take another look at the table next to the electroencephalograph.

In the darkness outside we lost our way and trudged for a long time through tall, wet grass, circling low, dark buildings, and following the metal fence, beyond which stretched the wet, dimly lit street. Briar shrubs caught at our raincoats and scraped revoltingly over their surface. When we finally emerged from the gate and stopped to catch our breath, our academician Fedya said:

"Induction. Of course. Induction from the grid current . . ."

With that comforting thought, we shook hands, and went off into the night, to our respective homes.

THE HORN OF PLENTY

by

VLADIMIR GRIGORIEV

VLADIMIR GRIGORIEV, *born in 1935, is an engineer. A partici-
pant in several scientific expeditions, including one to study
the Tungus meteorite, he began to write science fiction in
1962 and has since published many stories and one collection
(1967).*

YOUNG AND GROWN-UP,
TURN IN YOUR SCRAP!

You can still see this sign, crudely made by some humble
workman and warped with time, in one of the old Moscow lanes. Many years ago it was nailed to the gray, weath-
er-worn fence, with the idea that its bright colors would be
all the more striking against the dingy background. And, indeed, at first it caught the eye of every passerby. People
slowed their steps, shook their heads, and muttered:

"What will they think of next?"

The sign depicted a large horn made of pure sheet cop-

62

per. A little man in overalls shoveled rubbish and refuse into its narrow end, while from the wide end came a stream of useful and necessary objects—rolls of woolen fabric, bakery products, penknives, slippers, harmonicas, and even a bottle of vodka, the foil on its still unopened top gleaming in the midst of all those riches.

Nursemaids and young mothers walking their children through the lane would invariably stop before the picture and say to their charges, "A horn of plenty."

But years passed. Bitter frosts bent the geometrically faultless oval. The burning rays of the sun dimmed the polished copper. And the winds swept out of the picture the rubbish, the shovel, and many of the objects. Time simplified the picture's theme. All that emerges from the throat of the horn now is a phonograph and the bottle, with a jagged, broken neck. And the little man, robbed of his shovel, stands bending over the horn, peering into it through the narrow end. Soon, soon the little man will vanish with the wind, in the wake of his shovel. His days are numbered. And his entire woeful pose seems to say, "Now, isn't that a pity! The machine broke down. But how it worked, how it worked!"

In short, nothing is left of the old enchantment of the gleaming copper horn. It lost its character, it blended with the fence. Passersby no longer slow their steps in the lane. And even the policeman Petrov, whose post for the past fifteen years has kept him standing almost directly across from the sign, now skims over its tarnished surface with unseeing eyes as he scans the wide open spaces of the lane.

On the whole, of course, it doesn't matter whether the sign is or isn't there. What difference? Of the thousands of people who have passed the spot in the course of the years only a handful have been sufficiently moved by its message to bring their scrap to the collection depot. And even with those few, the action did not turn into a habit. It remained an isolated incident which they hastened to forget, as people generally prefer to forget trivial facts considered unworthy of mention in biographies.

Nevertheless, the horn was there. Forgotten, merged into the grayness of the fence, it seemed to wait for the one and only person who could appreciate the full significance of the artist's idea and be inspired by it to great deeds.

It was the early evening of a chilly autumn day when a short man, in a thick woolen coat of a style long out of fashion, walked down the lane. His felt hat, which had seen better times, was pulled low over his eyes; his hands were in his pockets; and his elbow pressed to his side two small dog-eared books, *Teach Yourself to Play the Seven-Stringed Guitar* and *Teach Yourself a Foreign Language*. The spot which specified the language was covered with a large ink blot.

This man, who had evidently not yet mastered all languages and who did not yet know how to play a seven-stringed guitar, strolled along the fence at a leisurely pace. His day's chores over, he had no need to hurry. At home he had the rented guitar waiting for him. And meantime, why not take a walk and look around?

He walked along the fence with the sign we have described earlier, and it caught his eye. He slowed his steps still further, and then stopped altogether. For a while he stood there, shifting from foot to foot; then he came nearer. Then he rubbed a part of the picture with his sleeve, glanced at it again, sighed, and prepared to continue his stroll. But suddenly his face lit up, and he slapped himself on the forehead. "Well, I'll be . . ." he said under his breath, snatched a notebook from his pocket, jotted something down, and almost ran to the end of the lane.

At home he did not even glance at the guitar, which gleamed invitingly with its delicately yellow sides. He looked for paper, took out an almost new indelible pencil, and feverishly set to work. Totally absorbed in his idea, he jotted down formulas, multiplied, divided, and made quick diagrams and sketches. When his stock of note paper ran out, he solemnly drew a large sheet of thick paper from the closet and tacked it to the wall. The indelible pencil was suspended in the air before the sheet for a few moments, then—presto!—a dot appeared on the blank surface.

An hour later the sheet was peppered with dots. The little man stepped aside, calculated something, then walked up to the wall again and with one sweep collected the dots into a single flowing line. Then he stepped back again, grunted, and rubbed his hands with satisfaction. The wall was now adorned with a picture of a horn of plenty exactly like the one that can still be seen in the old Moscow lane.

"Stepan Onufrievich, my primus stove is broken, I wonder if you'd take a look at it," a voice said through the partly opened door.

"Your primus stove? I'm sorry, I can't now, I'm too busy," he answered absentmindedly, still admiring his work. "You see, I'm inventing . . ."

"What a head, what a head, he's inventing again!" the neighbor said sympathetically and closed the door.

Stepan Onufrievich Ogurtsov was known among his neighbors as an eccentric, but everybody liked him. "A golden pair of hands," they would say, bringing him their broken primus stoves, locks, and sewing machines to repair. For the children in the yard he made snares and bird cages, repaired portable radios. No electrician was ever called to the house; replacing a burnt-out fuse or tube was a trifling job to him. He repaired cheap old television sets so well that people from neighboring houses came to see the programs.

"Ogurtsov himself repaired it!" his neighbors would boast. "It will last a lifetime."

He mended a doll for the house manager's daughter. When he got through with it, the doll suddenly began to speak and move its arms and legs, and exactly at eight every evening it would close its eyes and topple on its side, until eight the next morning. "We don't need an alarm clock," the manager told everyone enthusiastically and took to dropping in at Onufriev's for a friendly cup of tea.

Naturally, the policeman Petrov knew nothing of all this. Therefore he became suspicious when Stepan Onufrievich began to frequent the lane. Not that he disliked this mysterious man who could stand for a whole hour before the half-obliterated sign; the man was always sober, clean-shaven, and neatly dressed. Nevertheless, the policeman's professional sixth sense told him there was some secret behind his actions, something straight out of a detective novel. And so whenever the little man in the thick woolen coat of unfashionable cut would reappear in the lane, Petrov's chest, criss-crossed with straps, would heave, and his heart would beat more rapidly.

What attracted the stranger to the sign? It was impossible to answer this question. Yet Petrov did not venture to accost him directly and ask to see his documents; after all, his general conduct always remained within the bounds of decency and legality.

One day, choosing a convenient moment, Petrov glanced around and saw that the lane was deserted. He left his post and cautiously approached the sign. A detailed study of the picture, starting at the bottom, going on to the middle, and ending at the top, disclosed nothing that could either sadden or gladden anyone.

Ogurtsov, however, was now visiting the lane with increasing frequency. Whether it rained, whether the sun was baking hot or frost nipped the cheeks, he came and spent long hours contemplating the sign. He looked at it from one side, then from another; then he would step back, and come nearer, as if searching for something.

Sometimes everything seemed to be going smoothly, and Petrov saw the inventor walking jauntily, whistling merry tunes. The worn-down heels of his shoes tapped out a light, dancing rhythm. He whispered and muttered something, and the policeman's keen ear would catch such words as "direct current . . . copper mounting . . . what a beauty, what a beauty!"

There were also days when nothing came right. And the policeman would see Ogurtsov in dampened spirits, shrunk into himself. He would stand before the sign with his back hunched, his hands in his pockets.

Oh, no, it was not easy, it was not easy for Stepan Onufrievich to invent the horn of plenty. It wasn't anything like fixing a television set or putting in a new fuse.

But Ogurtsov knew himself. Never in his life had he undertaken a job he could not handle. Even with television sets, he would sometimes take a look, and think a while, and say, "No, I wouldn't tackle it." Stepan Onufrievich knew what he could or could not do. Therefore he would not give in. "If the idea came into my head," he said to himself, "it means I can do it."

At first he made the horn perfectly circular in every cross section. He mounted strong magnets all around it. He charged it with static electricity. The horn sent out sparks, but that was all. "The discharge is too weak," his intuition prompted him, and he made the horn rectangular. It began to look like a large, sharply bent phonograph horn. It sent out stronger sparks and, now and then, a small flash like a globe lightning. But it was still far from the real thing.

Ogurtsov's neighbors gradually stopped bringing him their broken machines and radios. Only the house manager still dropped in for tea. They drank glass after glass, and Ogurtsov heard as through a veil of dream:

"Quite a gadget! We don't need an alarm clock."

"No, no," the thought kept hammering in the inventor's brain. "It should not be round. Perhaps it should not be rectangular either? Perhaps oval?"

Soon the horn became oval. It stood on a large wooden trestle in the middle of the room, covered from curious eyes by wide folds of burlap. The inventor came home in the evening, ate hurriedly, cleared the table, and went to work. "Well, my dear little horn," he'd say aloud, "now we'll clear out your belly. Now we'll see how your throat will sing."

The burlap would be removed, and the room would come alive with the reddish glow of copper. The mirror-smooth sides of the horn flashed and glittered with rainbow colors. Each time he threw aside the burlap cover, Stepan Onufrievich went numb with ecstasy and stood, unblinking, for a long time, contemplating his magnificent creation. In its presence he saw himself as important, tall, almost great. The inventor had good reason to be proud. After all, it is no secret that many had tried to construct a similar device before, but no one had succeeded. And here, in this room, the crater of the horn had already brought forth real things. Once it threw out heavy leather boots, three of them at once, and, for some reason, all for the same foot. Another time a Persian rug slid out of it.

"You're on the right track, Stepan," Ogurtsov said to himself on that occasion. "A little more work, and the machine can be put to general use without blushing for it." The inventor's imagination obligingly envisaged all sorts of pleasant scenes. Ogurtsov saw himself standing on a high platform next to the horn, clearing his throat into his fist, and saying to the assembled audience:

"Here it is, citizens! I invented it. Now take what you wish and use it well. It works perfectly. But don't forget to oil it. And if anyone has a broken television set or bicycle, bring it over, I'll help you repair it . . ."

These were not idle dreams. The horn worked better and better every day. It rarely went wrong.

And one day Stepan Onufrievich smoothed out the brim of his hat, put on his good suit, polished his shoes to a high shine, and proceeded to the appropriate government office. Without a moment's hesitation he stepped across the threshold of the big building, full of busy people. He walked past the imposing, shiny signboard, introduced himself as an inventor, and was directed to the third floor, to Molotkov's office. Ogurtsov went up, modestly entered the office, and came into Molotkov's presence. The young man, in an elegant, stylish suit, sat at the desk and labored mightily. He turned the pages of some books, made notes, kept pulling out folders from the drawers, and smoked and smoked without a stop. Every few seconds the telephone rang, and he picked up the receiver, saying "Molotkov, yes."

Such was the man the inventor had been directed to. For a moment he hesitated, thinking that he might come another time, the man was much too busy to be disturbed. But the latter suddenly put down the receiver, smiled amiably, and asked: "You want to see me?" Then, noticing the visitor's embarrassment, he added: "Sit down, sit down, please, and tell me what it is."

Ogurtsov glanced at the window, then at the telephone, collected himself, and blurted out: "Well, it's about my invention. A machine, you might say . . . I mean, a horn of plenty."

And he sketched a diagram.

Molotkov's eyes simply glittered when Onufriev finished his description. He pulled on his cigarette, settled down more firmly in his chair; then, narrowing his eyes, he looked straight at Onufriev and breathed out with a cloud of smoke:

"Efficiency?"

"Eighty-ninety," estimated Ogurtsov.

"Let's go, let's go directly to your place," Molotkov said decisively. He picked up the telephone and barked out: "Postpone conference. Bring the car!"

The new limousine rushed at top speed, while Ogurtsov was suddenly overcome with doubts. When the car stopped sharply before a traffic light, he remembered that he had expended his entire stock of scrap. How would he demonstrate the horn?

It must be said here that the inventor had just recently moved to a new apartment. He was now living on the seventh floor, with a fine view of a beautiful, ideally tidy street. The garbage collector passed slowly along it every hour, collecting all the rubbish that chanced to be there. The lack of raw materials essential to his experiments drove the inventor frantic. He had to waste precious time on trips to less well-cared for districts. In especially urgent cases he had to run down to the janitor and plead with him for a single pail of trash, solemnly promising to return it. Without the promise the janitor would not give it to him. If he did, how could he prove to his superiors that he had done his work? And this, indeed, was the reason why Ogurtsov had been compelled to spend several extra days on reconstructing the horn. Now the machine could work in reverse as well. When you turned the handle to the right, the horn transformed scrap into valuables; when you turned it left, the process was reversed.

Be that as it may, at this moment there was no scrap at hand, and the janitor had gone with his wife to a concert at the conservatory of music. As he escorted Molotkov to his room, Ogurtsov looked utterly crestfallen. "He won't believe me," he was saying to himself, "he won't."

As soon as Molotkov saw the horn, he threw off his jacket and vest, rolled up his shirt sleeves, and plunged his hands into the mechanism's entrails. Stepan Onufrievich stood next to him, obediently giving explanations. "So the wave guide is grounded?" came from the belly of the horn.

"Yes, it is," answered Ogurtsov, astonished at the engineer's quick grasp.

"Falling characteristic?" came from the horn again.

"Yes," confirmed the inventor.

At last Molotkov straightened up, tidied himself, lit a cigarette, and walked around the horn once again. Then he went to the window, threw out his cigarette, and lit up another. He was agitated, and Ogurtsov stood silent, waiting for the verdict.

The engineer was at the window. A broad stream of cars rushed along the street below. The people behind the wheels hurried somewhere on their own business, suspecting nothing. Today they were still ignorant of the marvels transpiring there, in that room on the seventh floor. Tomorrow everyone would know everything.

He turned, went over to the inventor, and pressed his hand. "Congratulations, Stepan Onufrievich. You've done a great job. It's a pity we cannot see it in action now, but when we get the commission together, we'll bring you as much scrap as you'll need."

And after pressing the inventor's hand again, Molotkov rushed away down the stairs, skipping two at a time. The working day was not yet over; he still had to attend the postponed conference and take care of a number of other matters.

It was a dry, cloudless day when Ogurtsov was to demonstrate his invention. In his favorite checked shirt, smelling of triple strength eau-de-cologne, he went down into the street and walked toward the old lane. On such a day he could not omit a visit to the spot where chance had prompted the birth of the great idea.

Ogurtsov entered the lane. Everything was in its appointed spot. The yellow body of the horn was still visible on the fence; the policeman Petrov was still at his post. Ogurtsov approached the sign and stopped before it with a solemn air, as though he were about to take an oath. There was nothing extraneous in his solemn mood; he had no vain desire to put the sign into a golden frame or to exhibit it in a public place or to build a monument in the lane. The inventor and the sign were motionless before each other, like old warriors who had seen many battles, who had paid the price of experience, but had done their work! And neither the noise of passing trucks nor the hurried steps of passersby could shatter the excited, gala mood of this meeting of two victors, who had succeeded in turning dusty everyday realities into a straight road to triumph.

Petrov, as usual, devoted his attention to the traffic and the movement of pedestrians. Nevertheless, the daytime visit of his old acquaintance did not escape his eye. Neither did he miss the new elements in his bearing—the lightness and ease of movement, the calm confidence. He looked like a man who had thrown off a heavy load and stood light and free, as though ready to fly away. And when Ogurtsov approached the policeman, Petrov glanced into his gay, triumphant eyes and immediately understood that something of the utmost importance had happened and that he would now be initiated into the mystery.

"Well, Sergeant, let's have a smoke, shall we?" said Ogurtsov, taking a pack of excellent cigarettes from his pocket. "I've been coming to your lane for two years, but we've never had a talk before."

Petrov took one cigarette, brought it up to the oddly shaped cigarette lighter the visitor held out to him, and listened to the whole story, from beginning to end. The inventor talked unhurriedly, pausing now and then to think over his formulations, omitting facts impossible to explain without a pencil and paper. At times his gaze misted over, as if turning to the past, and a strange smile played on his face. At those times his thoughts flew to the most cherished moments of the past years.

"It's a good thing you've done," the Sergeant told him in parting.

Neither of them suspected that they would meet again that day, and in quite another place. Ogurtsov went to visit his friend, the house manager, and Petrov was summoned urgently to his precinct and told that he was being given an important and responsible assignment—to keep order during the tests of the machine invented by Ogurtsov. It was a truly fantastic coincidence!

"Oh, yes, I know," the Sergeant boasted. "Continuous action, with a copper casing, with a reverse lever. I know the inventor very well," he added.

"They're gems, those fellows in my precinct," his chief said to himself with satisfaction as he wrote out the assignment.

The test site was just out of town, near a gay birch grove. The sun shone brightly down on the platform; infrequent gusts of wind rustled among the birch leaves. As the members of the commission waited for the start of the test, they strolled under the young birches, enjoying the shady coolness. Molotkov, who had arrived first with a group of young research assistants, found a suitable spot and started a game of badminton. His strokes were agile and precise, firm muscles rolled under his tanned skin every time he swung, and he hardly ever left the spot he stood on.

"What a fine young bunch we have!" the older members of the commission said benignly, glancing at the players. "Such broiling heat, but they don't give it a thought."

Ogurtsov hurried back and forth over the experiment site, giving instructions. He had to keep an eye on everything. He took great pleasure in making the arrangements and was in an excellent mood. First, the horn had been delivered in perfect condition; there had not been a single hitch along the road. Secondly, he had unexpectedly met Petrov again—and the man was, after all, someone he knew.

"How did you get here?" he had asked the policeman.

"Oh, I've been assigned to guard you, just in case . . ." Petrov was suddenly timid before him.

"Who can be guarded against chance?" Ogurtsov said in

a jesting tone. "Take the way I first got the idea for the horn. I walked along the lane with never a thought, then I looked up—and there was the sign! Another day I might have paid no attention, but this time—wham!—and it came over me. Pure chance!"

"No, that was a lucky chance," Petrov insisted.

"Oh, well, stand guard, if you wish," Ogurtsov agreed, running off to receive the scrap.

It turned out that they had sent only one truckload.

"It's not enough," the inventor waved his arms.

"Do you really need more?" the commission member responsible for the delivery of scrap questioned doubtfully.

"It's a continuous action mechanism. No matter how much you put in, it wouldn't be enough."

"But how much do you need?" he was asked, and everyone stood still to hear his answer.

"Ten truckloads!" Ogurtsov said firmly, breaking into a sweat in his excitement. He had never had such quantities of raw materials to work with before.

When the tenth truck had left the site, the commission assembled around the horn, and Molotkov, who had already taken a swim and therefore looked especially fresh, delivered a short speech.

"There have been other instances in history," he began, "when individual inventors have outdistanced their epochs by a hundred, a hundred and fifty, or even more years. They have made discoveries that otherwise would have had to wait for their remote descendants. This is a remarkable characteristic, one might say, of human nature. Where the collective thought of society is impotent, the flash of the pioneer discoverer saves the day; where the flash does not work by itself, collective thought steps in! And so it is one for all, and all for one.

"It is to this breed of inventors that the bold experimenter Stepan Onufrievich Ogurtsov belongs. According to our estimates, such a machine could have been expected in a hundred and sixty years or so, but not any sooner. Even in the presence of the completed model, it is almost impossible, at the present stage of science, to fully comprehend the finer points of its action. Nevertheless, the model is here, before our commission, and is ready to operate."

Stormy applause greeted this introduction, and Molotkov stepped down from the dais. It was Ogurtsov's turn. He checked the electric contacts for the last time, shoveled scrap into the horn's narrow opening with his own hands, and turned the lever to the right. The horn shuddered, growled quietly, and the gray mass of trash crept into the bowels of the mechanism, as though of its own will.

For a few moments nothing came from the other end of the horn. The mysterious process of transformation went on within it. Then it whistled, sighed, and various objects began to tumble out onto the ground. It was difficult to tell what they were, for no sooner did an object appear than it was covered by the next one. The pyramid of finished goods grew as the assembled group watched. "Woolen socks," someone managed to notice. "And there's a samovar," came from the center of the group. But these were isolated voices. The great majority of the commission stood dumbfounded.

And the products still poured from the horn, astonishing everyone with their variety. At one point, a bicycle rolled out and came to a stop at the pyramid. The horn's construction was not yet ideal, and the inventor himself would have been hard put to say exactly what was to be expected.

Ogurtsov also stood before his brainchild, quite overcome. And who, indeed, could help being affected by the wonders taking place on the platform? Deep silence prevailed, even after the last splinters of wood from the huge pile of rubbish had rushed through the copper oval and emerged transformed into a long garland of pins. It was like the silence in a concert hall after a great conductor has waved his baton the final time.

And then everything burst into motion. People embraced

one another and the inventor. "Swing him, swing him!" everyone cried, and Ogurtsov flew up into the air for the first time in his life.

Only one man preserved utter calm in the midst of this pandemonium. Dressed in a large, wide coat, he stood there, pondering something with great concentration. His face reflected the intensity of his thought. "It needs verification, of course. A good deal of verification," his lips whispered. He was known among his colleagues for his extreme scrupulousness and assiduity. And also for the fact that even the most extraordinary events could not ruffle his absolute calm. It was said that he had once witnessed a severe earthquake. Buildings crashed all around him, and an abyss yawned only two feet away, but he merely commented, "How impressive are the forces of natural phenomena. When I get home, I shall have to tell the family about this."

His name was Parovozov, and his opinion was held in great esteem by many people.

As soon as the first outburst of rejoicing subsided, Parovozov stepped forward and asked, "Does the device contain a register to keep a record of the products manufactured?"

"No, I haven't invented that," Stepan Onufrievich spread his arms guiltily. "There wasn't enough time."

"Complete it, complete it, by all means," Parovozov admonished him amiably. "And now, the second point. This machine can evidently come to be of value to the economy. But to approve it, the commission must first check every aspect of its operation. Here, for instance"—he waved a slip of paper—"it is written that the construction has a reverse movement. In other words, that it can process the objects produced back to their original state. Can we see this with our own eyes?"

"That's the easiest thing," Ogurtsov smiled. "But what for?"

"Everything must be done properly," Parovozov declared.

"Well, in that case . . ." and Ogurtsov turned the lever to the left.

The other members of the commission, still excited over everything they had seen, did not pay much attention to the little interchange. "All right, what's the difference. Let's see." The victory was obvious in any case.

And the mountain of things began to melt away. Things flew clanking into the mouth of the horn in larger and larger quantities. The opening was much wider here, and could receive far more than the narrow end. Many objects rose into the air and floated around the horn, colliding with one another in response to the powerful force drawing them in. Clouds of dust rose over the area. Small twisters danced around, occasionally combining into a large, powerful one. And when a straw hat was snatched from the head of one of the observers and carried up into the clouds, the entire commission, to a man, dropped to the ground. Only the unbending Parovozov remained standing. He caught at the brim of his hat and was just about to make a pronouncement about the mighty forces of nature when a strong current of air raised him up and carried him irresistibly toward the roaring throat of the horn. His body whirled lightly in mid-air, pushed aside several smaller objects, and smoothly entered the machine with the general stream. Parovozov had not even had time to remove his hand from his hat.

No one saw this except Ogurtsov. All the others were lying pressed to the ground, trying to shield their heads with their hands. Desperately the inventor tried to pull the lever back to zero position. It was stuck! He bore down on the damned lever with all his weight, but it would not budge. "What a scandal! What a scandal!" he whispered with trembling lips, and beads of sweat rolled down his forehead.

Ogurtsov looked around. Parovozov was already half-swallowed by the horn.

"Dig in with your hands, dig in, you damned fool!" he

shouted in a voice he did not recognize as his own. Then he abandoned the lever and plunged into the stream of objects being sucked into the horn, where only Parovozov's legs were visible among the whirling armchairs, washstands, and bolts of fabric. He gripped those legs and pulled with all his strength, and both were swallowed in a cloud of dust.

Seeing that the situation was critical, the policeman Petrov covered half the distance between himself and the horn with one mighty leap, and then crawled on his belly across the dangerous storm-zone. But suddenly the horn grunted, boomed like a copper bell, and stopped by itself.

After a while the people recovered and gathered around the machine. There is no need to describe their dismay at the calamity. Besides, without Ogurtsov no one properly knew how to operate the thing. They tried to turn the lever to the right; it turned easily enough, but that was all. Only a trickle of molten metal poured out of the horn, congealing on the way. The members of the commission took out their cigarettes and silently lighted up. It was certainly a hell of a situation!

For days engineers and mechanics struggled to reanimate the horn. Their efforts proved almost totally useless. All they managed to do was restore the reverse action to some extent, so that the horn could process useful objects into scrap. Molotkov grew pale and lost weight. All those days he did not leave the horn for a moment. Someone began to revile Parovozov, but Molotkov cut him off sharply.

"It's our own fault! The Parovozovs should not be allowed within a mile of new developments. And we . . ."

Someone else blamed Ogurtsov himself for leaving no clear explanations while there was still time.

"Try and explain it," Molotkov countered wearily. "It's centuries ahead. As mysterious as human computers. They'll juggle millions in their minds, but how? Try and understand!"

The policeman Petrov suffered from the grievous loss along with everyone. Besides, it seemed to him that he alone was responsible for everything. He could not bear to meet the eyes of the commission members. How could he have permitted this outrage to occur? Such an idiotic request—to make the machine work backward! Parovozov now seemed to him one of those vicious hooligans who sauntered around idly in tight trousers. He almost convinced himself that he had once taken Parovozov to the precinct for disorderly conduct while in a state of intoxication. But he had taken pity on him, and let him go without reporting to his place of employment.

In reality, of course, no such incident had ever taken place. Parovozov had lived a most exemplary life, and no one could have brought any complaints against him.

As for the horn, it was turned over to a group of scientists for restoration. In the course of the catastrophe, however, it had been reduced to such a condition that to "restore" it meant to invent it anew. For the time being, alas, there is little hope of success. After all, not everyone is capable of an invention that only our remote descendants will be equal to!

THE USELESS PLANET

by

OLGA LARIONOVA

OLGA LARIONOVA, born in 1935, is an engineer. Her first published science-fiction story, "Kiska," apeared in 1964.

1

On the huge, faintly glimmering external viewing screen,
the city of the Geanites looked even more squalid. Especially
this section of it, spread out on the lower ledges of the hill.
No harmonious, columned temples here, no plazas paved
with violet-tinged stones.

This was the market place, one of the ugliest parts of
the city. Baskets, woven mats, more mats, more baskets, piles
of raw or semiprepared food products, covered with dust,
lying virtually on the bare ground, and everything touched
and picked up directly by hands. Fruit, vegetables, and fish
were transferred to the baskets of the buyers, and often

thrown back, if the price or the quality proved unsatisfactory. Wild gesticulation, endless curses, and filth, filth, and filth.

The Commander wrinkled his face squeamishly. Why did the two who had gone from the ship today choose to go to the marketplace? Crowds of bustling Geanites filled the screen, and it was extremely difficult to distinguish among them the two who resembled the Geanites only in appearance. Ah, there they were!

The Commander leaned forward, carefully examining the small white figure moving unhurriedly across the screen. She walked more slowly than the rest. Others overtook her, jostling her occasionally, and almost everyone who glanced at her face turned for a second look. How did she differ from the other Geanite women?

The one who had been sent out that morning to control her followed her at a distance of fifteen or twenty feet. His loose gray garment, his staff—a genuine one!—and his tousled beard attracted no attention. The girl glanced back at him occasionally, and he slowly lowered his head as if afraid of stumbling on the gravel path—a sign that everything was proceeding correctly.

And yet they looked back at her.

She herself was probably unaware of it. Now she entered a fenced-off portion of the market, lifted the edge of her tunic, and stepped across a basket with small, dark red fruit. A little old Geanite with a beard dyed a bright orange ran out with tiny steps to meet her. He must have been standing under the awning of the money changer's shop. Bending low, he spoke to the girl, offering her some ornaments. To buy? No. It seemed that he was offering to give them to her. Now he took her by the hand, gently but insistently drawing her after him. He pointed at the enclosed litter. The girl refused with gestures—evidently uncertain of the correctness of her pronunciation. That was wrong. When the collector cyber gave her instructions, he stressed that in public places,

such as streets, market, or harbor, there were often people
who spoke languages other than that of the city and its envi-
rons.

But in every other way she behaved correctly—offering
passive resistance, which did not attract the attention of the
Geanites around her.

Her control should intervene now.

Yes, there he was. Feigning blindness, he bumped into
them, sending the redbearded Geanite sprawling against the
clay wall. While he was getting up, the girl disappeared
through a gap in the fence.

And yet, what was it that attracted the redbearded
one? Why did he choose her of all the women in the marketplace?

The design for her was created by the collector cyber
after long study of the Geanites' appearance, way of life, and
customs. The details were developed under the Commander's personal supervision, and he could not discover a single
error. Why, then, did everyone look back at her, and why did
the redbearded one try to detain her?

The Commander pressed the outer communications button: "Twenty-seventh, return to the ship at once!"

One of the numerous CPs, made in the shape of small
flying creatures and positioned almost over the entire city, received the order, swooped down and dashed past, right over
the head of the Twenty-seventh. The girl stopped, then she
turned sharply and walked toward the exit from the city.
Soon she would reach the brush-covered mountains where
no more Geanites were to be seen, and switch on her levitator.

The Commander shut his eyes, allowing himself a moment's rest.

2

"Your hands," the Commander ordered.

The girl raised her hands, palms up, awkwardly pressing her elbows to her sides, and stood motionless, with her head thrown back a little, as though weighed down by the enormous knot of black, gleaming hair.

The Commander took her hands into his own, brought them nearer his eyes, and carefully examined them on every side. No, everything was correct. The oval nails, and the network of veins faintly visible through the delicate skin, and the fantastic pattern of lines on her warm palms, like tiny cracks in pink marble.

Everything was correct.

And even if it were not, could it be noticed at a distance of several feet?

The Commander let her hands go, and they dropped inertly along her body.

"Walk three steps."

The girl threw up her head still higher and took three light, gliding steps.

"Turn. In profile."

She turned.

"Walk to the wall and back, slowly."

And again: "Now, a little faster."

And again, and again, and again: "Stop. Walk. Stop. Walk. Slower. Faster. Forward. Back. Your head!" cried the Commander.

The girl started and straightened her neck.

"Could it be this?" asked the Commander.

"No," said the girl. "No."

"Why are you sure?"

"I don't know. I cannot explain it, but I feel that it's not it."

The Commander sighed, rose from his chair with an ab-
rupt movement, and approached the girl. Carefully, as if
afraid of breaking them—they were genuine, collectors'
pieces—he undid the bronze clasps on her shoulder and took
out the pin that held her tunic at the belt. The white, blue-
bordered fabric fell silently to the floor. The Commander held
the bronze ornaments in his hand for a moment, as though
weighing them, then placed them carefully on the table. Then
he picked up the white garment, went to the internal service panel, and selected the code signals for his order:

"Central storeroom. Samples of genuine fabrics."

Almost immediately the door of the horizontal chute in
the wall clicked, and the gray ribbon of the conveyor brought
out a folder with neat squares of varicolored fabrics. As he
closed the door, the Commander looked at the girl again
with close attention: wearing nothing except her wooden
sandals with their fantastically interwoven thongs of white
leather, she stood three paces away from his chair, her head
once more thrown back at a slight angle and her eyes half-
closed. But the sandals could not account for it either: like
the bronze ornaments, they were genuine.

The Commander sank into his chair and opened the
folder with samples.

If he had had the right to fatigue, he would have admitted to himself that he was dead tired.

Failures, failures, and failures. From the greatest (not a
single one of the expeditions under his command had brought
any positive results) to the pettiest, which seemed to pour
down on his head with astonishing consistency—like the present one, when the Twenty-seventh, out on her first expedition,
was recognized by the aborigines, seemingly without any reason.

Perhaps it would be best to suggest to the Twenty-seventh
that she assume the appearance of some animal, like the One
Hundred and Fortieth, who had chosen the shape of the

small black animal which often accompanied the Geanites both in their walks in the city and on their longer journeys. Yes, he should have taken her inexperience into account and advised her to choose the role of an animal. Of course, this would have narrowed her field of observation and the time she could devote to it, but the most important things were already recorded by the CPs, designed specifically for Gea in the shape of small flying creatures, which emitted piercing, through relatively rhythmic, sounds. The black and dark gray CPs hung in the sky, flitted and circled over the city, got into crannies under roofs, hid in the foliage of trees, and constantly transmitted reports on everything that came within their field of observation. The CP recorder in the ship had a separate tape for each of the mobile reporters.

The Commander placed his hand on the thermo-tumbler of the inner communications panel.

"Send Number One Hundred and Forty to me."

A black, shaggy beast entered the ship's central cabin, his claws clicking on the resonant floor. If he stood up on his hind paws, he would be as tall as any Geanite. Slowly waving his tail and dripping saliva on the gleaming floor, he went up to the Twenty-seventh and stopped motionless beside her without looking up at her.

The Commander was silent again, looking at them. And again a feeling like resentment, that vague and scarcely acknowledged feeling that rose infrequently and unexpectedly from the subconscious, swept over him. And he was no longer Captain of a ship of Collectors, no longer the Commander on his sixteenth expedition, but simply Number Four, simply an aging Logitanian, who did not have many more expeditions to look forward to. And he tried desperately to suppress this uninvited sense of grievance, which stretched into the past with bitterness, and with anxiety into the future. And he could not suppress it.

The Law of the Collectors said: "A Collector who has

prepared an exact description of the planet under study can consider his duty fulfilled."

When they leave the planet, all the members of the expedition will forget it. The Commander, however, must draw up a report and submit his preliminary conclusions on what the planet can give Great Logitania. If he does this with precision and complete accuracy, supporting his arguments with facts, he will have done all that is expected of him. His report will be studied by the Supreme Commission on the Civilizations of Other Planets, and no one except those who were with him will know what they achieved. But no, what he is saying, they will forget. They will forget everything. They will begin to prepare for their next trip, without a thought for the last.

It was ever so. But he had never felt this bitterness about it before.

The Commander carefully banished these thoughts. When he finally eliminated all feelings except concern for the fate of the expedition, he turned to the One Hundred and Fortieth and the Twenty-seventh. Two strange figures, never seen by anyone in Logitania, stood motionless before the Commander: the naked Geanite girl with her head slightly tilted back, and the black, gloomy beast. The Commander did not look at each separately but somehow at both or, to be more precise, at the space between them. And again he could not understand why the bitterness should have arisen in him precisely at this moment. Perhaps simply because those two still had flights and flights ahead of them?

"One Hundred and Fortieth," he said, once again driving away the uninvited thoughts. "Are you ready to go out?"

The One Hundred and Fortieth nodded his head, made a queer, indeterminate sound, and nervously clenched his front paw. The shape he had chosen was an excellent disguise for the Geanite city, but on the ship it was very difficult for him to eat or speak. However, discarding the disguise each time he returned to the ship and reassuming it again to go out would take up too much time and energy, and he could not allow himself the luxury.

"Any time!" the words came out hoarsely from his maw.

"You will be the control tomorrow. As always, you will leave the ship before dawn. The use of the levitator and of weapons in areas accessible to observation by Geanites is still forbidden. That's all."

The girl turned and walked to the exit, the wooden soles of her sandals tapping lightly on the resonant metal floor. Why does she walk so lightly? The walk of the Geanite women is much heavier. And she differs from all the real Geanite women, even though the collector cyber created her image on the basis of several hundred photographs. Neither the Fourth, nor the Ninety-third, nor the Hundred and Fortieth can distinguish her from the other Geanite girls. The Geanites do from the very first glance.

The Commander turned away. The door closed with a soft thud, and he was once more alone with his thoughts. And once more these thoughts carried him back to his distant homeland. He did not think about Gea. It was clear to him from the very start that it was a planet from which nothing could be expected—a useless planet.

3

Ge-a—like a bit of yellow fluff that sticks in the throat when there is not enough breath to push it out and blow it away from the lips. This frustration of the inability to pronounce it; this refusal of the simplest of the alien words to be mastered; this body, turned into a taut string, stretching from the toes which barely touch the ground to the fingertips, which lack a mere two hand-widths to reach the faceted crystals of the stars; this head, thrown back, and the

black nocturnal sky falling on the face; this rosy, transparent
mist of the spring gardens and the flowering of the sky at
dawn, reflected endlessly in one another; this guttural cry,
born of the echo in the gorge and caught up by a flock of
birds, frightened off by the appearance of the Yellow Star
and sweeping northward—Ge-a . . . Ge-a . . . Ge-a . . .

Gea is a flood of never imagined concepts, of sensations
coming in the wake of the consonance of strange words, too
soft and fluid for the Logitanian tongue—words like *Despair*,
numbing and alienating one from light and sound; like *I
Want*, unquenchable, pulsing like her two hearts; and this
strange new word, *Fear*, which came just recently, this very
evening, stopping her breath, making her want to disappear
—a word just barely discovered, not yet experienced to the
end . . .

Fear was born today, and its first cry sounded today,
when the steps of four soldiers, like the stamping of two
four-legged beasts, grew louder and louder behind her. Fear
arose somewhere outside her, distant, and yet present everywhere. It started all around, as on the line of the horizon,
and quickly spread and closed over her head, like the cupola
of a protective energy field. But this field did not protect. On
the contrary, it paralyzed all thought, stopped the flow of
blood. It made her want to do something incomprehensible
and altogether illogical—to scream, to fall on the ground. . . .
But instead the word itself came to mind, and the simplicity
of its sound instantly swept out both the newly aroused feelings and the chaos of thoughts, leaving only infinite astonishment. How had it happened that she, the Twenty-seventh, a
being subject to the strict laws of the Logitanian's inner
world, had suddenly permitted herself to descend to the level
of the Geanites, those semianimals whose conduct was gov-
erned not by reason but by hereditary instincts?

Fear, she repeated to herself. Animal fear, bequeathed by
the instinct of self-preservation. Fear of those stamping feet,

of the clanking metal, the whistling breath of the Geanites, gasping in the cool night air. This fear had driven her, and in those moments she was neither a Collector nor simply a Logitanian woman. She was a small, frightened Geanite girl.

When she understood this, she stopped.

The four who pursued her could not stop as suddenly; they ran a few more steps, and finally stopped, slipping on the clay of the hillside and squatting down with feet wide apart to halt their motion. No more than a few steps separated them from the Twenty-seventh, but they continued standing motionless, gasping from the long, fast run, greedily swallowing the air, and for some reason none of them seemed in a hurry to take those few steps.

The Twenty-seventh stood immobile, facing her pursuers. There was something inhuman in this immobility. Only a Logitanian could stand like that, without moving a single muscle, frozen in some strange pose that would seem extremely uncomfortable to the Geanites. But the Twenty-seventh was too inexperienced to notice her own mistake. Therefore she calmly looked at her pursuers, unable to understand what had driven them to follow her and why they were now timidly shifting from foot to foot when three long leaps would bring them to her.

The girl looked at the soldiers now without a trace of fear. She even felt a little sorry: the sharp sensation, newly experienced and not likely to recur, was gone. Should she report it to the Commander? This was a part of the Collector's duty. But the reports were always on feelings arising in them—feelings of Logitanians, and in those last few minutes she was not a Logitanian. What was to be done with these four? They stood and stood; they were breathing. You could always see the Geanites breathing. Ordinarily only the upper part of their torsos rose, and their lips parted slightly. But these four were breathing with their whole bodies. The air broke from their throats with snorting, gurgling sounds, and

rapid shivers ran up their bodies, starting with the legs and
rising to their bellies; then their chests swelled up and their
jaws dropped. Then a hissing intake of air by four throats,
and the bodies drooped weakly, as though the muscles were
slipping off their skeletons, and again the painful gurgling of
escaping air. But these were warriors, they were Geanites
with special training and the endurance of pack animals. Perhaps she had been wrong to run so fast?

She thought with chagrin about her control. The One
Hundred and Fortieth, the huge black beast she had lost on
leaving the tavern. Unable to follow her inside, he remained
to wait for her in the faintly lighted street. But four soldiers
broke into a fight. Then fragments of white stone were
flying, and lumps of earth, and bones fished out from the garbage bin that stood inconveniently near. And then those four
caught sight of the girl and ran after her, driving her along
dark alleys and further, beyond the city limits, toward the
sea. But the One Hundred and Fortieth was not next to her.

And now those four were standing before her, and she
could not understand: Why had they pursued her if they had
no wish to come nearer?

Perhaps she ought to say something to them. Or perhaps
she ought to turn and run again. But it was absurd to continue standing there and staring. Stupid, really. Perhaps the
best thing, for want of any other, was to switch on the levitator and rise into the air?

Suddenly she saw that the expression on the faces of the
four was gradually changing. First there was a kind of ex-
pectancy, as if they were saying to themselves: We'll catch
our breath for a moment, and then . . . This was followed
by confusion, puzzlement, and finally, fear. The same fear
that she herself had felt just before. What could they be afraid
of? She was standing in an open field; her face—the face of
an ordinary Geanite woman—was brightly lit by the moon;
she did not move. Why, then, were they afraid?

And now she heard from the distance the faint clicking of claws on the stony path. The Geanites, of course, did not hear it yet and would not see anything even if they turned. But the Twenty-seventh knew: it was her companion, and now this foolish, incomprehensible incident would at last come to an end. The Geanites turned at once, but it was too late: the beast leaped over them and, dropping at the girl's feet, instantly froze into immobility, as though it were carved in black gleaming stone. The girl still did not move.

The Geanites stood where they were a few moments longer, then one of them let out an inarticulate howl and all four dropped flat on the ground, shaken by violent, rhythmic tremors. Their teeth chattered loudly, but through this chatter she could clearly distinguish a word never before heard by a Logitanian—"Hecate!" Their trembling gave way to convulsive movements, and she saw the Geanites, their heads still down, crawling away toward the nearest copse.

A cloud obscured the moon, and in the dark she heard the rapid stamping of their feet. The erstwhile pursuers were in full flight. The moon emerged reluctantly, slowly, much more slowly than it had hidden, and it was only then that the two who remained on the sloping hill stirred. The girl lowered her head and looked at the dog. So everything turned out well, after all; there were no violations of instructions, and now they could fly back to the ship and report to the Commander. The animal raised its head and a shiver as of disgust ran through its body, causing the fur to stand up and lose its gloss. Yes, everything was straightened out, but how many stupid things had been done! And they'd have to report all of them.

The girl turned and slowly walked down. She would report everything that had happened. But she would not give away the feeling that had come over her when the copper armor of the soldiers was clanking behind her. This would not be named or pronounced aloud; it would remain with her forever. Whether it was good or bad did not matter. It was a feeling inaccessible to Logitanians, and there was no reason for them to know about it. It was a little piece of the fantastic world of Gea which she would not give to anyone.

She returned to the ship and reported in detail everything that could have been observed and understood by her companion. But she kept fear to herself.

The Commander listened to her with bowed head. How weary he was of this absurd, troublesome Gea!

If he could only give the signal now . . . A general signal for an emergency start, abandoning all the apparatus on Gea and soaring away through this stupid blue glow, going home at last, to the black peace of interstellar vacuum. That was a good way of putting it. With marvelous precision. Though somewhat prematurely.

In the gleaming white pantheons of Great Logitania there were many graves, each one like the other. But those were the graves of ordinary Logitanians. None of the Collectors, that upper caste of the Logitanian population, was lying there. Even when a Collector chanced to die on his own planet, his body was encased into a gleaming capsule and thrown out into space, far from the itineraries of the Logitanian ships.

This was where the Fourth derived the once sarcastic, then bitter, and now indifferent designation "home."

But he was not yet allowed to go "home."

There were laws and regulations, prescribing the fixed time-span of every possible type of Logitanian. Gea was a useless planet, a planet that could give them nothing, but even here it was necessary to conduct a number of investigations, to utilize the situation in training the young Collectors, to load exhibits confirming the conclusion that the planet was useless. Only then could they fly back, after first eradicating all traces of their visit. The training of young Collectors . . . Laws and regulations. Regulations and laws.

"Tomorrow we shall make the last attempt to go into the city. Control will be assumed by the Ninety-third."

4

The Commander summoned only the Twenty-seventh, and the One Hundred and Fortieth remained outside. It constantly seemed to him that his clawed paws and his matted fur defiled the gleaming whiteness of the ship's interior.

The One Hundred and Fortieth shook his head with anger, as if driving away a troublesome insect. In the daytime they plagued him mercilessly. Now it was night, and they all hid themselves somewhere. But his thoughts, persistent and monotonous, gave him no rest.

They are all doing the wrong things. This wretched girl will never become a real Collector. She looks much too attentively at this vile, disorderly world; she is drawn into the labyrinth of foul-smelling lanes in this dirty settlement. She does not and will never feel that holy hatred for everything that is not Great Logitania and that holy greed for everything that may be useful to it, which are essential for the Collector. And the old man? And even the Commander himself? Can any of them be compared to him in that infinite, blind devotion to his distant homeland which filled him during his endless wanderings?

The One Hundred and Fortieth raised his muzzle and uttered a long, anguished sound. The sound was born of itself; it meant nothing either in the Geanite language or in the language of the Logitanians. But it came from the heart, and the One Hundred and Fortieth could not determine which heart had prompted the sound—his own or that of the wretched black beast whose shape he had assumed.

He met many such beasts in the alleys and squares of this city; they differed from one another in color, size, voice, and ways. But after a while the One Hundred and Fortieth realized that there was one important thing that divided these beasts into two entirely different camps: some were home-less, others belonged to one of the Geanites.

And now, as he looked at the gleaming body of his ship, he felt sharply the vast distance between him and his master, his own Great Logitania, huge, calling him powerfully. And the moonlit bulk of the ship was but a tiny grain of sand, a minuscule part of this distant master. Overwhelmed by sudden pity for himself because he had been granted so lit-tle of the longed-for happiness of serving, he howled again and crawled on his belly toward the ship, tearfully blinking his whitish lids.

5

The next day the Ninety-third awakened in an excellent mood because this would be the last time he left the ship on this charming, absurd planet.

The Ninety-third was old and wise. The shape he had chosen was traditional with him: he always assumed the semblance of an aged, infirm native—of course, if there were any natives on the planet visited by his ship and if their shape could be copied. He knew very well that he was considered one of the best Collectors in all of Logitania, and he smiled to himself quietly about it. However, he smiled to himself about everything, and particularly about his colleagues. Even the Commander seemed amusing to him, with his constant scruples and demands upon himself and others, his ambition to be an ideal Collector, and his attempt to attain it by slavish obedience to every paragraph of the Rules for Collectors. He was also amused by the One Hundred and Fortieth, with his fanatical dedication to Great Logitania—a mythical home-land which they were permitted to see only as a reward for special achievements. He laughed without malice at that youngster, too—the Twenty-seventh, with her unspoken en-thusiasm about the first planet she has ever seen. Then will come a second planet, a third, and her transports will give way to dull indifference and then, perhaps, even to embitterment, as with the One Hundred and Fortieth—that hypertrophied sense of one's own transience, adventitiousness, and unimportance, which inescapably develops in each one of them. Planets and flights, flights and planets, and the miserable crumbs of knowledge which they stealthily appropriate for the greater glory of Logitania, without giving anything in return.

Poor youngster, he thought, following her with wide, shuffling steps along the narrow rocky lane, with its malodorous puddles of slops thrown out by busy housewives from behind the mud fences. Poor youngster, she goes into transports at the sight of the colonnades of the remarkably proportioned temples, the faultless symmetry of the whitish narrow leaves of the small trees, which look as though they were covered by a layer of powdered metal, and the generous arrangement of the little dark-blue fruit in heavy, geometrically perfect clusters. And all because it corresponds to the ideals of formal discipline maintained in Great Logitania. How many of you there are, poor youngsters, who will never learn to understand that there is only one way out—to lie and to betray. Lie to your comrades, and betray your work.

Only the Ninety-third himself knew to what extent and how long ago he had ceased to be a Collector. Upon arrival on a new planet, he was instantly able, thanks to his wealth of experience and intuition, to immerse himself in the life of its inhabitants, discovering unerringly the sources of the simple joys of the ordinary native. He did not seek refined pleasures. No, he consistently experienced all the uncomplicated, everyday delights available to the creature whose shape he assumed.

Thus, on the third planet of Remizanga he caught the forbidden blue spiders and, closing his eyes, crushed them on his stomach, causing them to give off an ineffable aroma, which plunged him for three small Remizanga cycles into a state of blissful prostration. On Nii-Naa, the sun's only planet, which had become a wasteland under the pressure of its implacably mounting population of half-wild creatures who are born eight and ten at a time, he crawled from cave to cave, leaving behind him a slippery thread of his own saliva as he searched for yellow-eyed infants. And when he found them, he snatched them up and let out a triumphant howl, calling the entire pack to the feast. Even on Copper Mountain, from which the Logitanians fled after losing half the crew, he had managed to violate four of the Six Commandments of Defense, and even to copulate with the white pteromouse Sheela, which defied classification under any laws at all.

True, this went beyond the limits of the ordinary pleasures of the average native, but the Ninety-third made an exception for himself while on the alien planet. Aboard the ship he was a Logitanian, and Logitanians generally admitted of no exceptions: it was not in their nature. Clear, immutable laws—every Logitanian was trained from infancy to obey them. And exceptions only corrupt the mind and awaken the imagination.

The Ninety-third was afraid of nothing. Along with the alien shape, he acquired alien instincts, whose call he yielded to without hesitation and even somewhat demonstratively. He knew that every move he made was observed by the numerous CPs, suspended over the entire area of action, and he did not try to conceal even his slightest move. He consistently went through every stage of pleasure, and the ship's apparatus obediently recorded all the details of his bestial state. Undoubtedly, if he were to plunge into such behavior all at once, the horrified and disgusted Commander would immediately expel him from the rosters of Collectors and annihilate him physically. But his entire secret was that he had gradually accustomed the Commander to regard his exploits as acts of selfless service to Great Logitania. Exhausted and full of protestations of self-loathing, he would appear before the Commander, and without concealing an iota of what the CPs could have observed, he would describe with utmost exactness the inner world of the aborigines. And invariably, as compared with the inhabitants of Great Logitania, these turned out to be stupid and carnal animals, corrupted by their second signal system. With implacable sacrificial zeal, he recalled in carefully chosen words all the most shameless aspects of the pleasures he had experienced, abominable from the point of view of both the natives and the Logitanians. The resulting portrait of the native was always vile and convincing.

And the Ninety-third himself had long acquired the unshakable reputation of an expert in the psychology of sapient creatures of other planets. It must be said that the preservation of this reputation required no special effort on his part.

Now he was following the Twenty-seventh in wide, measured steps. As he walked, his sharp knees outlined themselves so clearly under his shabby garment that it seemed they must cut through it at any moment.

The lane they were ascending circled a steep hill. Fragments of violet-tinged stone rolled down underfoot. The cross-streets running downhill breathed morning freshness, mingled with the smells of newly caught fish and the large striped fruit that grew directly from the soil. The rays of the rising luminary, called Helios on this planet, gave almost no warmth, but the dreary clay fences covered with fantastic stains of diverse origin suddenly turned a delicate golden pink. Helios would rise, and this astonishing hue would disappear. But the Ninety-third had only a short distance left to go, and until he reached his destination, the morning Helios would spray his path with the petals of yellow and red roses.

The old man clicked his tongue. He was on the way to a tavern.

This dim, barnlike structure opened at dawn, or perhaps

was never closed at all. No one cleared the rough wooden tables. The sleepy harlots returning from the lower streets passed their hands over them in search of leftovers before retiring to their cellar.

The old man chose a place near the door, which commanded a view of the well-trodden area before the tavern and the narrow lanes running down to the sea. Until now, he had followed the Twenty-seventh at a distance of several steps; it was time for her to get accustomed to act independently. True, he would still be nearby and ready to come to her assistance, for every time she came out into the city the Geanites literally would not leave her alone, a circumstance which constantly puzzled the Commander, that—the old man carefully sought for a most suitable epithet in the Geanite language—that cretin.

For a time Ninety-third watched the girl ascending the hill, her hand holding down her garment to keep it from flying up in the wind. Then he took a plain clay bowl from his canvas sack and placed it before him. He knocked on the table with his knuckles and craned his neck. The Twenty-seventh was still visible. A stocky slave, his bare feet gripping the stony hillside, was evidently taking a shortcut to the sea, where the quavering bell of the fishermen was already calling the first buyers. The slave kept turning his head, throwing hurried, greedy glances at her, as all Geanites on her way would do. The Ninety-third gathered his scanty beard into his fist and narrowed his eyes. He understood very well why this happened. In fact, *understood* was the wrong word: he was simply drawn to her himself, and it was the call of an instinct unknown to Logitanians.

Everything proceeded as it should, and the old man rapped the moist boards of the table again.

The mistress appeared in the doorway, shutting out the light: there were no windows in the tavern, and the lamps were not lit. The old man opened his fist; a small coin clung to the wilted brown skin. The mistress leaned forward and snatched the coin; she was certain that the beggar had stolen it somewhere at night. The money was instantly transformed into a bowl of yesterday's fish and a small cup of light-colored wine, smelling of damp, rotting grass. The old man drank and tugged at his beard again. The wine was poor. Wretched. And once again he rapped the table impatiently. And another coin, a larger one, disappeared in the folds of the woman's garment, and the woman suddenly began to move lightly and rapidly. Then more wine. And another coin. And still more wine.

The coins had, naturally, been stolen the previous night (forging them would have taken too much time). In the Commander's eyes, this was an act of extraordinary courage in the name of the purity of the experiment and the glory of Great Logitania. To the old man, it meant the satisfaction that any Geanite pauper would feel at coming into a pile of money without the expenditure of much effort (it was obtained with the aid of the Logitanian levitator and silent plasma cutters).

Today he was spending that money.

That was luck again.

He sipped cup after cup, slowly getting drunk. Space gradually shrank around the bowl of roast fish, wrapping the old man in a gray, dull, humming cocoon of intoxication. His head dropped lower and lower, and when the Twenty-seventh ran past the tavern back toward the ship, as though escaping from invisible pursuers, he did not even notice her.

6

The door of the cabin creaked, and the Twenty-seventh turned around. The Commander stood on the threshold.

"When did you return?"

The Twenty-seventh did not answer. The Commander

frowned; it was an unnecessary question. Of course he knew better than anyone else at what moment she had left the ship and when she had returned. But that was not the main thing.

The Twenty-seventh had changed her clothes.

She wore the same tunic she had worn that morning, and the same sandals, but now everything was dazzlingly white. And not only her clothes. How was it he hadn't noticed it before? Her lips, skin, eyelashes—everything was white. An unnatural, inanimate whiteness, not dull, but gleaming and brittle, as if the Twenty-seventh were carved of a large piece of ice. The face was utterly white, as were the eyes, and in this lifeless mask the pupils were like black sparks, now shrinking, now widening, alive.

"Why did you change your appearance?"

The Commander looked at the Twenty-seventh again and realized that she simply had no intention of answering him. "Last night you ran from four Geanites and could not tell me why. This morning you returned without carrying out your assignment, and again you cannot tell me why. During the day, you've made this clothing, although you could have worn the regular expedition uniform, like the other Collectors," he went on, pointing at his clothes. "Why?"

The girl did not stir. Even her pupils were no longer alive. The Commander turned, circled the small cabin several times, his shoulder brushing against the walls. Rhythmic movements should aid the thinking process. What could he do with the Twenty-seventh now? He tried to remember the regulations. "The planet, which cannot offer anything to Great Logitania, should be utilized as a training ground for young Collectors." He could recall nothing else. But training required maximum activity of the entire organism, and the Twenty-seventh seemed to be in a strange state of shock, although her controls insisted that there were no reasons for it. Hence, it was necessary to bring her out of this state.

"This Gea," he said, "at which you look with more attention and interest than your duty as a Collector requires, is doomed to perish in the near future."

The girl raised her chin and looked straight at the Commander, and her glance went through him with such astonishing ease that he had an impulse to turn and see what it was that she was scrutinizing through him.

It gave him a strange, disturbing feeling.

Neither the dignified hypocrisy of the Ninety-third, nor the all-encompassing and inexhaustible hatred of the One Hundred and Fortieth, had ever troubled him. But now, under the direct gaze of those eyes—not even eyes, only pupils —he paused and for the first time did not believe what he himself was planning to say. It was logical, wise, necessary. But it was a lie.

The Commander turned away. This was delirium. He had thought things over carefully; his ideas were harmonious and logical; they even had a certain elegance. Everything was right. He must speak, he must destroy Gea in the soul of this stubborn brat while they were still there.

If he did not, she would carry Gea with her. She would not be able to forget it as she went to another planetary system, on a new assignment. The rules and regulations were clear on this point: a Collector must collect but not remember. When a ship leaves an alien planet, all information about it must be recorded on the CP tapes; all the samples of the material culture must be stored in the special containers designed for this purpose. But the minds of the Collectors must be free of memories about the planet just abandoned and ready for work on the next one, where, according to the theory of probability and the data provided by the innumerable past missions of the Logitanian ships, the Collectors would face entirely different conditions, forms of life, and civilizations. Although, in fact, the latter would in most instances be lacking.

The Commander walked along the wall again, carefully thinking over his next sentence, and suddenly, without turning, he said, quite unexpectedly to himself: "But Logitania was once so very much like Gea . . ."

It is difficult to imagine how blasphemous this was—comparing Great Logitania, even in the distant past, with the savage world of the ignorant Geanites!

But no, he thought, it never really reached this stage. What we observe on Gea is not a lower stage of civilization but its premature decline. Logitania was rescued in time. Here, on Gea, the government is too dispersed and therefore too weak to subjugate to itself the entire economic and political life of the planet. The population of Gea is divided, and there is no power that can subject it to a single goal and a single law.

What is it, though, he asked himself, that determines the inevitability of the end of civilization on Gea?

The information cybers sent into numerous orbits around the planet indicate that the levels of development of the various local tribes are extremely varied.

But not only does each tribe, each center of civilization have its own government; each government is subdivided into a number of sectors—state authority, military authority, religious authority, spy systems maintained by each sector against the others. What can be the future of such tribes?

Without a strong, centralized government, they are extremely warlike. Each seeks to swallow the other. And every time an active individual comes to power, each tribe rushes to expand its lands at the expense of its neighbors, never wondering whether it would be able to keep the conquered group in subjection. Seizure is preceded by peaceful espionage, in the form of trade.

And so, the leader, the king, or more rarely the head priest, launches a war, and does it in his own interests. This is logical. But returning with his spoils, he divides them between himself, the state treasury, which is not always entirely at his disposal, the priestly caste, and the numerous nobility. In other words, he quite illogically strengthens the elements, to the subjugation of which he devotes the greater part of his energy.

In case of victory, the troops also enrich themselves outrageously, which leads to their disintegration, corruption, and loss of maximum efficiency. The warriors acquire slaves, and every erstwhile subject—even the lowest subject of his king —begins to feel a master over his own slaves. This leads to a sense of independence in the thinking of the lower castes.

Besides, we encounter on Gea phenomena entirely unknown in Logitania—the creation of so-called works of art. This is a useless and logically unjustified expenditure of energies and resources. From the point of view of the Logitanians, all the servants of the arts and their works ought to be exterminated for the good of the Geanites themselves. But Logitania is not concerned with philanthropy. Hence I devote almost no attention in my report to the problems of art and take only a few samples with me.

What, then is taking place on Gea? The lowest strata, involved with their families, their slaves, their possessions, get out of the habit of absolute obedience. The upper strata become much too numerous, fat, dull, and utterly corrupted by art. The masses of slaves resent their position only because they can compare themselves to the poorest freemen, who live better than they do, and are therefore always ready to rebel. Such a society is obviously ready to be wiped off the face of Gea by neighboring savage hordes.

And this is what will surely happen.

It will keep happening until all civilization on Gea totally destroys itself. Is there any natural means of preventing this? No, for the Geanites multiply too rapidly, the land will not be able to sustain their ever increasing numbers, and expansionist wars are inevitable.

Could Logitanian civilization be implanted on Gea by forcible means?

Of course it could. Several hundred large Geanite cycles under Logitanian control, and we could have a young and satisfactory civilization along the Logitanian model. But then, Logitania is not interested in philanthropy.

Well, then, let us leave Gea with its just-born but already dying civilization to its own destiny, without helping it in any way and without taking anything from it. After all, it is a planet that has nothing to offer Great Logitania, anyway.

The Commander stopped. He had not spoken or thought so long and so passionately for quite some time. But everything was true, everything was correct. He acted in full accordance with the regulations.

Point One—the most important—said: "The main task of the Commander is to preserve the integrity and efficiency of the ship's entire crew."

This he would fulfill.

"Now go," he said simply.

She did, but not toward the door. She went up straight to him and stopped before him.

"I want to remain on Gea."

There was a long silence. The Commander looked at the girl, sensing with horror the irresistible apathy that was coming over him. A moment longer, and he would say, "Remain." Or even worse, "I don't care."

"Go!" he said as sharply as he could. "Straight up!"

He followed her out into the central corridor. The lounge. The central compartment. The exit platform . . . Past it.

"Upstairs!"

The first level. Storage chambers for the exhibits. All were filled.

"Upstairs!"

The second level. How lightly she walked! The women

of Gea did not walk like that. But it was no longer important.

The Twenty-seventh slowed her steps. Another door. Past it. And another. Past it. And yet another. The Twenty-seventh stumbled and fell to her knees. But there was no need to go any farther. These chambers were empty. They would no longer have time to fill them. This one, then.

"Go in."

The door shut after the girl. It could not be opened from within.

The Commander walked rapidly to the central compartment. The entire crew was on board. He switched on general communication:

"The crew will assemble in the central compartment. All CPs are to be returned on board ship. Send out the last group of transport cybers for exhibits. Rush the loading of exhibits already delivered. As soon as they are loaded, we start."

7

The floor was rough and not at all cold. The chambers were designed for storage of inorganic exhibits at the temperatures at which they were taken. The Twenty-seventh pulled up her knees to her chin and clasped her arms around them. Night had just fallen. There was still so much time before dawn that even the slowest and heaviest of the transport cybers could make twenty journeys to the city and back.

Everything was not yet lost. Nothing was lost as yet. It was lucky that the Commander was in too much of a hurry to take her to still another level. Then all would indeed have been finished. But she had fooled the Commander so cleverly, and so easily. As easily and cleverly as if someone had taught her. Miracles! For it was impossible, it was logically out of the question, for a Collector to fool his Commander. But this had not been done by a Logitanian woman. She had felt like a little Geanite girl, just as she had when the four soldiers were chasing her. And this girl had played a sly trick: she chose the door she needed, and the Commander trustingly allowed himself to be tricked. It was true that this door could not be opened from within, but from without it could be opened even by a cyber.

Something rustled outside the door.

No, this was not it; it was probably a lightweight ionizer on an elastic caterpillar track. And now came the special, gulping hum of the sending mechanisms, throwing out heavy transport cybers one after the other. The first group was gone. Now they would leap softly across the mountains and suspend themselves over the city, seeking out the "snails." Together with the Ninety-third, she had scattered two or three hundred of them every day. Inside each "snail," fashioned exactly along the model of the Geanite land mollusk, there was a tiny transmitter which began to work on a specific frequency as soon as night fell. There was also a simple memory device. Before attaching the almost unnoticeable "snail" to the exhibit chosen for shipping to Logitania, the Collector dictated to the device the number of the storage chamber it was to be taken to, as well as the physical conditions required for storing the exhibit. This precluded confusion in loading.

The transport cybers found the transmitter with their locators, picked up the exhibit together with the "snail," and brought it to the ship, delivering it precisely to the specified chamber.

As he had ascended to the second level, the Commander thought that the reserve chambers of the inorganic exhibit section could not be used without his permission. He did not know that the only thing chosen by the Twenty-seventh that morning for transfer to the ship was to be delivered precisely to that chamber.

Now all she needed was to wait patiently until the cybers opened the door.

The Twenty-seventh prepared to wait.

But now the air was filled with clanking, the vibrating sobs of planetary motors, the clatter of metal feet—above, below, from the corridor, ever mounting and drowning out one another. The doors of chambers slammed, something was dragged hurriedly along the corridor, brushing the walls. The gulping hum rose and fell, rose and fell. Then it was quiet for a while.

It was clear that the ship was being readied for the start.

The Twenty-seventh pressed herself to the floor—her forehead, her palms, her whole body. But how could one distinguish the rustle of a creeping transport-cyber in this infernal clatter? Too late. Too late. She should have thought of it earlier. She should have thought of it in the morning. She should have thought, instead of speeding madly back to the ship! No, it was not even thinking that was needed. She should have listened and obeyed the voice of the Geanite girl, which had so often taught her what to do.

But that morning for some reason it had not told her that she must run away from the ship, not to it.

And now it was too late. No other group of transports went out. The loading was being completed.

There was a dull thud against the door. The Twenty-seventh jumped up to meet the sound and straightened up, dropping her arms and tilting back her head.

8

The Commander did not turn in response to sounds. The red glints of the indicators danced on the control panel. All the mechanisms were aboard ship. A door slammed, and there was a clicking of claws on the resonant floor: the One Hundred and Fortieth was back. Energy was fed into the central levitator. Excellent. The levitator would consume

enormous energy, but it would not do to rise directly on the
planetary levitators near a populated point. A flash in the sky
was something else: it would be taken for a flash of lightning. The door opened and shut again; it was the goat-
bearded Ninety-third. Zero readiness.

The Commander paused a moment, then his hand went
to the inner communication switch. No. They must start
first. He withdrew his hand.

"Start!" he said loudly and turned on the antigravitators.

The ship slowly separated itself from the surface of Gea.
The Commander switched on the external viewing screen.
The black mass without a single spot of light was dropping
away from the ship. On the right, the sea glimmered faintly.
It seemed as though the ship were leaving behind a wild,
entirely uninhabited planet. It might be useful for the Twenty-seventh to take a look at it. There could be no regret at the
sight of this lifeless blackness. The Twenty-seventh must see
it.

He shifted controls to horizontal flight and went out of
the cabin without a glance at the other members of the
crew. He ascended to the second level and found the door.

"Come out," he said to the girl. "Come out. We are
aloft."

She did not move from the spot.

"Gea is still visible," he said. "Black Gea, which had
nothing to give us. Go take a look at it."

The Twenty-seventh was silent.

"I am ordering you to come into the cabin!"

The girl did not stir. She stood with her hands along her
sides and her head slightly tilted back. The Commander
stepped across the threshold and approached her.

"You . . ." he began, and broke off. Her pupils were as
white as the rest of her face. They simply were not there.

He raised his hand and cautiously touched the high,
smooth forehead, then passed his finger down the neck and
the arm.

Stone.

For a long time he stood, trying to understand it. Then he started. What was he thinking of just now? He could not understand it at all. His mind was in confusion. She had turned to stone? Nonsense! One could assume the semblance of stone, but turn into it?

9

The girl stretched her arms, palms forward. It was completely dark, and without the pallid infrared radiation of the stones, giving off their last bit of warmth before sunrise, she could hardly have found the road she had followed yesterday with her goat-bearded escort. Before her there was still a steep ascent, sharp pebbles, which got into the sandals, and —along the edge of the hill—the dark cypresses aimed at the night sky, as though waiting for the signal to shoot up, toward the ship that was silently, stealthily moving away from Gea.

The girl passed her hand along the rough surface of the wall and found the gap of the doorway. Inside, someone growled and gurgled. There was no reason to fear: someone was making these sounds in his sleep. But she must be careful not to waken anyone. Her white dress could be seen from far; she might be pursued and lose her way. And the most important thing to her now was to find the way. With great difficulty, she had found the tavern where she had separated from the old man the previous day. He had dived into this dark, stuffy entranceway. After that she had gone on by herself.

The girl continued, retracing yesterday's path step by step. Here was the high tree-stump where women put down their jugs to rest on the upward climb. Here she had turned to a narrow path, steeply ascending the hill. Here she had seen the slave with the rush basket for fish and had quickened her steps after meeting his eyes.

And here was the hilltop where she had caught sight of that man.

There was something about him that distinguished him from the rest of the Geanites. Not his face. She did not remember his face, although she retained the memory of the pleasure she had felt in looking at him. Nor his clothing: it was quite ordinary and therefore left no impression. But the man himself conveyed a sense of some oddly hopeless, despairing calm; it could be seen in the tightly shut lips, in the light, slow gait, and in the way he had walked past her, not only without staring at her with the usual greedy, envious look of the Geanites but simply without noticing her.

What was he doing on the hill? Yesterday she could not understand it. But today, seeing before her the ashen glimmer of the predawn sky, she knew: He had come up to see the distant, cold sun rise from the sea. Yesterday she had not known it, but something impelled her toward him, anyway, and she had followed him.

They looped in and out of the narrow, damp labyrinths of the seaside lanes. The girl did not know whether they were approaching the center of the city or going away from it. The man she followed never speeded up his steps. She followed him at the same pace. But strangely, the longer this slow, calm progress lasted, the more violently she was swept with the premonition of something extraordinary, and she wanted to push him on, to make him walk faster. If she had been able to, she would have made him run. But she had to restrain herself and slow her steps, and she felt within her a growing childish anger, a distressing confusion, and a desperate fear that compelled her to shut out all thought of what would happen when they finally reached the end of their journey.

Now she walked fast. She did not walk, she flew, unerringly finding the right turns and crossings, descending lower and lower, at times almost falling in the dark gaps of the streets, until her hands recognized the damp cleft in the stone that supported the gates and the warm roughness of the vine over it. These gates, unexpectedly huge, had surprised her yesterday. The rest of the walls along that street had tiny doors, through which a tall Geanite could pass only bending his head. Yesterday she had walked into the gateway, but now the gate was locked, evidently for the night. The girl turned on her levitator. She rose silently over the vine-grown fence and descended in the courtyard. There it was even darker than in the street outside, and she found with difficulty the moss-covered stone well. Summoning all her strength, she moved the slab over its opening, then took off her belt with two flat tiny boxes—her portable viewing screen and her battery-powered levitator.

All of this, tied together, disappeared in the water with a hollow splash. Nothing more was left of the world of Logitania.

The girl came out onto the sandy path. Dawn was already beginning to brighten the sky. The light came quickly here; before you looked around, it would be day. The birds —the domestic birds that did not fly—began their morning chatter from one end of the city to the next. If that man wished to see the dim Geanite sun rise again from the sea, he would leave the house very soon.

The girl walked away from the little house with tiny, blurred windows on her left, and hiding, as she had yesterday, behind the dense wall of shrubs, she approached the shed, which loomed darkly in the depths of the garden.

When she had realized the other day that this was simply the workshop of one of those people who made unnecessary objects for decorating streets and buildings, she felt vaguely disappointed. While she was following the man she kept hoping that she would finally discover the marvelous secret of the difference between Geanites and Logitanians. She sensed with her whole being that such a secret existed and that its main charm lay in the fact that the Geanites for some reason needed one another. Until now no one had ever needed her, just as she had never needed anyone. They all belonged to Great Logitania. Their relations proceeded only from the fact that the more experienced were obliged to teach the less experienced how to use their energies and effort more efficiently and productively in the course of their service.

But here everything was different. With her very first steps on this strange planet she had realized that its inhabitants had an acute need for one another, that they were seeking for someone, and that their choice was free.

She also realized that she herself was needed by them, that each one of them needed her. And this desire of theirs to make her their property overwhelmed her and filled her with the instinctive desire to escape.

But yesterday she had met a man from whom she had not the slightest desire to escape. He was indifferent and inattentive. His face was impassive, but as she followed him she tried to imagine what would happen if this man were to behave like all the rest. With astonishment she searched herself for fear, and not finding it, she transferred to the man that greed that she was accustomed to see in the eyes of the other Geanites. She realized with wonder that the expression of carnivorous greed was simply incompatible with his face. He was a man created to possess the whole world, a kind and magical world, and, most important of all, one that submitted to him of its own free will.

She had stood behind him, with all the wonder and strangeness of a creature from an alien star, with all the goodness of a child who did not know the meaning of the word *evil*, with all her trusting readiness to learn at last why one Geanite needed another.

But she did not see herself as a part of the Gean world; she was a stranger, alien, unnecessary.

He might leave in a moment, and she would not dare to call out to him.

But he did not leave. Hidden in the shrubs, she had looked at him as he stood on the threshold of his workshop. The floor was littered with fragments of stone. Along the rear wall could be seen white vases and figurines of animals molded from warm lilac-brown clay. In the center stood a statue, covered with a light-colored cloth.

It seemed that the man was trying to see its features through the coarse fabric, and yet afraid of it, as though this swathed figure was indeed the source of his deeply hidden sorrow. So that was what made him suffer—a stone idol, an unknown divinity, a crude imitation of the human figure!

The man took a step forward, lowered his head, as if forbidding himself to look at his work, and thus, without looking, he took off the covering.

It was not a goddess. It was she, the Twenty-seventh.

The man dropped on his knees before the statue, pressed his head to its feet, and the girl saw his face.

The man was crying.

Shaken, disbelieving her eyes, she stepped back. And again. And again. This world, so unattainable to her, a world where people cried before stone figures, this world, it seemed to her, was pushing her out—a creature alien and un-initiated in its secret.

And then she began to run. Suffocating with the bitterly sharp awareness of her own alienness, with the pain of homelessness, of the impossibility of this newly born hope, and most of all with the knowledge that she meant nothing to this man, who was the only man in the whole world to her, she raced through the city, to hide in the corner of her cabin, to be alone at last. Without Geanites, without Logitanians.

But even here, in solitude, she could not calm herself. What she had seen was too incredible. How could her statue

have gotten into the workshop of the unknown sculptor?
The girl knew that making the statue had to take much more
than the three days she had spent in the city of the Geanites.
Therefore it was not her likeness that the artist had carved.
But then, whence this resemblance? Could the collector cyber,
who had gathered all the information about the Geanites before the members of the expedition had emerged from the
ship, have seen the statue and suggested to the Twenty-
seventh that she assume her shape?

No, that was impossible. Cybers never make mistakes.
The program stated clearly: On the basis of all the known information about the appearance of the women of this planet,
they were to create a composite image of a young woman
answering all the basic expectations of the Geanites. A cyber
did not simply create the average. If he encountered any deviation, anything that was regarded by the aborigines as a
flaw, he avoided it in his synthesis. As a result, the Twenty-
seventh turned out to be the ideal young woman that a
Geanite could have imagined, just as the One Hundred and
Fortieth was the most excellent dog in the city, and the
Ninety-third the most wretched beggar.

But that meant that the unknown man had also striven
to create an image of the perfect young woman?

What for?

And then the girl noticed that the "snail" she had carried
in her hand all morning was missing. The "snail" with the
number of the out-of-the-way room that had never been
used. The girl had wanted to take something with her as a
memento of her visit to the sculptor's garden and never noticed in her haste that she had dropped the tiny apparatus
near the statue.

Good. At night the feelers would wrap themselves
around the figure, lift it carefully, and deliver it to one of the
reserve chambers, where no one would think of looking. She
merely wanted to look at it—at herself, in stone. And then,

perhaps, she would grasp the elusive difference which made the man carelessly pass her by on the hilltop and later cry bitterly, with abandon, as one can cry only in total solitude, at the feet of her marble double.

He needed the stone more than he did the living being. It was beyond understanding, but she would accept it. She would turn into stone herself, as far as she could. Her garment, her sandals, her adornments. This did not take much time. Now she would drain her body of color. So. Now no one could distinguish between them.

And this was when the Commander had looked at her again. He suddenly began to speak about Gea. He remarked that she had made herself new clothing, but she did not answer his questions. And then he had launched into a logical and consistent talk about the transitoriness and the corruption of Geanite life. And the longer he muttered, the stronger became her conviction that she must remain on Gea. He spoke of their distant and great homeland, but to her there was a single corner of the universe for which she gladly would have given all her life, drop by drop. She knew that she would probably never become a true Geanite; something distinguished her from them, some unrevealed, mysterious quality, perhaps. But she did not expect that much. She agreed to become simply a thing, a motionless thing, if only she were needed by this man. The Commander spoke about distant worlds that had submitted to Great Logitania, about the infinite expanses of Space—and she laughed quietly at him, at his poverty-stricken wisdom. And she pitied him because she could not tell him everything that filled her to the brim. He would not even understand what happiness it was to be a thing, a dead, inert thing that the man from the hill would need for a moment at dawn.

She repeated it to herself for the thousandth time—only a thing that he would touch once a day, in the morning, removing the veil, a thing near which he would kneel on the

wooden floor littered with fragments of stone, with his hair
on the white marble of the pedestal . . . And then those unfamiliar dreams made her weary, and she waited unhappily
for the Commander to finish. But he spoke and spoke, as
though all he was saying still had any meaning for the girl.

He finished, and she told him, to end it once and for all:
"I want to remain on Gea."

Then came the storage chamber, the clatter and excitement before liftoff, the interminable waiting for liberation,
and the flight, so hurried that she had not even managed to
take a look at her stone double. And then the night journey
across the mountain, through the dark maze of streets, to this
courtyard, to this threshold.

10

She entered the workshop, and her feet stepped on
something soft. She bent down and picked up the linen
cloth. It was rapidly growing lighter, and the white pedestal from which the statue had been cut with silent super-
sonic knives was clearly visible in the center of the room.
The girl slowly mounted it. Now it would be her place.
The place of a thing. All morning, all day, and all evening she
would be an inanimate, motionless thing. Only at night
would she silently slip out into the garden to pluck some
fruit and get a handful of icy water from the well.

It was growing still brighter. The sun had probably lit
the summits of the nearby mountains. In the street, behind
the stone wall, somebody screamed something piercingly in a
strange, alien tongue. She must hurry.

She threw the cloth over herself and, dropping her arms,
tilted her head back just a little, standing as the statue did before her. And with her whole body she felt that the pose
was a familiar one. This was how she had stood before
those from whom she had now parted forever. It would

be easy for her to stand like this. The only discomfort was the lack of air under the dense cover. Now she must remain still and breathe as only the Logitanians could, without quivering a muscle. And then the warmth. She must lose all human warmth and become as icy as stone at night. This also only Logitanians could achieve. But she must hurry, before he came and touched her.

A door slammed in the house. The girl stood motionless. He would now walk past her into the street, on his way to the sea. What a pity she could not see him.

But today he did not go to the sea. She did not expect it, she did not want it to happen so soon. But despite her will, his steps ran quickly into the workshop, his violent hands tore away the covering with such force that she was barely able to retain her balance, and his hot human lips pressed themselves to her feet—just where the narrow thongs of her sandals crossed over her narrow, still warm ankles.

It was over, she knew. It was over. She had not had time enough, she had not expected him so soon. Now he would realize her deception, feeling the warmth of her body.

It was impossible not to feel it. He recoiled and jumped up to his feet. And now it was over. She had failed, she had not even succeeded in becoming a motionless, inanimate thing to him.

She sighed, quietly and guiltily, and made a step forward, descending from her marble pedestal.

EPILOGUE

On the right of the path there was an endless row of fantastic stone beasts. Carved in varicolored jasper, they stood with their blunt, horned heads bent low, and each one's hind paws rested on the head of the preceding one. Their polished rears were raised to the sky, from which solitary dry snowflakes fell here and there, lit horizontally by the newly risen, utterly white sun. The white flakes lay on the path, and it could be seen that someone had already passed here. Two pairs of footprints, very close to one another.

"This way," said Bina, because the footsteps on the path turned left.

Sergey released her hand. Squeezing themselves through between the violet jasper idols, they went on along the path which lost itself in a labyrinth of ruins and fragments. It was a gigantic, indescribable heap of confusion. Mysterious machines, pieces of apparatus of unknown purpose, shreds of half-decayed paintings, fragments of statues and columns, dummies and stuffed creatures, perhaps even mummies—all of them covered with a thin layer of dry snow and interwoven with clinging tendrils of creepers.

"Just imagine," said Bina, turning her head as she walked so that the wind would carry her words to Sergey. "Just imagine, all this was considered unnecessary to our Great Logitania."

"To begin with, it must be protected by a system of synthericlon cupolas. With a stable microclimate. Whatever is left must be saved. Later it should be sorted out."

"We have not gotten to it yet," Bina said apologetically. "You can see for yourself how much we must do."

Sergey was silent. Yes, they had other things beside jasper rams on their minds. Even if the rams had come from distant, alien planets.

"Here," said the girl, stopping. "Take a look."

The path was narrow, and Sergey could not stand next to Bina. He stepped behind her and put his arms around her shoulders.

Bina threw her head back, and Sergey felt with his lips and cheek the nearness of her warm, lovely face.

"But look," she repeated. "Look."

He glanced up.

Before him, directly on the snow, without any pedestal, stood a marble statue. A statue of an earthly woman of extraordinary beauty.

"It is the Twenty-seventh," said Bina. "Remember?"

"Oh, no," Sergey exclaimed. "She is one of us, an earthly woman. Only . . . Only there is no one like her on earth. Such beauty can only be imagined."

Bina laughed.

"She is a Logitanian. A most genuine Logitanian, one of the Collectors' caste. There were still castes at that time. This statue was found by their commander, I think he was called the Fourth. And then the first detachment of those who had resolved to fight for the right to a human life, for freedom of the heart came here. They needed her, you see. She was like . . . Like a symbol, like a banner. Do you know on Earth what a banner is?"

It was Sergey's turn to smile.

"We on Earth know it well. When you go into battle, it's somehow easier with a banner. True, when it comes to hand combat you sometimes forget it. And when everything is over, you get up and shake yourself, and then it must perform the saddest of its tasks—cover the dead."

"How do you know this?" asked Bina. "Do such things still happen on Earth?"

"Not on Earth. But I am a cosmonaut."

"Yes. I cannot forget it for a moment. Because of all the vast meaning of the word *cosmonaut*, I know only one—that you must leave."

"But . . ."

"Be still," Bina said quietly. "Please. Let us stand here awhile, without speaking."

They stood silently, and there was nothing around them but the slanting rays of the rising sun, the scattered snowflakes, and the white marble woman standing directly on the snow—and Sergey's hands, so huge in comparison with Bina's

slender shoulders, and her two hearts, beating with a frightened, discordant rhythm under those hands.

There were steps behind them.

"That's all," said Bina. "That's all. Let's hurry. They are
waiting for us."

She pulled him by the hand. They went around the
statue and rapidly walked down the path, but Sergey halted
and looked back.

"Bina," he asked. "Why do people come here now?"

Before the statue two young people stood still, just as
they had a moment earlier. The young man's arm was around
the girl's shoulders, and both were silent. Those two had such
faces that Sergey repeated: "Why do they come here?"

Bina turned away. Then softly, so that Sergey could
barely make out her words, she said: "It is our custom . . ."

Sergey looked at those two, standing, solemnly hushed
before the statue of the Twenty-seventh, and he knew what
the custom meant.

"Bina," he said, "I am a fool, I am a total idiot, forgive
me . . ."

He kissed her small, warm face. She closed her eyes as
though she wanted to cry, but in reality she was simply very
happy and very ashamed in the warm darkness of her closed
eyes. And when she opened them at last, there was no one before the statue. Only the snow was falling. And she laughed
happily because there was sun and mushroom snow at the
same time, and said:

"It is a mushroom snow, it makes mushrooms grow, you
see!"

"I don't see," said Sergey. "I don't see anything, and
there is no such thing as mushroom snow."

"Silly, where did you learn all this vile logic? Here?"

"No, I haven't learned it. I've lost it altogether. That was
the last drop."

Steps were heard once again behind them, and two others
stopped before the statue of the Twenty-seventh.

"Come now," said Bina.

"Yes," Sergey agreed. "But we must come here again before I start. Perhaps she'll want to send a message to someone
on Earth."

"Why are you so certain that she remained on Earth?
There are no documents on that flight: all the archives
burned down during the uprising. All that is left is the statue
—and the legend."

"You know, we have a similar legend on Earth. . . . I'm
trying to recall it, but it escapes me. Only fragments. But
there is such a legend. And then the stone is earthly, ordinary
earthly marble. And the beauty is miraculous but earthly too."

"No," said Bina. "It's simply that you have a strong wish
for all this to have happened in your homeland. But think of
it yourself: the planet where the Twenty-seventh remained
was classified as a useless planet, a planet that had nothing to
give Great Logitania. Think of it, could it have been the
Earth?"

"I guess not," Sergey agreed reluctantly. "Then it was not
the Earth. What a pity . . . But I guess it wasn't."

THE ULTIMATE THRESHOLD

by

HERMAN MAXIMOV

HERMAN MAXIMOV, a young writer who lives in Alma-Ata, in Kazakhstan, began to publish science-fiction stories in 1965.

> On orders from Lak-Iffar-shi Yast, a House of Death was erected. This House existed one and a half periods. When a Ling who wore the red badge testifying that he had attained his majority wished to cut the thread of his life, he came there. And he was never seen by anyone again . . . This House had been built by a Master Mechanic by the name of Velt. And it was he who destroyed it.
>
> —*History of the Planet Sym-Kri,*
> Section 76, Paragraph 491.

"Is your decision final?"

The inscription ran across the width of the door, from right to left. The letters, once painted yellow, had peeled and darkened. The all-pervasive dust had settled on them in a thin crust. The plastic-coated door frame was covered with hurried notes and names, scratched out by those who had entered the door, never to return. In the corner there was a pile of things discarded by the thousands who had passed through—devices for telling time, bracelets, metal pillboxes for cana grains.

"Is your decision final?"

He had to answer the question. A single word. Velt hesitated a moment, trying to still his hammering heart. Then he breathed, just audibly:

"Yes."

The door did not stir. Its green electric eye watched every movement he made. The tunnel smelled of damp. The light bulb, shrouded in cobwebs, burned dimly. A lifeless silence hung in the stagnant air. Only up above, somewhere along the circular road, the one-seat chitoplatforms were chattering far, far away: clack, clack, clack . . . Against his will, Velt strained to catch the faint sounds penetrating into the underground passage from the surface. They meant movement, and hence, life. Clack, clack, clack—as though someone pitiless were driving nails into his head, his breast, his heart. Velt stood, listening to the distant sounds of life, and felt that he was almost drained of resolve. In a moment he would back away, turn from the dreadful door, and run. Run, driven by terror. Run until his heart was bursting with blood and he had flung himself upon the sun-warmed grass and smelled the welcoming earth.

And then? Then the past would come back. While he was here, the pangs of conscience, the waking nightmare, the nights filled with thoughts as heavy as stone—all these were behind him. The tears of mothers, the cold hatred of fathers and brothers, the last curses of those before whom this door, and the twenty other doors to the House of Death had opened—all these were behind him. While he was here. But all of it would return with daylight, with life. And something new would be added—self-contempt for the moment of weakness.

Velt stretched his hand and touched the raised, discolored letters. They were cold and rough: "Is your decision final?"

"Yes!" he said loudly and distinctly, although every nerve, every cell of his body shrieked "No." "Yes!"

The steel door noiselessly slid up, opening the way. A cold light spilled into the passageway. Velt tore his disobedient feet from the ground and entered the bright space. The heavy door slid softly down behind him.

It was difficult to guess the dimensions of the room. It was seen at the same time as infinitely vast and infinitely small. This effect was produced by mirrors. Space, compressed and endlessly reflected by the mirrors on the walls, floors and ceilings, became an illusion. It seemed that even time, weary of tossing from wall to wall, stopped still and thickened, thrown back to the center of The Room of the Last Confession. Velt's reflections stared at him from all sides—thousands of Velts, with gaunt faces and bewildered eyes. A clumsy, incorporeal host, they crowded the smooth walls. Broken, they hung from the ceiling and crumpled themselves underfoot, as though fused into the floor. Velt was alone with himself. The mirrors splintered him into a multitude of fragments, and each fragment—he sensed it almost palpably—robbed him of another minute of his life, another particle of his dreams and fleeting hopes. So little remained in him that there was no longer any reason for regrets or fears. And this sensation of sudden emptiness within passed over into calm indifference. The calm of the doomed. Velt walked to the corner and lowered himself into the single chair by a low metal table. The chair was shabby, with a sagging seat.

And the confessor machine began at once:

"Life will go, but the holy fire of the great Chimpo will continue to burn," the machine uttered the ritual formula.

"Who are you, who have stepped across the ultimate threshold?"

The voice was soft and gentle and so familiar that Velt started and involuntarily glanced around, looking for the only one to whom this voice belonged. His senses lied to him: the room was empty, and only thousands of silent reflections looked back at him. His senses lied, but he could not and did not wish to resist the deception. He leaned back against the chair and plunged into the bottomless pool of memory. The cold squares of the floor dissolved, scattered into the soft, warm dust of a country road, and Velt himself became a small boy in a short ati, just above his scratched knees. His mother was calling him, and he ran, hopping and skipping, to his house, raising fountains of dust.

"Who are you?"

He ran up to her, threw his arms around her, and hid his face against her warm, soft stomach. And she stroked his disheveled head and spoke to him. He could not remember what she said, but her words were tender and a little sad.

"Who are you?"

By an effort of will he shook off his numbness. The ghosts of the past melted and vanished. Childhood disappeared in the abyss of time.

"I am Velt-Nipr-ma Gullit, Master Mechanic, Honorary Ling of Sym-Kri."

"Where and when were you born?"

"In the village of Ikht, on the seventh knot of the Great Canal, in the year of the blooming of the sky blue rea. It was four periods and seven revolutions ago."

The machine was silent for a moment, as though weighing his words. Then something squeaked and quavered in the apparatus concealed in the vault of the ceiling, and the mechanical confessor . . . broke into song.

> This little ling
> Has twelve misfortunes.

> He laughs,
> But don't believe him . . .

The machine sang in a gruff, old man's voice, shouting the words with reckless abandon. Frenzy, animal terror, despair and devil-may-care gaiety were all mixed up in the hoarse flow of song blared out by the mechanical throat. In the belly of the machine something cracked, squeaked, crunched, as if someone invisible were driving over broken glass. Velt felt as though someone had punched him on the chin. He jumped up and stared at the ceiling with terror-stricken eyes. Thousands of reflections jumped up with him, staring up. The machine sang. It was unexpected and absurd. It was like delirium. The machine could pray with the one preparing to die, it could weep with him, console him. But it should not sing. He knew that very well.

> He has no other home
> But the House of Death . . .

The song broke off, and the machine asked in the official tone of an interrogator: "Did you say good-bye to those with whom you are bound by blood ties?"

Velt could not speak. His lips trembled. He stood in the middle of the room and saw the doomed rushing about in terror in this mirrored crypt, hammering their fists on the steel door, forgetting that it could not open while they were alive. And the machine, gone berserk, howled street songs intermingled with sacred psalms. Confession, turned into torture.

"But how could I have known it's gone out of order?" he said aloud, as though justifying himself before his reflections. "How could I have known?"

The reflections were silent. Velt felt in his pocket, brought out several grains of cana, and threw them into his mouth. The narcotic acted immediately; a light veil dimmed his consciousness, his nervous tension subsided, and his muscles relaxed.

"How could I have known?" he repeated, sinking into the chair.

"Did you say good-bye to your relatives?"

"I have no relatives," Velt replied wearily. "I am the last of the Gullits."

"Your friends?"

"There are few honest Lings left in Sym-Kri. I have no friends."

"Friend, friendly, friends," said the machine. "To make friends, to befriend, friendship . . . Whom shall I notify?"

"The Supreme Keeper. He will be pleased."

Yes, the Supreme One would be pleased. He did not know how to forgive insults. And the letter that Velt had sent him was demanding, and therefore insulting to a tyrant. Velt's imagination, stimulated by the narcotic, obligingly painted for him a picture of the short fat Lak-Iffar-shi Yast examining a small black cardboard square with the symbol of the House of Death and Velt's name punched on it, then turning with feigned sorrow to the officials accompanying him: "What a loss! Our best Mechanic, Velt, has killed himself." "It should have been expected," one of the officials, most likely the lanky Kut-Mu, would respond. "He behaved rather strangely of late." And everyone would smile. Just faintly, so as not to violate propriety.

"What good did you do in life?"

The confessor machine calmed down, as if it, too, had chewed some of the red cana seeds. Its voice was soft and intimate again, despite the occasional notes of concealed anxiety.

Velt shrugged his shoulders, forgetting that the machine would not understand his gesture. Had he done anything good? He must have. It is difficult to live through four long periods without having done anything worthwhile. But what? Velt closed his eyes: it was easier to remember that way. Well, for example, he had designed the "hard triga," a whole system of machines that made it possible to extract the rich deposits of the Second Material. That was good. Or why would they have raised his statue on the shore of the White Lake, next to the statues of the great thinkers and mechanics of Sym-Kri? He had discovered the Law of the Wave. His work had been appreciated: he became the three hundred and seventy-sixth Honorary Ling of the Planet. He had staged a colossal experiment with Flying Darns and had won in the debate with the Dogmatists, who had brought the Science of Things to a dead end. But this was not the main thing. He was simply evading the question, trying to deceive himself. The main thing . . .

"I created you!"

"Me?"

"Yes. You, and the whole House of Death."

The silence lasted an eternity. The machine was thinking over the answer.

"Are you telling the truth?"

"No one lies at the last confession."

"They lie," the machine said with conviction.

"But I am telling the truth. I, Master Mechanic Velt of the Gullit family, built this House."

"Very well," the machine said in a conciliating tone. "If this is so, you must know what awaits you."

"I know."

"Tell me."

Velt thought, with a wry grin: It's testing me. Like a teacher, with a bragging schoolboy.

"When the confession is over, you will open the door to the Stairway. Forty-two steps. One of them—I don't know which one you will select this time—carries a high electric charge. A sudden shock, and you will throw me, no longer alive but not yet dead, into a pool filled with a solution of Quatre. In seven seconds, nothing will remain of the Honorary Ling."

"The plastic buttons will remain," the machine said, and it seemed to Velt that its tone was aggrieved. "They don't dissolve. I've had to clean my drain pipes three times already because of them."

Velt suddenly wanted to laugh. He felt more gay than ever before in his life. He was simply bursting with merriment. He felt the tickling lump of laughter roll irresistibly from chest to throat, from throat to lips. So it had worries too! Plastic buttons! It cleans its drain pipes and probably grumbles at its task like an old woman mending her grandson's old ati. It isn't concerned about the destinies of those who knock at the doors of the House every day, it doesn't give a damn for them at all. . . . If only their buttons aren't made of plastic.

"You laugh," said the machine. "This happens with many. I understand—nerves."

Something gulped again in the mechanism. Some incomprehensible struggle went on inside it. Inarticulate sounds—muttering, whistling, hissing—were trying to break out of it. The machine almost shouted the next question, trying to drown out the noises.

"And now tell me, what were the evil things you did in life?"

The noise mounted. The sounds came in waves and, finally, spilled out into the room. They filled it to overflowing, they screamed out some pain of their own and beat against the mirrored ice of the walls. And suddenly there was silence. The sounds died out all at once. And only a single gong was striking brassily.

"They are always like that," said the machine. "They won't lie peacefully in the repository."

"Who?" Velt asked, puzzled.

"The diagrams I make of everybody after confession. There are too many of them, and they are always trying to break into the speech circuit. Sometimes I cannot control them and they scream through the speaker. But you did not answer my question."

"Yes," said Velt. "I have done evil too."

"What?"

"I created you."

"I don't understand it," said the machine. "You contradict yourself. You have just called it a good act."

"Good can be evil, and evil can be good."

"This is contrary to logic."

"But it is so."

"I cannot understand," said the machine. "I am tired. Every Ling is a new problem, and two blocks are out of order in my problem-solving mechanism."

"You will not understand this even if you have a thousand functioning blocks instead of six."

"But I want to understand."

Velt found the last grain of cana in his pocket. Stupid machine. What, in fact, is it seeking to understand? Life? But life is above logic. Love and hate, joy and sorrow, happiness and disillusionment—can these equations be solved without error? Who can determine where one ends and the other begins? In the tangle of thoughts and feelings one can lose his way as easily as in the forests of Katonah. And wander, lost, for an entire lifetime. Like himself. And, finally, come out upon the open road and realize that it leads to the House of Death. Stupid machine.

"I want to understand," the machine repeated.

"What?" asked Velt.

He bent over the table and pressed the yellow button on the side. A round lid flipped open in the center of the table, and the automat served up a tall slender goblet. It was filled to the rim with the juices of wine fruits and the tuck tree.

"Why you said that you had done a good thing when you created me?"

Velt took his first sip and listened within, waiting for the moment when the pleasant warmth of intoxication began to spread through his body.

"I was convinced that I was doing something good and necessary. I felt that it would help Lings . . ."

"To die?"

". . . to live."

"I don't understand."

Of course. It was useless trying to explain this to a machine. How could it ever understand that true freedom was, first and foremost, the freedom to dispose of one's own life? Why should a Ling go on living if he no longer wanted to? Why could he not follow the example of the sainted Chimpo who, when his work was finished and his life was no longer needed by anyone, mounted the bonfire? These were his thoughts when he, the best Mechanic of the Planet, was developing the project. And these were his thoughts for some time after the House of Death had been built. And others constantly supported and reinforced him in this view. The Supreme Keeper himself had discussed this subject with Velt many times. He spoke of the crisis plaguing the Planet's economy for almost six periods. He spoke of the millions of unemployed Lings who would have chosen to commit suicide but dared not for fear that their funerals would place too heavy a burden of expense upon their loved ones. To them and others like them, he said, the House of Death would be a blessing. And the aged? The helpless old with trembling hands and eyes expressing nothing? They were like a stone around the neck of their families, extra mouths supported by society. "When I am old," Lak-Iffar would say, "and my hands tire of holding the Sacred Sceptre, I shall go to the House of Death myself." And he also said, "A Ling who has lost interest in life but goes on living is not only useless but is also harmful to society. Such Lings sow the seeds of disorder: they do not value their own lives, and therefore they do not value the lives of others. The forty-two classes into which our rational society is divided are a ladder by which generations enter history. And each successive rung of this ladder rests on the preceding one. Those who have lost interest shake the foundations of our order, hoping that the ladder will collapse over their heads. They want to die, and we must help them." Velt nodded in agreement and marveled at the wisdom and humaneness of the Keeper.

But not everyone understood the Supreme One's wisdom. Many were against the idea. They condemned it.

They said: it is a lie.

They said: it is blasphemy.

They said: it is a crime.

Perhaps there was some truth in these words, but it was the petty truth of those who are unable to look into the future, the truth of cowards. It did not declare itself loudly and in everyone's hearing. It slipped into the ears as a timid whisper, it clothed itself in the transparent vestments of hints, it retreated and hid itself as soon as one attempted to take a closer look at it. It was too fragile, this truth, and the Supreme One destroyed it with two words—*social demagogy*.

Lings spoke. They whispered from around corners. And he, Velt, went on with his work. He chose a good place—a little valley among the Obsidian Cliffs. He carved the House in the heart of the black rock, with twenty-one tunnels leading into it from the surface. He built an automatic circular road that precluded the possibility of anyone meeting another seeker of death at the ultimate door. He foresaw everything. He surrounded the house with a protective field, he devised foolproof machines; together with psychologists, he developed the program for the confessional. He was building for the centuries, hoping somewhere deep in his heart that he was building a monument to his genius.

"Did you make life easier for the Lings by building the House?"

Velt started. He had forgotten the machine. He had forgotten where he was and why he had come. Very little juice remained in the goblet. He shook it, and a grayish, muddy sediment rose from the bottom.

"No," said Velt. "Everything turned out contrary to expectation."

Yes, everything had turned out contrary to expectation. Fighting for a false humaneness, he had challenged true humaneness. The appearance of the House of Death legitimized suicide and even encouraged it. The promise of an easy end tempted Lings who were oppressed by the burdens of living. And they came to the steel doors and said "Yes." And the doors to nonbeing opened before them. Many came—not only those who were driven by suffering but also those who were led by petty grievances and momentary delusions. And then death became fashionable.

The House became a symbol of fate, a symbol of defeat. Its existence paralyzed the will and robbed struggle of meaning. It drew a sharp line between desire and possibility of realization. It brought, not freedom to live, but only freedom to die. A lie instead of hope, confession instead of food, indifference instead of hatred. That which he had hoped would be a healing balsam for sufferers had turned into salt corroding their wounds.

And the timid truth that had been trampled into dust raised its head and filled Velt's nights with ringing whispers. Whispers that were screams, whispers that were weeping. So cries the night bird Shoon over the roof of a house visited by misfortune.

It cried: a lie!

It cried: blasphemy!

It cried: crime!

It cried that he, obedient to an evil will, had brought the Planet sorrow, that he was living like a blind man, afraid to open his eyes.

It is terrible to lose faith in oneself from day to day. It is the same as walking toward an abyss blindfolded. The letters he received burned his hands, thousands of letters filled with curses. And the mountains of black cardboard squares delivered to him daily by pneumomail. He did not know the names stamped on them. But they screamed at him, those silent cardboard squares, neatly engraved with two letters known to everyone: "HD." It was impossible to hide from them.

He tried to hide. He escaped to the Second Continent, buried himself in the wildest, remotest region, worked to the point of stupefaction. He put space between him and the black squares and shut himself off behind a dozen secretaries. But he could not escape from himself and from his Shoon bird.

A period and a half away from society. He should have been forgotten: time erases a great deal from the mind. But the first person to speak to him when he stepped out of the superplane and walked down the ladder reminded him of the House. It was an old woman with a face that was all wrinkles. She touched his sleeve and asked, "Tell me, most respected sir, it isn't frightening?"

"What?" he did not understand her question.

"Oh—out there, in your House . . ."

He recoiled from her. But she clung to his clothes and spoke rapidly.

"He was just a boy, he had just received his red badge . . ."

He broke away and ran, pushing others aside.

And in the evening he had a visit from Uram-Karakh, who had told him about the tablets. "They're infinitesimal," Uram whispered, "like specks of dust. One is enough to produce an irresistible longing to die. Var-Lush, Kam-Dan, Fot-Grun—you didn't think they went voluntarily? Who can tell Lak-Iffar now that he violates the Nine Rules? No one. Do you understand?"

Velt finished the juice, carefully placed the goblet back on the table, and said to himself, It's time to finish.

"You still have four minutes," said the machine. "The time for confession is not up."

"Let eternity which awaits me be four minutes longer."

"You are in a hurry to die?"

"No, I am in a hurry to destroy you."

"Destroy me? But you cannot do it."

"I created you."

"You have no weapons."

"I am myself the weapon."

He rose, smoothed his clothes, and smiled: force of habit.

"How do you intend to do it?"

He knew that it would not be able to prevent him. If he had carried weapons, it would not have opened the door to him; it would have foiled any attempt to destroy it from outside. The House was too well protected from without. But by letting him in, the machine had signed its own death warrant. The program did not provide for defense against a living bomb, and he had turned himself into one.

"Before coming here," he said, "I swallowed two small portions of Sitane."

"What is Sitane?"

"A substance. A powder. When I fall into the pool, the Sitane will come into contact with the Quatre, and . . ."

"Explosion?"

"Of colossal force."

"I see," said the machine. "You have devised a clever plan. But there will be no explosion; I will not let you out upon the Stairway."

"Everyone who comes here must go down the Stairway. Even if you do not want him to."

He approached the inner wall and said loudly, "I am ready!"

The mirrors slid apart, opening a narrow passage. Directly beyond it was the first step of the Stairway leading down. Velt raised his foot.

"Wait," the machine almost shouted. "Wait! It is so terrible to die. If you want, I'll let you out of here."

"You cannot do this. I know it."

"That is true. Good-bye, then. I have switched on the Planet-wide Requiem. After all, you are an Honorary Ling."

"Good-bye."

He glanced back and waved his hand to his reflections. They answered him with his own gesture.

INVASION

by

ROMAN PODOLNY

ROMAN PODOLNY, *born in 1933, is a historian and editor for the popular science magazine* Znaniye—Sila (Knowledge is Power). *He entered the field of science fiction in 1962 and is the author of many short, usually humorous, stories.*

One fine spring day in the year 2074, She and He sat on a bench in the midst of a tropical forest, preserved as a sanctuary. Their little go-everywhere plane dozed quietly under a nearby palm.

Even the wind was still, not to disturb them. And there was not another living soul for a hundred kilometers around. But at the moment when His lips came close to Hers, there was a strange hiss, some unknown force thrust them apart, and on the bench between them appeared, from heaven knows where, a bearded little old man.

Instantly grasping the situation, the stranger said in a frightened voice:

"Forgive me, I had no intention . . ." But he quickly recovered his self-possession and changed from apologetic to solemn tones. "You will, of course, forgive my intrusion when you learn that I am a visitor from the distant past . . ."

He had not finished his sentence when the young man crossed his arms and clasped his own shoulders, whispering in despair:

"I must be cursed! Another one!" He turned to the girl. "I swear I had nothing to do with it."

"I understand," she said coldly.

"But I don't!" protested the visitor. "Why don't you welcome me?"

The young man mastered himself sufficiently to answer:

"For the six millionth time? It's enough that we welcomed the first one."

"But I have invented a machine for traveling into the future! I was the first to test it!"

"Congratulations," he said drily. "We studied you at school. . . . But your machine . . . well . . . I mean, those who left later came earlier. It happens. Don't upset yourself. Better tell me something," and the young man's gloomy face brightened. "Why is it that visitors from the past always appear in the most inappropriate places and at the most inconvenient times? After all, this sends the whole theory of probability into the antiworld! Even the Council of the Wise cannot make head or tail of it. Couldn't something be done about it?"

"It's the fourth time he was interrupted just as he was going to say he loves me." She sighed resentfully.

"Again, forgive me . . . As for your question . . . If you studied me at school, you know that the time machine does not travel with the passenger. It merely shoots him forward, across so many years—approximately, of course. And the properties of space-time are such that a man who travels in time also moves in space, and it's impossible to foresee . . ." The great inventor was now speaking in the manner of a lecturer.

"We know it without you," said the young man, evidently losing all interest in his neighbor.

"Um . . . excuse me, but what about me now? I'm sure you have already invented a machine for traveling back into the past? I would like to go home."

"Ah, if we had! All the six million of you only wanted to take a peek at the future and then go home. If they didn't, would so many have come? Every one of them was desperately eager to go back to his relatives and friends as soon as possible. Eight years ago, after the first visits, the Council of the Wise transferred forty million physicists and mathematicians to work on this problem. True, some of them felt that such a machine was impossible because it would violate the law of cause and effect, but we're used to manipulating natural laws. And meantime, until the problem is solved, the great Nurden suggested sending our guests further into the future—into a time when people have learned to travel back and forth in time. We've sent on nearly four million. But then a poet suddenly asked a question: 'If travel into the past is possible, how is it that no one has come to us from the future?' And so we had to liquidate the whole project. And we stopped sending our visitors into the future: that would have meant merely shoving our own problems onto someone else's shoulders."

"What problems?"

"What problems? Don't we have to console you, and give you medical care, and spend decades retraining you? . . ."

The great Nurden stepped onto the podium and looked at the audience with his kindly eyes.

"I think," he began, "that I can bring you good news. According to our calculations, the last of the six million, twenty-four thousand, five hundred and thirty-three persons sent into our era from the year 1974 has just arrived. The second invasion will take place about two centuries hence. We must ac-

cept those who have been sent three hundred years into the
future. But in the next two centuries we shall have time to
prepare . . ."

The podium on which Nurden stood rocked violently.
And the physicist received a most painful jab in the side as a
badly embarrassed young man appeared next to him.

"You, Nikolay?" the great man gasped. "But you were
the first to arrive from the past, eight years ago, and we immediately dispatched you into the future . . ."

"Forgive me, they must have miscalculated," the uninvited guest whispered miserably. "I never meant . . ."

WHEN YOU RETURN

by

IGOR ROSOKHOVATSKY

IGOR ROSOKHOVATSKY *was born in 1929. A teacher by training, he works as a correspondent for a Kiev newspaper. His first science-fiction story appeared in 1959. He has since published several novels and story collections.*

1

What struck her was not what he said. The girl could not recall his words; it seemed he asked her why she was crying. But his voice . . . It was unlike any other. . . . And so tender that it made her cry all the more. As through a wet glass she saw his smile, full of concern. It seemed to the girl that she had seen him somewhere, long ago. But she could not remember where.

"Did anyone hurt you?"

The girl shook her head. He added quickly, "I don't mean to pry into your affairs. I simply felt lonely strolling here by myself. And then I saw you coming, crying . . ."

She recalled her teacher saying, "Vita Leshchuk, you are guilty before Kolya, you must apologize." She had stubbornly bitten her lip and said nothing. "Very well, then, you won't come to the outing. Stay home and think it over." But she could not tell him how it really happened. Vita Leshchuk was no tattletale. She'd rather be punished.

"Look, little girl, I know that the fault was Kolya's, not yours."

How does he know?

"The day after tomorrow I am flying to Prague for a day. Would you like to come with me?"

The girl stopped. Delicate and light, with fluffy hair, she was like a dandelion, and one wanted to shield her from the wind.

"The day after tomorrow my class will fly to Prague, but they won't take me . . ."

Vita raised her head and looked at the stranger attentively. He was tall, with disproportionately broad shoulders, like two stone cliffs. Perhaps this was why he stooped a little. In his triangular face with a powerful, prominent forehead everything was angular and sharp. Even his eyebrows looked like the runners of skates. But the eyes were kind and anxious.

"May I walk with you part of the way?" And he added quickly, "I feel sort of lonely by myself."

Vita was silent, and he spoke again, "I'll tell you my problem; perhaps you'll want to help me."

This proved irresistible.

"All right, tell me."

And she walked on, slowly, looking up at him encouragingly. He walked by her side, trying to keep step with her.

"You see, I have a great many things to do in Prague. I'll never get them all done by myself. But if you come with me and take care of my business at the toy factory, I'll be able to manage the rest. Well, agreed?"

"I must first ask my mother and grandmother," said Vita, and the stranger seemed delighted for some reason.

"Of course. But make it quick."

"My house isn't far."

She was so reassured and trusting by now that she held out her hand to him when they came to the escalator. There were many people here. The stranger pressed her hand so hard that the girl cried out.

"I'm sorry, Vita."

How does he know my name? Why doesn't he say anything about himself? What is his name?

"It's time for me to introduce myself," he said at once. "My name is Valery Pavlovich. I am a biophysicist. I am on vacation now, but it's almost over."

For a while they rode silently. And every time they stepped from one escalator to another, Valery Pavlovich took Vita's hand. His fingers were dry and hot, as though he were ill and had a high fever.

When they came to Vita's house and the door opened automatically, Valery Pavlovich hesitated for a moment at the threshold, as if he did not quite dare to enter.

2

They were met by Vita's mother, a small, round-faced woman with the same fluffy red hair as her daughter's. She stared with surprise at the stranger.

"Oh, we have a guest!"

The woman looked closely at Valery Pavlovich, and it seemed to her that she had seen him many times before. But when? Where?

"Ksana Vadimovna," she introduced herself.

"Valery Pavlovich," he said, and immediately turned away his eyes.

Where did I see him? the woman strained to remember. At first she thought he might be one of her husband's colleagues. But then she would remember him, as she remembered everyone connected with Anton, her Ant. She strained her memory but could remember nothing. And then, when she gave up, her memory brought up a recollection to the surface as lightly and effortlessly as water brings up a bit of straw. She remembered a theater lobby. An exhibition of paintings by young artists. She was tugging at her husband's sleeve. "Come, Ant, come now! They rang the second bell!" But he could not tear himself away from a painting done in ringing colors. In it, a face with sharpened features emerged from darkness—all of it impetuously thrusting forward. Ant had said to her then, "That's how I'd like to be." His wife glanced sideways at his plump, kind face with the slightly pouting lip and smiled to herself. "Childish fantasies!" And now that portrait was before her, come to life.

Perhaps he had been that artist's model. Incredible!

"Mama, Valery Pavlovich invited me to come with him to Prague!" the girl announced. "He's going on the same day as our class."

"Well, then you will meet there," said Ksana Vadimovna without much attention to her daughter's words. She looked at their guest, thinking, As if he has just come out of that portrait. This face . . . I will never forget it now. I think it's only now that I am beginning to understand what Ant saw in it. But it is too mobile, its expression changes so fast that I can't follow it . . .

"Mama," the girl was impatient. "They won't take me on the trip if I don't apologize to Kolya."

"What happened?"

"I hit him."

"And you won't apologize?"

"Never. He said that heroes are fools and cowards are clever. And that people say differently because it's to their advantage."

"You should have explained to him . . ." Ksana Vadimovna tried to calm her daughter down.

"Explain to whom? To Kolya?" the girl said, so expressively that her mother could not help smiling. Then she frowned again to show that she disapproved of her daughter.

"He's a miserable creature, your Kolya. He'll have a dull life if he doesn't change," said an elderly but still strong woman, coming in from the other room. She had gypsy eyes, and her short black hair was combed in such a way that it seemed disheveled.

"I am Vita's grandmother," she said to the guest, and turned to Vita again. "You simply should have laughed at him."

She nodded meaningfully to the guest, as if to say that there was something else behind all that, something unsaid. But Ksana Vadimovna asked tactlessly, "It's because of Daddy, isn't it?"

The girl became taut as a string.

"Your mother is right. In such cases it's best to stay away from personal matters," Valery Pavlovich put in hastily, either trying to explain something to the girl or in order to help out Ksana Vadimovna.

Vita turned away from the guest with a sharp movement.

She cannot understand it yet, he thought sadly. There will be many bruises before she does.

"You see, my child . . ." Ksana Vadimovna began once more, but Vita resolutely shook her head.

"I will not apologize to him. Never!"

"Well, you don't have to," her grandmother suddenly came to her support. "What we have told you is for the future."

Ksana Vadimovna shrugged her shoulders and left the room.

Vita stole a glance at their guest. How was he reacting? She was very, very anxious to go to Prague. The guest sat huddled in a chair, his head lowered, but Vita saw that his eyes were smiling.

"Come to the table, please!" Ksana Vadimovna invited her family and guest.

They went to the dining room, where the blue lights of

the synthesizers were already burning on the control panels before each chair.

"I've programed them already. See how you like my new menu," Ksana Vadimovna said to the guest.

"Thanks, but I am not hungry," he said with some embarrassment.

"But just a little, just try!"

Before Valery Pavlovich knew it, a plate of salad appeared before him. The synthesizer chute was open, and he knew that another dish would appear in a moment. The guest's long finger pressed the stop button. The indicator light went out. Ksana Vadimovna turned an astonished face to her guest, who spread his hands in an oddly helpless gesture and said:

"Really, I am not at all hungry."

The grandmother fixed him with her quick black eyes, frowning. It was obvious from her expression that she was thinking intently.

Valery Pavlovich glanced at her. I must help her, he thought. This might be best for all of us. And he prompted her mentally: Yes, you are right. This is why I seem strange to you, this is why I don't have to eat.

"Excuse me," the grandmother said to the guest, and turned to Ksana. "Can you come with me for a moment? I need your help."

The women went out into the other room, and the grandmother said reproachfully, "Let him alone. Don't you understand it yet?"

"What am I supposed to understand?"

"Haven't you noticed anything unusual?"

"Well, he seems odd somehow . . ."

"Odd," the older woman mimicked her. "He may seem odd to us. But how do we look to him?"

Ksana Vadimovna shrugged in puzzlement. Her gesture meant: You'll always invent something!

The grandmother gave her a long look and shook her

head: How did you ever get along with Anton, you're both so different! Her memory immediately brought back her son. She only had to call him silently, and he always came, and she could have long talks with him. But this time she had not called, yet he came. Perhaps no one else would find anything strange in this, but the mother knew: something must have happened. But what could happen now? He had perished three years ago. Then perhaps it meant that something was yet to happen?

She thought anxiously about Vita. Was it all right to let her go with him alone? Her voice was irritated as she said to her daughter-in-law:

"But didn't you guess that he is a synthehomo, a synhom? I think that's what they called them. You saw such beings recently on television. They said, 'This is a step into the future of mankind, a great experiment,' and other things of the kind."

Ksana Vadimovna recalled it and reproached herself. Why hadn't she realized it at once? That powerful brow, the rocklike shoulders, where additional organs were probably concealed. A man synthesized in a laboratory. Superhuman in his potentialities. And yet, both then and now she thought of a synhom as a machine rather than a man. She had read that this was a prejudice, akin to racial prejudice, stupid human arrogance. She understood it with her mind, but her heart rejected it. She felt indignant when she heard that many of the first synhoms would become doctors. She wondered, Who will consent to being examined by a synhom? And what if he decided that the fragile human creature did not deserve to live? Poor synhoms—it won't be easy for them to get their first patients . . .

And suddenly—a synhom at her own house! But of course he needs no food: he is charged up by sunlight batteries and some other devices. And he stores energy in accumulator organs. But what does he want here?

She felt a chill when she recalled what he wanted; he

wanted Vita to go with him to Prague. Perhaps he plans to study her like an experimental animal?

"Vita will not go anywhere with him!" she said decisively to her mother-in-law.

"But what reason do you have to distrust him?" asked the other. At the same time, she thought, Perhaps it's better this way.

"You always like to contradict, Mother," Ksana Vadimovna reproached her.

The older woman said nothing. Of course, she thought, we'll spare ourselves worry if we don't let her go. But why deprive Vita of the pleasure?

They returned to the dining room, pretending that nothing was amiss.

The guest gave them a quick glance.

Could he have noticed something? the older woman wondered, and remembered that synhoms had telepatho-amplifiers. They sensed the psychic state of others and freely read their thoughts. Synhoms could talk among themselves over vast distances with the aid of telepathy. This meant that Valery Pavlovich knew what they had talked about and what they were thinking. But why, in that case, did he not suggest to them the thoughts he needed in order to fulfill his plans?

Her certainty that their decision was right was shaken. The mother-in-law was frightened. What if he was suggesting this doubt to her? She looked at the guest, expecting to meet a heavy, hostile stare. And she was ready to fight him with all her strength and passion. But Valery Pavlovich was not looking at her. He was looking at Vita. His sharp features softened. And though no wrinkles gathered around his eyes as he smiled, his face no longer seemed so strange.

He looked at the dandelion girl and smiled to her. And the girl responded with an answering smile.

3

"You are a big girl now, you ought to understand it yourself," Ksana Vadimovna began almost immediately after the guest had left. And Vita understood everything.

She looked pleadingly at her grandmother, but the latter turned her head to the window, pretending that she was looking at something.

"Mama!" Vita cried reproachfully. "Why won't you let me go? Why don't you like him?"

Ksana Vadimovna was somewhat at a loss. "He is not a man, Vita. He is a synhom. Do you remember, they were shown on television?"

"So what?" asked the girl, as though she had known it before and thought nothing of it.

"We don't know why he invited you," Ksana Vadimovna tried to explain, but Vita clapped her hands with indignation.

"Mama, don't you remember? I told you that some of our girls were saying that synhoms were dangerous. And you explained to me that they were only repeating the words of foolish and ignorant people. And now you're talking like them yourself!"

I think she is blushing for me, thought Ksana Vadimovna, and her eyes begged her mother-in-law for support.

And the other immediately came to her aid: "Still, Vita, he is not human. And we cannot guess his intentions."

"He is good," the girl said with conviction. "Why are you all against him? If Papa were alive . . ."

Her lips twisted and her chin trembled. But her eyes threw out a challenge.

Ksana Vadimovna once more recalled the portrait her late husband had liked so much. And now the being who had stepped out of the painting had won the affection of her daughter. Was it an accident?

4

"Are we taking a graviplane?" Vita asked, and hastened to add: "I've been up in every kind of a plane except a graviplane."

"And did anyone ever carry you in his arms?" asked Valery Pavlovich.

Her lashes rose tensely, like the wings of a bird ready to fly away at the slightest noise.

"When Papa was alive . . ."

But even before he heard the answer, the synhom realized he had made a mistake, he had hurt her.

"I'll carry you to Prague," he said.

"Good," Vita agreed.

At first she thought it was a game, but then she remembered what her teacher had told them about synhoms. She had never thought that anyone except her father could have a hand as tender and as strong as the hand that lifted her up now. Valery Pavlovich picked her up as gently as one picks up a dandelion. Two jets rose from behind his shoulders, wrapping him and Vita in a firm, transparent sheath. The girl saw the green earth receding and chains of light, fluffy clouds like flocks of cranes running to meet them. She imagined the synhom flying here alone, plunging into clouds which wrapped him in this cold white murk. She felt sorry for him, so strong and so lonely. And she said:

"Thank you, thank you so much. I'd never be able to fly like this if it weren't for you."

She felt a pleasant warmth on her head, as though someone had put a hand on it and rumpled her hair.

"Look down, Vita!"

Chains of hills were floating back beneath them. They were covered with mist, and only their chalky summits were visible through it.

"Just like a fairy tale," the girl cried, and he guessed from her voice that she was always ready to encounter wonders.

"Can you fly like this into the cosmos too?" she asked.

"I can." The synhom smiled.

"And what other marvelous things can you do?"

He smiled silently, deep in thought.

Vita decided to help Valery Pavlovich.

"Can you dive down to the bottom of the sea?"

"Yes."

He was thinking now simultaneously about the girl, about her mother and grandmother, about himself and what awaited him:

I am carrying her in my arms, but I need her more than she needs me. Even my creators never suspected how much I'll need her.	It was hardest for them. And now? How worried they are, suspecting me of evil motives! And they must still find out the truth. . . . Will they be able to understand?	There is no need to gather speed. Velocity is instant, like a burst of light. This is the only way to break the barrier.

People are always breaking barriers. The very fact of life is the breaking of a barrier. And especially the fact that they were able to create us. This is perhaps the greatest barrier they've overcome. And we have our own barriers before us. But it is easier for us than it is for them, although we try to help, to lift some of their burden onto our shoulders. They gave us all the things they were deprived of—omnipotence and immortality. And the only thing we have given them is hope. And now this girl is giving me her warmth and admiration. What can I give her in exchange? And does she need what I can give?

The answer had to come from the girl herself.

"And can you dive through time? Our teacher told us . . . You know, I could do it too, if only I had such organs. And first of all I'd dive into the past, about four years ago . . ."

He understood that she was revealing to him her deepest secret. She spoke approximately, "about four years ago," but she was thinking precisely, "Four years." Her father was still alive at that time.

The synhom felt his emotions rising and interfering with thought. He was able to grasp his state of mind in its entirety and to see all the nuances that merged into a single powerful current beyond the ken of ordinary man, whose nervous system was hundreds of times poorer than his inner communications system and whose emotional capacity was hundreds of times smaller. Such a gust of feelings would break man as a storm breaks a dead tree. But the synhom did not try to decode the stream of emotions flowing through him. He switched on the will stimulator, and it seemed to him that he was hearing the threatening roar subsiding gradually in his brain.

"Guess what this is."

The girl's hand pointed down at the green bristling mass of a forest.

He wanted to say "a forest," but he caught the mysterious glitter of her eyes and said in a whisper, "A green monster."

She looked at him with astonished admiration, as if to say: You are so clever, not at all like an adult. It is interesting to talk with you. And she asked:

"Is he evil?"

"No, he is only pretending. In reality he is very good."

"That's right," she said, and looked at him for the first time neither patronizingly nor with admiration but as one looks at an equal, a friend.

"Look, there is Prague on the horizon."

A diamond horseshoe gleamed at the spot he was pointing to. It was the new laboratory district. When they came nearer, they could see that the horseshoe consisted of two levels—one on the ground, the other in the air. Many of the laboratory buildings floated in the sky, at a height of three to five hundred yards. Everything had a geometric shape—rhombuses and spheres, cubes and triangles. They met several people flying from building to building. Someone waved to them and followed them with his glance for a long time.

And now old Prague was spread beneath them—a museum raising the spire of the old Town Hall and the medieval churches. The synhom and Vita landed in the square before the Town Hall.

"The ancient clock will strike in a moment, and you'll see the apostles," said the synhom.

"What are apostles?"

"Toy figures. They will appear in that window."

At Vita's request they watched the apostles twice. Then they crossed the Charles Bridge over the slow Vltava. The girl stopped near every statue and finally concluded:

"They used to like dolls more once upon a time."

"Yes," the synhom said seriously. "At that time grown-ups also played with dolls."

They stopped before the famous toy factory, and the synhom said, "You'll look over the factory, and I shall leave for a short time and come back for you."

5

He returned earlier than he had planned, although the time organ in his mind showed that he was making inefficient use of time. He did not try to justify himself. He thought about Vita, recalling how she had asked: "And can you . . . ?" At the factory she would be invited to select a toy. And the synhom, refusing to turn on his telepatho-amplifier, tried to imagine what her choice would be.

He was escorted to the office of the chief designer of toys —a gay, tall man in a sport suit. The designer sat on the small chair meant for visitors, and Vita was settled cosily in his soft antique armchair. The synhom saw her profile—a burning cheek, a cloud of fluffy hair, a curious eye.

"Oh, that's for me," she said to the chief designer when she saw the synhom.

She gave him one hand, and with the other she clutched a plastic box.

"Guess what present I chose," she asked Valery Pavlovich, with a conspiratorial look at the chief designer.

"That's difficult," said the synhom, trying to frown, but he did not succeed: the plast-albumen skin refused to wrinkle. "Would you help me?"

And then, without waiting for her answer, he asked, "New or old style?"

"New," and her eyes were saying: You are sly!

"A machine or a living creature?"

"A living creature."

I was not mistaken, thought Valery Pavlovich, recalling the synhom doll, the latest product of the Prague factory. The doll walked, sang, could speak several words. In its forehead there was a tiny projector covered with a shutter. She will think of me whenever she sees the doll.

He asked, "Does it look like me?"

"A little," the girl said slyly.

"Is it a synhom doll?" he asked slowly, as if pondering it.

"Oh, you didn't guess!"

Vita opened the box. It contained two Czech dolls— Papa Schpeibel and Gurvinek.

"But you said it was a new toy."

"I said the truth: Papa Schpeibel plays, and Gurvinek dances. The old ones didn't."

The synhom and Vita said good-bye to the chief designer. They left his office and crossed the hall where all the toys were exhibited. At the very exit the synhom halted for a moment and asked Vita:

"Wouldn't you like to have the doll I mentioned too?"

The girl shook her head.

"You won't remember me?"

"What has the doll to do with it?"

"It looks like me."

"No," said the girl. "A doll is a doll. And you are you." And she ran, hopping, to the door.

"Not so fast, Vintik, you'll fall!"

The girl stopped short and pressed herself to the door. He had said "Vintik." Only one person in the world had called her that—her father. What did it mean?

The synhom walked up to her, put his hand on her shoulder, and pulled her close to him. And this was how they walked out—a giant with massive shoulders and a dandelion girl. Questions were racing like birds through Vita's head, but she asked nothing.

They walked along the old embankment rising over the Vltava, and Vita tried not to step on the synhom's big shadow. Leaves rustled underfoot like yellowed paper, like fragments of old letters that were never delivered.

They came to Vaclav Square. The synhom was explaining something to the girl. He was telling her about King Vaclav, but she was not listening, occupied with her own thoughts. Suddenly she raised her head and asked, looking into his eyes:

"When will your vacation end?"

"In two days," he answered. Guessing what she meant, he said, trying to make his voice as firm as possible, "I'll come to see you afterwards too."

"A man's word of honor? Yes?"

She looked at him intently—a serious little woman who would not forgive a lie. And she confided to him something she had never spoken of to anyone.

"My father always kept his promises. But once . . .

When he was leaving for the Experiment, he promised to come back . . ." She turned away. "I don't want you to think I am a cry baby. But other children have fathers . . ."

He was afraid to meet her eyes, he knew what they would be like now. And the girl pressed herself to him with all her strength and whispered, "He promised to come back."

The synhom felt that the will stimulator could no longer control the lump rising in his throat. It was as if something had broken down in him, some irreplaceable part; neither the third nor the fourth signal systems, nor even the system of Highest Control could do anything. For a moment he had become again what he had been a long, long time ago, before he had died—an ordinary, weak man. The words broke from his lips:

"I've kept my word, Vintik."

"Papa . . ."

"I'll explain it to you later . . ."

"Papa! . . ."

A strong gust of wind ruffled the girl's hair, blew up her dress like a bubble. Her fluffy hair tickled the synhom's lips. He wanted to explain something to the girl, but he thought: She would not understand. Even I cannot define exactly how much there is in me of Ant and how much that is new. Did I tell her the truth?

6

"Ant," whispered the woman.

He turned his face to her, and she saw that there was no trace of sleep in his eyes.

"You haven't slept all night!"

"But I don't need sleep. I don't get tired."

What remains in him of the man I loved? the woman thought. But she said something else altogether.

"You seem to me a higher being, a kind of ancient god."

The synhom smiled, and she saw that Vita had not been mistaken: It was the former Ant's smile.

"If you feel good, then everything is fine."

The words were also Ant's.

He added, "You know I dreamed of becoming as I am now."

But what remained in him of the man she loved? She stroked his hot shoulder. The other Ant's shoulder was never so hot. She said, "I have a feeling that it's you and not you . . ." And finally she dared to ask, "But what remains in you of the old Ant?"

"You have just answered your own question."

He knew that she was suffering; she felt that there was something blasphemous in his return. Both she and his mother; they were both tormented, searching for answers to questions that must not be asked. Vita alone had joyously accepted everything as it was. To her the main thing was that he had returned.

The synhom did something he had forbidden himself to do from the very beginning. He switched on the telepatho-amplifier and immediately turned it off. Then he said, answering Ksana's unspoken thought:

"I could have returned as I was—exactly as I was before I died. The Experiment, you know, was very dangerous, and my organism was recorded on viotapes. It would have been simpler for them to restore me according to the master tape."

"Then why . . ."

"When I came to, it seemed to me I was sleeping. Then I heard a familiar voice. Professor Ives Kuhn called me by name. I wanted to turn my head but could not. I wanted to look at Ives but could not. He was asking me, 'Do you hear me, Ant? Answer!' I said that I heard him but could not see him. And he said, 'I'll explain it in a moment. You died. Oleg died too. Try to recall.' And I saw again how Oleg moved the lever—and the flash. . . . 'Do you remember?' I answered

'Yes.' Ives said that they had started to restore us. This was the first stage. For the time being I was only the model of Ant's brain, created by the computer. Ives said, 'You have the organs of speech and hearing, but you still have no vision. And I want to ask you before I start the second stage . . .' I knew what he was going to ask. You know that I expressed my feelings very strongly back when the first synhom was created. And we often spoke about it afterwards, so that he knew exactly what I wanted to become. He merely wished to know whether I had not changed my mind . . ."

Ksana raised herself on her elbow, looking attentively at his face, which no longer seemed strange.

But why am I astonished? He was always like this, she thought. We never understood each other very well. What seemed like sacrilege to me and to others was normal and clear to him. Will I ever understand him?

"But why did you choose to become like this, and not your former self?"

How can I tell her? he thought. It would offend and sadden her, and anyone else like her.

"I had to carry out the Experiment, and I could not have done it as I was before. I lacked the scope of memory, the speed of thought and response, the control and protective organs I now have. I had only two signal systems; now I have five. And I also have a system of higher control."

The synhom remembered something that had happened long ago, when he was still a man. His friend was dying in a satellite, nailed under the smashed radiotelescope, and he had not been able to help him, he could not raise his hand. His nose was bleeding, and grinding wheels seemed to be turning in his head, crushing his memory. He had cursed his weakness and that infernal gyration that spun the satellite for some unknown reason, as though it had fallen into a whirlpool. Through the grinding of the wheels, he heard his friend's screams, "Help! Help me!" Then everything was quiet. . . .

The synhom passed his hand over Ksana's hair, her cheek, her throat. His fingers felt some wrinkles. He remembered her fear of old age. He took her hand and pressed it gently.

"What are you thinking about?" she asked.

"You."

He was thinking:

She asks why I decided to assume another shape. The trouble is that it cannot be explained; she has to feel it. And this is almost impossible. Of course I could switch on the amplifiers and suggest it to her. But I have forbidden myself to make use of such advantages in dealing with people. And I was right. With them, I must be a man—not more, and not less. That's the whole difficulty . . .

Mother is probably up by now. Will she understand? I told her once that the limits of the human organism are exhausted sooner than we had thought, and that, if man wanted to move further, he would have to create for himself a new organism, with a different life-span and different capacities. She agreed with me then. But at that time I was the old Ant.

Three minutes before the start of the Experiment I'll have to switch over the higher control system, so that it operates only in the power sheath. It is also important to maintain constant control of the temperature in the Delta-7 sector.

"Are we going to the beach today?" the woman asked, her heart beating anxiously as she waited for his answer. The old Ant loved the sea.

"An excellent idea," the synhom answered. "I'll carry you. Do you remember, in Capri you asked me to carry you into the sea?"

For the first time in those two days since she had learned

the truth she felt truly untroubled and gay, as though everything painful was already behind her. And she laughed, asking, "You will carry all of us, your three women? All the way
to the sea?"

"Of course," he said. "I'll carry you faster than a graviplane."

"Do you know how much we weigh together?" Ksana
went on, thinking that he was joking.

"At any rate, less than a thousand tons . . ."

"You can carry a thousand tons?"

"Yes, and more too," the synhom answered, and she realized that he was not joking.

Ksana fell silent and drew away from him involuntarily.
He had become a stranger again.

There was the melodious sound of a bell.

Vita, thought the synhom, with a happy smile.

"Come in, if you are not an ogre!" he cried, covering his
face with his hands and spreading his fingers wide.

"Papa, Papa! You're back to your old jokes! But I am not
three years old any more." Vita skipped into the room, wag-
ging her finger at him.

The synhom heard his mother's voice: "Good morning,
children!"

She entered with her quick, elastic walk, and Ksana
looked at her searchingly. Hasn't she thought about it at all?
Hasn't she wondered how much remained of her son in this
strange being? Was it easier for his mother than it was for
her?

"Mama," said the synhom. "Ksana and I have made
plans for the day. We shall all fly to the seashore."

"Hurrah!" Vita shouted, and threw her arms around his
neck. Her eyes gleamed with pleasure. "And you'll carry us,
just as you carried me the other day? Yes?"

"And will you be obedient?" he asked.

"I won't!"

"I reduce your offense by half for your honesty," he pronounced solemnly, and felt Ksana's hand on his shoulder.

"Enough fooling around, Ant. Just like a little boy . . ."

7

Two days passed.

"Time for me to go."

What else could he say to them, the synhom thought without looking at his mother. If only she would not cry.

Tattered clouds moved slowly across the sky.

"Will you come back soon?" asked Vita.

"Yes." And he added: "A man's word of honor."

No one smiled.

What could he say to his mother? It must be hardest for her.

He could think of nothing.

The clouds lumbered across the sky like an endless wagon train of times long past.

"Good-bye, son. I wish you success in everything you do."

Her voice was steady and calm, and the word *son* came out quite naturally. He understood. His mother accepted him as he was and did not torment herself with questions of how much remained in him of the son she bore. She could not have grasped his transformation by logic or even erudition, although she was not an ignorant woman. What was it that helped her, then? Perhaps it was maternal wisdom, he thought. So he did not really know his mother, after all.

"Good-bye," said the synhom, embracing all three of them and already imagining how he would soar upward now, break through the clouds, and fly across the blue.

"Be careful, Ant," Ksana begged timidly. "You're so reckless. Don't . . ."

She did not finish. And the unsaid words hung between them like a falling stone about to hurt someone.

Ksana is afraid for me, as she was that time. She has forgotten that I have become invulnerable. I am the old Ant to her . . .

Death . . . Once upon a time we were so accustomed to it that it seemed an inalienable part of human life. But even then we fought against it. We recorded voices on magnetic tapes, we preserved likenesses in photographs and portraits. We created a memory for mankind through books and films. A memory that could no longer die. And thus we came to understand what was the most important thing in us and what must be kept from dying.

Ant smiled as though he had caught the stone and thrown it aside. He said, "If I perish again, I will return anyway."

"ONE LESS"

by

IGOR ROSOKHOVATSKY

The truck came out of the gates and sped down the street through the puddles, raising fountains of spray. Pedestrians hurriedly shied away toward the buildings. And the driver bared his tobacco-yellowed teeth in a jolly grin.

The front door closed with a soft thud behind Victor Nikolayevich. He took six slow steps, down to the sidewalk. A laboratory assistant ran past him, skipping three steps at a time. Victor Nikolayevich smiled indulgently. There had been a time when he never noticed the steps either. He too had been one of the "promising young men." And now, at forty-nine, he was still no more than a research associate, who had not yet defended his doctoral dissertation.

Victor Nikolayevich slowly walked down the avenue, thinking about the series of experiments just concluded.

Mikhailov's position, he said to himself, is certainly unenviable. All those months, all that work, and the results don't bear out his theory. Perhaps it's the right moment to offer my hypothesis?

163

His glance slid down, and he halted for a few seconds. There was a dark strip of mud on the cuffs of his trousers. His wife would grumble again about his habit of shuffling like an old man. It was something he could not help; as soon as he started thinking, he dragged his feet.

Victor Nikolayevich shuffled on, and his thoughts returned once more to the laboratory. On that day it had been established that stimulation of the group of neurons known as "group K" results in the feverish excitation of the entire organism and a tenfold increase in strength.

Why was it then that preparations that counteracted the stimulation of "group K" failed to affect violent patients in mental hospitals? The laboratory workers had asked themselves this question, had discussed it at length back and forth, and found no answer, no way out of the apparent dead end.

And only he, Victor Nikolayevich, took another approach to the problem. He asked: Whence came the tenfold increase in strength? This question led him to a very interesting hypothesis.

Clattering, the truck turned the corner to the avenue. The driver stopped for a moment and ran across to the store for cigarettes. He opened the pack as he hurried back to his truck. Settling down on the seat, he flipped the cigarette over to the corner of his mouth with a practiced movement of the lips, and the truck roared on.

If I tell them, they'll probably laugh, thought Victor Nikolayevich. It's too much like a fairy tale, like skipping ten steps at a time. Yura will say, "I smell something burning." But the second series of control experiments points in that direction. And if we are to believe the Indian professor . . .

He stopped before a store window, admired a new television set, and sighed. Even if he bought it on installments, there would not be enough money left for his wife's vacation.

After he defended his dissertation, then . . . But if he was to have no problems with it, he had better avoid getting the reputation of an idle dreamer.

If I tell Mikhailov that the organism must have an untapped source of energy which is controlled by a specific nerve center, he'll screw up his eyes, bend his head to the side, as if preparing to peck, and say, "You think so?" If I ask: "Where does a man find superhuman strength at moments of extreme danger? How does it happen that a dying man who has been given up by the best doctors performs a miracle and recovers by the sheer force of will, of a powerful desire to live? Will power, the desire to live belong to the sphere of the spirit. They must find reserves, then, in the material sphere, in the organism. Evidently, these reserves are kept under the severest control and manifest themselves only at the most critical moments. In fact, our organism is like an overcautious general who cannot make up his mind to bring the reserve regiment into action, who keeps saying it is still too early until the very last opportunity is gone. But in violent insanity control by the nervous system is weakened, the energy reserves are liberated, and the man acquires the strength of ten, from heaven knows where . . ."

Ah, you talk too much, Victor Nikolayevich said to himself with a smile. There's not much sense in rushing in with arguments. Mikhailov won't listen, anyway. He'll cut you off in the middle of a word and drawl out negligently, "That's philosophy, not science." And what can you say to that?

I can show him the results of the experiments I carried out with Arkady. There you have science, not speculations. I can say: "From all evidence, 'group K' controls the untapped energy reserves. This is why its stimulation produces the symptoms of violent insanity without mental disturbance. The animal twitches, writhes in convulsions, destroys everything around simply because the liberated energy seeks expression. And, incidentally, we must remember that this nerve center is very difficult to arouse. Let us also remember the burst of energy which occurs in the organism at the moment of death, known as 'necrobiotic radiation.' This is lost energy. Why not try to utilize it while the organism is alive? Just imagine the results—extension of life, victory over any disease . . ."

But wait, wait! Victor Nikolayevich cried out mentally. What if the hypothesis should be offered as a fantasy? Say, as a science-fiction story read in some anthology? And then, if I ridicule it, Mikhailov will, as usual, take the opposite side and begin to defend it. Tomorrow I'll do it!

Victor Nikolayevich's lips moved as he carried on his silent monologue, and a faint smile brightened his face like a reflection of distant light. Deep in thought, he stepped off the curb . . .

The truck roared out from around the corner. The driver caught sight of the figure crossing the street. The brakes whined agonizingly. Too late. The driver's lips turned blue and twitched. The unfinished cigarette danced at the corner of his mouth.

A crowd assembled instantly, long before the ambulance arrived. The doctor jumped out and ran toward the accident victim. A few moments passed, and the man in the white coat straightened up slowly.

"He is dead."

The attendants laid the corpse on a stretcher.

The crowd still lingered. An elderly woman pressed her hands to her heart, and a man tried to calm her:

"What can you do? One less . . ."

Eyes turned on him angrily, and he snapped:

"There are three billion people on earth. Even if a million disappear, no one will notice."

He was in a hurry to get to the clinic for treatments. The doctors had not told him that his illness was incurable and that he had very little time left to live.

No one could know as yet that there was, after all, a way of curing his disease—by liberating his untapped reserves of energy. And the one man among the three billion inhabiting the earth who knew how to do it was no longer there.

"WE PLAYED UNDER
YOUR WINDOW"

by

VLADIMIR SHCHERBAKOV

VLADIMIR SHCHERBAKOV, born in Moscow in 1938, is a radio engineer who works in a radiotechnical research institute in Moscow. Author of several scientific works, he first began to publish science-fiction stories in 1964.

He walked rapidly, his eyes half-closed against the sun and the wind. The dandelion leaves and flowers by the roadside merged into bright spots, and the clouds hung over the houses like billowing white smoke. He stopped for a moment, to drink the lemonade from the bottle rolling in his traveling bag. The only things that remained in it now were a razor and a soft towel. An hour and he'd be home. But it all seemed unreal to him, like a dream seen over and over again. He felt that he had looked upon this endless ribbon of the road, had walked along this asphalt and these grassy paths many times before. He tried to reconstruct the details of his return, but

168

they blurred in his memory, as though wrapped in mist—the voices, the faces.

For thirty minutes or so he had rested, trying to collect himself, in the room for new arrivals, and the only face he remembered was that of a young woman who sat at the opposite table. She was evidently waiting to meet someone.

It occurred to him now that her face seemed familiar, and he strained to recall where he had seen it. Then he laughed. She probably wasn't even born when he flew away. A fine face, he thought. One could envy the man she was waiting for. The odd thing was that the girl had looked at him also with surprised, questioning eyes, as if she had remembered something. But he did not deceive himself about his appearance. Even those who had known him in the past would not recognize him now. Little remained of the old Sergey. He would soon be sixty. In three months. They might not let him fly again, quoting some point in the regulations. He would plead with them, of course, but he might walk on his head for all the good it would do. They'd merely shrug and say, "We would be glad to, but we have no right. Read it yourself."

At moments it seemed to him that all he needed was to take a rest, have some sleep, shave himself unhurriedly, and he would be his former, forty-year-old self, young-looking but sufficiently experienced. But did he really want to fly again? He knew very well what it meant: days, nights, years, and then—nothing like the miracles once dreamed of, no paradisiac gardens, no promised land. . . . All you see is a distant star getting bigger and bigger until it's like the sun. You hear the clicking of photographic cameras. The apparatus, the indicators go on, sparks flicker on the panels of the telemeters. And you—you must be careful, alert, and turn back in time. He had flown these long missions before. But this last time he had been caught by the gravitational forces of a star and barely managed to get away. Officially, this is called investigation of the stellar field.

Sergey nearly stepped into a puddle: he leaped across, but the puddle was wide, its bottom grooved with bicycle tracks. It had rained last night, and now the air smelled of wet grass and clover, and the asphalt had not yet dried completely. Bumble bees flew out of the dandelions and buzzed over the pathway. The mirrorlike window panes of the houses he passed reflected the road, the grass, the flowers, and the clouds, and therefore the windows turned from blue to white, to indigo, to green. Like a long row of bright chessboards, they marched forward together with Sergey, and near the houses children leaped, ran, shouted.

He stopped to console a five-year-old boy running after a girl who had taken something from him. Sergey spoke to the boy, but that was the last drop that made the cup run over, and the child burst into tears. "A dead beetle . . . my beetle," he repeated, sobbing. He had found the May beetle on the grass. The girl was bigger than he. Sergey gave the boy a large white shell. The boy continued to sob. Sergey waited a little and told him that the shell was from Mars.

He had gone about fifty steps when another boy, with a dog, caught up with him. In his hand he had a willow switch. His dog stopped a small distance away and wagged its tail. The boy said something, but very quietly, and lowered his head, poking the earth with his switch. He also wanted a shell from Mars.

"I am so sorry," said Sergey. "I had only one. . . . What? Next time? No, I won't fly again. Never. *The Swift* was my last rocket."

The dog came nearer and wagged his tail even more energetically. The boy traced lines on the ground with the switch.

"You see," said Sergey, "I always used to bring many pebbles and shells for the kids in my house, but this time it somehow turned out . . . I haven't been home for a long time, and the children have grown up. That's how it is . . . Well, I must go."

Actually, that shell had been meant for his son. It had lain in his traveling case for a long time. He had it with him when he came home last; he picked it up near the base on Mars. His son was seven at the time. But at home he found a brief note. His wife had taken the boy and left. All the furniture and the floors in the rooms were immaculately clean, as if someone had polished them only the day before—not a speck of dust, not a spot anywhere. He never heard from her again —as if she had vanished from the world. And some time later he flew away. He expected to be gone about eight years, but the eight stretched into twenty. He loved his wife and therefore compelled himself to forget her. But he could not forget his son.

He had remained alone. He had hoped to find them, to see the boy. But he never searched. He never got around to it; he thought it might be best not to. Waiting for the day of his departure (he had entire days free to himself), he made friends with the neighborhood children. He built toys for them—jumping rabbits and frogs, rockets that flew higher than the houses, butterflies harnessed to little carriages, made of paper and thread.

The yard would be ringing with voices when the children gathered in the evenings. Neighbors objected. The children were not allowed to shout, to break the branches of trees, to throw pebbles at cats, to run over the lawns with butterfly nets, to jump on the parking lot. In fact, they were altogether forbidden to play under the windows, only at the playground. Everyone chased them away. Sergey alone did not. He did not scold them and did not complain to their strict young mothers. He liked their noisy games under his windows. At least, he was not lonely then. But their parents tried to spoil even that little pleasure for them. They demanded that their children politely ask Sergey's permission every time they wanted to run and jump under his window.

And when he'd come home, the children would leave

their games for a moment, as though on command, and shout: "Sergey is here!" (Found themselves a playmate!) And the long-legged Elka, the eldest of the group, would run up to him and ask, "We played under your window. All right?"

There was a rustling of tires. A car drew up alongside and slowed down. Behind the wheel sat a man; next to him was the young woman Sergey had seen at the airport.

"Can we give you a lift?" asked the man at the wheel, smiling for some reason.

"No, thank you, I don't have far to go," said Sergey.

"He'll take you right to the house," said the young woman.

"They offered me a car at the airport, but I refused. I'm tired of machines, and I have no place to hurry to. Have you been far?"

"Mars, Jupiter-2," answered the man, and smiled again.

The girl looked attentively at Sergey. It was beginning to annoy him.

"I've been farther out," he said.

"We know," said the girl. "Did you miss home?"

"Not a bit. I've almost forgotten where it is."

"And you?" she asked her companion. "You haven't forgotten?"

"No," he said. "And I didn't have to remember: you promised to meet me."

They drove away. He tried to remember where he had seen her before. Had he seen her?

He walked along his street and recognized his house, the one before the last on the block. He entered the courtyard and found his windows. The house was the same, but not quite, as though it, too, had aged. The trees that had been planted before he left had grown enormously, and this made the house seem a little lower.

In the yard the woman he had spoken to on the road was sitting on a bench, as if expecting him. She saw him, bent down, said something . . . and he saw the children running to meet him. Sergey stopped. He recognized her. Two faces had finally merged in his memory. Elka, who used to jump rope under his window . . . Elka with the short fluffy pigtails and long legs . . . Could she really remember him? He stood indecisively, looking at her, at her husband, at the children surrounding him. He had to say something, if only to greet them. He saw that they were happy, they were enjoying the moment.

"Hello, Sergey, hello!" cried the children. "We were playing under your window!"

He was awakened by the doorbell. At first, he could not understand what was wanted of him. The trees, shrubbery, people, cars on the distant road—everything he glimpsed as he opened his eyes seemed the continuation of a dream, the beginning of which was lost in his faraway childhood. Then, too, there had been people, faces, the cloud-swept sky. The soft light in his room. Steps outside his door, in the kitchen. A voice—his mother's, or his grandmother's. Morning. A bell. Time to go to school. He was hurried on. Faster, faster, you'll be late! . . . How he hated to get up—if only he could sleep a minute longer! But his grandmother's loving hand pitilessly pulled off the blanket.

While he was dressing, someone impatiently pressed the bell. From the street came the sounds of voices, the low purring of motors, distant whistles.

Sergey opened the door and invited the man to enter. The visitor hesitated a moment, as if undecided, then rapidly came into the room and, after the usual apologies, launched at once into the business that brought him.

"You see," he began, "we are not clear about some of the details of your return. It may seem strange to you, but I must ask you some questions. My name is Volin; I'm from the cosmodrome."

"Go ahead," said Sergey.

"Do you remember the exact time of your landing?"

"Ten twenty."

"You landed in *The Swift?*"

"Yes, in *The Swift.*"

"Landing strip number?"

"Number Nine. Has anything happened?"

Volin was silent, as if trying to collect his thoughts. Sergey was irritated by his tone, although he realized that Volin must have come for a good reason. But to come without telephoning first? It suddenly seemed to him that the man had wanted to surprise him, without warning.

"What is it?" Sergey asked a second time.

"The point is," Volin said slowly, "that strip Number Nine is empty."

"Where's the rocket?"

"Nowhere. It isn't there. It disappeared."

"You're joking . . . look in my valise."

"It's useless. There has been no rocket."

"What do you mean, there has been no rocket?"

"*The Swift* never landed."

"Then I must have come on foot."

"You're in a better position to know."

A strange feeling came over Sergey. Fragments of memories, impressions, thoughts whirled in his brain. He looked at Volin attentively. The man's face seemed to recede; his voice came from far away. After yesterday, Sergey's head was still going round. If he had not been awakened, he probably would have slept for a long time. By an effort of will, he banished the remnants of sleep. Volin's face came nearer. Calm and collected, with deliberately slow gestures, Volin seemed to study Sergey. His attentive eyes were half-closed. As though in ambush for the time being, they were the eyes of a man who could turn the flow of events in one direction or another, throwing all his strength and intelligence into one powerful effort.

". . . imagine this," Volin spoke slowly. "A cosmonaut arrives. At any rate, it accidentally becomes known in the morning that he is at home. The rocket disappears. We look for traces of the landing—there are none. Physical and chemical analyses of the surface of the landing area indicate that there has been no rocket at all. No one has recorded the landing. No one has seen the rocket. Not a single human being. Not a single radar instrument. Are there any hypotheses or explanations? There are none." Volin fell silent, turning his back on his host.

Sergey seemed to listen to his meaningful silence. Suddenly he wanted to laugh. To lose a rocket? Have they all gone mad? Restraining his smile, he asked Volin, "So *The Swift* did not land? Let's go to the landing field."

Sergey walked up to the platform. Volin stopped at the narrow staircase. It was an ordinary working day. A short distance away men in overalls were preparing someone's rocket for launching. Sergey heard the regular electric buzzing and the sharp metallic sounds.

Dusty grass pushed up between the stone slabs of the rocket field. Warm air rose from the power tubes. The wood in the distance quivered as a faint gray line on the horizon. Strip Number Nine was empty. A light breeze rolled some straws across the cement.

Sergey realized that circumstances had drawn him into the center of events that for the time being could not be explained. But where was their beginning? He was regarded as lost. An unforeseen deviation from the set trajectory, and the rocket had been drawn to a star. He had seen the red spurts of the protuberances quite near, almost as near as that wood on the horizon. And a fiery stellar wind drove luminescent clouds past the ship, hot coiling cyclones like golden snakes being burnt in fire-breathing ovens. Could his return itself be considered the first link in this chain of events? Evidently, not.

He remembered very well what it had cost him. He remained alive because he had survived the pressure.

But after that . . . this vanished rocket. Sergey recalled how he and Volin had looked for the boy who had asked him for a shell. It had not been difficult to find him. Sergey had remembered the approximate location of the house, and many people knew the boy and his playful little dog. The boy immediately recognized Sergey. But when Sergey had tried, half-jestingly, to remind him of the conversation about the rocket (he was still in a cheerful mood and he bantered with Volin on the way), the boy only stared wide-eyed. "A natural reaction," Sergey said, as though to himself. Volin was silent.

And yet the theory of a misunderstanding had to be abandoned. The rocket was not on any of the cosmodromes. Sergey walked slowly toward the spot where he had stepped down from the ladder yesterday. Volin shouted something and pointed with his hand.

"What, what?" asked Sergey.

"Come back," he heard, "don't walk over the strip!"

A desk of some dark wood, two or three chairs, a bookcase as wide as the wall, an open window—the Professor's study. Sergey stopped at the door. Professor Kopnin offered him a chair, apologized for the disorder, and quickly brushed the cigarette butts overflowing from the ashtray onto a sheet of white paper. He crumpled the sheet and switched on the light. ("It turned dark so quickly, I hadn't noticed.") An absentminded glance at Sergey from under the glasses, the voice calm and quiet:

"You know, we calculated the trajectory by your data. You were only twenty thousand kilometers from the photosphere. *The Swift* inevitably had to plunge into the star, do you understand? To burn up, to vanish. How did you manage it? Tell me, how?"

Sergey mumbled something. What could he tell him?

Was it possible to tell about years of hope and anxieties, about love and death and life? About the minutes of expectation? The seconds won, and the meters which had given him the gift of life? And about nerves that rang like taut strings, and hands clenched so hard that the knuckles turned white? Words would be so pallid, so unlike the truth.

Kopnin offered a rather complicated hypothesis to account for what had happened. He referred to recent astrophysical studies of the structure of stellar specters.

"Think of a drop in the ocean," he said to Sergey. "We have studied the drop thoroughly, we have weighed it and measured it, and stand astonished before nature, which has created such a masterpiece. But of the ocean we know very little and therefore regard it merely as a large puddle or, at best, as a mechanical aggregation of multitudes of drops. The drop is Earth. The ocean is a star. Some people think that a star is a virtually eternal accumulation of fragments of atoms, something like a giant bonfire, a kettle in which you will not find a single whole molecule. In part, this is true, but only in part.

"We must not discount evolution. Why is it that a single drop contains mountains and plains, people, rockets, love, dams, revolutions, artificial synthesis of nuclei, mathematics? But the ocean is assumed to contain nothing—zero. Is this entirely indisputable?"

Sergey listened absently. He wanted to walk over to the open window and be silent. Now, when the light burned softly over the desk, when the noise of the city was subsiding and the grass and shrubs and trees exhaled the fragrance of young leaves, he was filled with deep joy. This was his second evening. Lights swam down the road—red, yellow, green. Stars quivered over the warm earth.

He did not understand much of what the Professor was saying. He would far rather talk to him about flowers and apple trees, about the old house where he had lived as a boy, about movies, books, fishing. But every time he spoke, Kopnin tactfully turned the conversation to the topic that interested him. Nucleons and electrons, those bricks from which matter was built, could be arranged, he said, in such a way that their combination would be stable and capable of resisting the fiery hurricane of a star. And, once this combination occurred it did not disappear, did not dissolve in fire because it was itself like a tornado, a fiery whirlwind. Such a tornado originated by pure chance and the probability of its occurrence was negligible. But then, stars existed billions of years, and their mass . . . but, of course, there was no need to say this to Sergey. Figures showed that such stable tornadoes were not a fiction. They drew their energy and renewed their force from the stream of radiation.

Professor Kopnin was outlining a strange theory. From the well-known fact of the material basis of thought, he was drawing far-reaching conclusions. Moving ions, electric potentials, biocurrents—thought was connected with all these. But, in Kopnin's view, the swarm of elementary particles, with its immeasurably higher power, its clear-cut structure, determined by titanic forces, and its lightning-fast neutrinos, was in no way less suitable as a nutrient medium for thought.

Kopnin held out an envelope to Sergey, who glanced at him questioningly.

"Photographs. Take a look at them."

Sergey took out two photographs—one large, the other smaller. The large photograph showed the night sky, and, in the right upper corner, a faintly luminous spot. On the second photograph the spot was larger.

"Accidental photographs," said Kopnin. "They were made about five hours before your return."

"The tornado you were speaking about? You don't imagine it all happened without a rocket?"

"It's almost self-evident to me."

"But oxygen . . . and all the rest?"

"Ah, those are trifles! Out of a single liter of nucleons

and electrons you can have enough oxygen for all of humanity."

"Of course. All you need is to arrange them in a certain order."

"Evidently, they can do it."

"Living tornadoes? On stars? Bringing a cosmonaut to Earth? But for that they would at least have to be capable of reading thoughts, and that is not so simple—analyzing the biocurrents of the brain. Do you really believe that?"

"I believe facts," Kopnin said dryly.

"But even if there had been something of the kind, why don't I remember anything?"

"Oh, that's a matter of technique. Suggestion, hypnosis, what have you. It has to be so, you understand? Why? Well, if only not to traumatize the psyche. You were flying in a rocket. But this was mere illusion. There was no rocket. This has been firmly established . . . What? Both you and the rocket? Transporting a rocket is much more complex. For purely economic considerations, if you wish."

Sergey feverishly sought for counterarguments. His whole being resisted the desire to believe what he had heard. So he was indebted to someone for his survival? But to whom? That was entirely unclear.

"Very well," he said. "Let's assume they are sufficiently perceptive. But this brings us immediately to a contradiction. After all, what I wanted was not simply to return. I wanted to see my son. What would it have cost them? If everything was as you say, it would have been the easiest thing for them, and I . . . try and find him now. I saw him when he was two, you understand? My wife surely did not speak to him about his father. . . . And, also, how did you learn of my return so quickly? After all, as you say, the rocket had not landed. I was considered lost, is it not so? And the only person who remembers me here is Elka. She was a little girl when I left, yet she recognized me."

"We learned about you from her husband. She told him about you, and he wanted to help you—to spare you the usual formalities. He returned on the same day, and next morning he came to the cosmodrome, to take care of his own formalities, and of yours, so that you would not have to be disturbed. . . . Hmm, yes, a son, you say . . . I never knew you had a son. But you will have to find him yourself. Perhaps this is beyond their powers. And, incidentally, this . . . what's his name . . . Dobrov, Vladimir Dobrov, had some trouble returning, too. Reactor failed. Without any visible cause. Two extraordinary landings at the same time—a rare case in our practice . . . Did you want to ask something?"

"Yes. This Dobrov—has he been flying long?"

"No. His first flight. A fine fellow. His mother died about ten years ago, and he doesn't remember his father . . ."

Sergey turned his back to the astonished Professor and unbuttoned his collar, as if it were choking him.

"You say his name is Vladimir Dobrov?"

Again and again he saw with his mind's eye a woman with a child in her arms, the laughter, tears, smiles of days long past. There she was before him—Anna Dobrova, his wife. He had but to give his memory free reign, and she stood again before him, as if alive. Here are her hands, so near, and in a moment she will raise her eyes . . .

He returned too late.

He had imagined that he had forgotten her, and, to forget her still more firmly, he had flown away. And only somewhere, almost below awareness, he sometimes felt a slight, almost imperceptible, pain—on the left, in his chest. She stole into his dreams all those years. And then he seemed to wander again in waist-high grass. And somewhere nearby, her familiar voice. Yellow-edged evening clouds. Shadows of trees on the damp earth.

With his hands over his face, Sergey once more went

over the details, afraid of making a mistake. His return. The
boys in the street. Elka. Volin. His talk with the Professor.
Vladimir Dobrov. He had his mother's name. A strange coincidence? Chance? No, that was out of the question. They had
returned at the same time. Kopnin was right.

Pressing his head with his hands, Sergey tried to cope
with the torrent of feelings that caught him up. And he could
not. He thought about his son. It never would have occurred
to him . . . though he was so much like his mother.

Their children—his grandchildren. Could that be possible? He longed to see them, but it was night outside. He tried
to recall their faces. The features were familiar, known, yet
they eluded him, dissolved in the darkness, and all he saw in
the night beyond the window were the street lights, like glimmering fireflies, and the long wet rays that spread in all directions around them.

PRELIMINARY RESEARCH

by

ILYA VARSHAVSKY

ILYA VARSHAVSKY, born in 1909, is a designer-engineer and a former sailor. He began writing science fiction in the early 1960s and has published many stories and several collections.

"Look here, Rong, I have lots of patience, but, really, sometimes I am tempted to pick up something heavy and knock you on the head with it."

Danny Rong shrugged.

"Don't think I like it myself, but there's nothing I can do. If the series of control experiments . . ."

"What the devil did you need these control experiments for?"

"But you know that the methodology we followed in the beginning . . ."

"Don't be an idiot, Rong!"

Thorpe Kirby got up from his chair and began to pace the room.

"So you did not get the point of it at all?" said Kirby in a voice that was all honey. He was always very effective in those theatrical transitions from a superior's stern reprimand to a friendly, heart-to-heart talk. "Your work is purely theoretical. No one will draw any practical conclusions from it, at least within the next few years. You will have enough time, oh, say in two years or so, to publish the results of the control series independently and, so to speak, refine and clarify the theory."

"Not clarify but refute it."

"Oh, Lord! Very well, refute it, but not now. After all the expectations we raised . . ."

"We?"

"All right, I. But can't you understand that, after all, there's something more important than your stupid vanity. There are the interests of the firm to consider."

"It isn't vanity."

"What is it, then?"

"Honesty."

"Honesty!" Kirby snorted. "Believe me, I've seen a thing or two in my lifetime. You've probably heard of the preparation called 'tervalsan.' Well, then, do you know that . . ."

Rong closed his eyes, preparing to listen to one of those staggering tales, in which Thorpe Kirby's resourcefulness, his skill in overcoming the intrigues of his enemies, his erudition and intelligence, were to serve as an example to the flock of sheep under his supervision.

Where does he get this assurance? wondered Rong, listening to the purling baritone of his chief. He doesn't know a thing. A windbag and a braggart!

". . . I hope you are convinced now?"

"Absolutely. And if you publish the results of the work without the control series, I shall always find the means . . ."

"Oh, how I would like to give it to you straight from the shoulder! But what's the good, you don't even take offense. I've never seen such a thick-skinned . . ."

"It surprises you that I don't react to your rude-
ness?"

"Well?"

"You see, Kirby," Rong said quietly, "very often we guide
ourselves in our actions by some example. My attitude toward
you has been determined, in many respects, by an incident I
witnessed as a child. It occurred in a zoo. I saw an old man
near the monkey cage, throwing candy to the monkeys
through the wire fence. He must have done it with the best of
intentions. But when he had no more candy left in his pockets, the monkeys flew into a rage. They gathered by the fence,
and before the old man realized what was happening, they
had covered him with spittle from head to foot."

"And what follows from that?"

"He laughed and walked away. And it was then that I realized that a real man cannot take offense at a monkey's insults."

"A lovely story!" said Kirby with a grin. "What I liked
best in it was that, after all, he went away covered with spittle.
A most instructive example. Be careful, Rong, or you may
. . ."

"It's all quite clear, Kirby. Now tell me how much longer
you'll be able to tolerate my presence. The point is that I
would like to finish the last series of experiments, and this will
require at least . . ."

"Well, let's not be petty! I am in no hurry, I can wait
even until tomorrow morning."

"Clear enough."

"Listen, Dan," and a heartfelt note reappeared in Kirby's
voice, "please don't imagine that this is due to any personal
animosity. I think very highly of you as a scholar, but you can
understand yourself . . ."

"I understand."

"I know how difficult it is nowadays for a biochemist to
find a decent job in Donomag. Here is a telephone and an ad-

dress. They pay very well, and, I believe, you work entirely on your own. As far as we are concerned, you can count on the best references."

"I'm sure."

"Incidentally, you have not forgotten that when you came to work here you signed a promise to keep the work in confidence?"

"I have not forgotten."

"Fine! Good luck! If you ever feel like dropping in at my house some evening, for a friendly chat, I'll be delighted."

"Thanks. If I ever feel like it."

"Dr. Rong?"

"Yes."

"Mr. Latiani is expecting you. I'll tell him you're here."

Rong looked around at the waiting room. Everything was in grand style. They didn't try to save money furnishing the place. Evidently . . .

"Come in, please!"

Stepping on the soft, thick carpet, he walked past the door, which was politely held open for him, into the inner room. A tall, baldheaded man with a chalky-pale face rose from behind a desk to greet him.

"Delighted, Dr. Rong! Sit down, please."

Rong sat down.

"If I understood Dr. Kirby correctly, you have nothing against coming to work for us?"

"You understood Dr. Kirby correctly, but I would first like to know the nature of the work."

"Certainly. If you don't mind, we shall talk about that later. In the meantime, I would like to ask you several questions."

"Of course."

"Your work with Dr. Kirby. Did you leave because the results of your work did not meet the initial expectations?"

"Yes."

"Was the idea itself, perhaps . . ."

Rong frowned.

"Forgive me, but I am bound by a pledge, and I would not like to . . ."

"Heaven forbid! I am not interested in the firm's secrets. I should merely like to know whether the idea was not somewhat premature, considering the present level of science. Somewhat fantastic, perhaps?"

"The initial hypotheses were not borne out. In this sense, if you wish, you may consider them fantastic."

"Excellent! And now the second question. Do you indulge in alcoholic beverages?"

An odd way of interviewing future employees, thought Rong.

"I have not vowed abstinence," he replied sharply. "But I don't drink at work. You need not be concerned on that score."

"By no means, by no means," cried Latiani, somewhat overenthusiastically, it seemed to Rong. "There's nothing better for the imagination than a stiff glass of cognac. Even at work. Believe me, this doesn't trouble us at all. But, perhaps, narcotics?"

"Excuse me," Rong said, getting up. "I believe that further conversation in this tone . . ."

Latiani jumped up.

"Oh, no, oh, no, my dear Dr. Rong! I did not mean to offend you in any way. It's simply that the scientists who work for us on the Problem enjoy the fullest freedom. We don't forbid the use of alcohol or narcotics during work hours. Indeed, we encourage . . ."

"You encourage what?"

"Whatever stimulates the imagination. This is the nature of our creative method."

It sounds like a clumsy hoax, thought Rong.

"Mr. Latiani," he said, "perhaps it would be better if you acquainted me first with the nature of the Problem and then we can see if there's any point in discussing the details."

Latiani smiled.

"I would gladly do it, my dear Dr. Rong, but neither I nor any of the scientists working on it have the slightest idea of what the Problem is."

"How do you mean, they've no idea?"

"It's very simple. The Problem is coded in the computer's program. You produce ideas, the computer analyzes them. Whatever is useless is rejected, what can be utilized later is memorized."

"But what is it all for?"

"Well, you see, no matter how perfect the computer, it will always lack the most essential quality—imagination. Hence the machine is helpless when it's a question of finding new ideas. It cannot go outside the bounds of logic. Otherwise, the result will be nonsense."

"And you want . . ."

". . . the machine to make use of the human imagination. For imagination never loses its value. Even the schizophrenic's delusions are composed of entirely concrete concepts, however fanciful their combination. Do you understand me?"

"The quantum of thought," Rong said with a wry smile.

"Exactly!"

"And you expect to solve a complex biochemical problem by this method?"

"Did I say it's biochemical?"

"But if it isn't, then why . . ."

"Why did we invite you?"

"Precisely."

"Oh, we employ scientists of all disciplines—physics, mathematics, physiology, psychiatry, cybernetics. We even have one astrologer."

"A scientist, too?"

"In his own manner, in his own manner."

Rong rubbed his forehead in confusion.

"Still, I don't understand, what will my duties be?"

"You will have to come here by eleven in the morning and remain in your study for four hours. All this time, you must think. It doesn't matter what you think about as long as it has bearing on your field. And the bolder the hypotheses, the better."

"And that is all?"

"That's all. You will start at three thousand sole a month."

Well! This was three times Rong's former salary.

"In the future your salary will automatically increase, depending on the number of ideas accepted by the computer."

"But I am an experimenter."

"Splendid! You can conduct mental experiments."

"But how will I know their results? This needs actual experimentation."

"You need it. The machine employs analytic methods which can determine the results without the actual experiment."

"But will I know these results?"

"Never! The machine will not yield any data until the entire Project is completed."

"And then?"

"I don't know. This is outside my jurisdiction. There is probably a group of people who will be informed of the results of the research on the Problem. I don't know who these people are."

Rong thought about this for a few moments.

"Frankly speaking, I'm puzzled," he said. "All this is so extraordinary."

"Unquestionably."

"And I doubt that it can lead to anything, anyway."

"That, Dr. Rong, is nothing for you to be concerned

about. What is asked of you is to produce ideas. And I repeat, it does not matter what they are—the bolder the better. The rèst will be done by the machine. Remember, you are not the only one on the project. Furthermore, we are now only in the stage of preliminary research. The work on the Problem itself will start somewhat later, when sufficient material has been accumulated."

"One last question," said Rong. "Can I continue my usual scientific work while I am here?"

"That is undesirable," Latiani answered after a moment's thought. "You must not do any systematic work. We want nothing but hypotheses, fragments. In the future, however, you shall be free to utilize them at your discretion. We shall not ask you to sign any pledge."

"Oh, well," Rong sighed. "Let's try it, then, although I don't know . . ."

"Excellent! Come, I will show you to your room."

The giant octopus spread its feelers over an area of several square meters. An opalescent pink liquid pulsed in the transparent tubes, illuminated by blinking lights. Red, violet, green flecks of light tossed back and forth amid an agglomeration of fantastic apparatus, flashed on the dull surfaces of screens, disappeared in the chaotic tangle of antennas and wires.

The cybernetic Moloch was digesting the offerings of its subjects.

Latiani tapped his knuckles on the transparent wall that screened off the machine room.

"It's stronger than steel armor. Not a bad protection against all sorts of eventualities, is it?"

Rong nodded silently, struck by the scale and the fantastic character of the device.

On the other side, there were numerous doors covered with black leather. Latiani opened one of them.

"This is your study," he said, affixing a small plaque to

the door. The plaque had a daisy painted on it. "Many of our staff are, for various reasons, reluctant to advertise their work here; and we ourselves are not interested in it. You will have to guide yourself by this plaque. Here is the key. Entry to other studies is categorically forbidden. The library is at the end of the corridor. And so, tomorrow, at eleven."

Rong glanced in through the doorway. It was an odd setup for scientific work. The room was small, with pink wallpaper. A lantern suspended from the ceiling and decorated with dragons provided dim light. No windows. Along the wall, a Turkish divan with a mass of cushions. Over the divan, a strange contraption that looked like a trough. Next to the divan, a low table with a multitude of bottles with bright labels and little boxes containing what looked like pills of some sort. Not even a desk.

Latiani noticed Rong's puzzled look.

"Don't be surprised, dear Doctor. You will get accustomed to everything very quickly. All this is determined by the special nature of our research."

Think, think, think! What about? Anything at all, but think, this is what you are paid for. Formulate hypotheses, the bolder the better. Well, go on, think! That swine Kirby! If he dares to publish the results without the control series . . . No, that is the wrong subject! Think! But what about? Damn it!

For five days Rong had regularly reported to work, and every day it was the same.

Think!

It seemed to him that even under threat of torture, he could not possibly squeeze a single wretched idea from his mind.

Think!

In despair, he got up from the divan and went to the library.

Chaotic disorder on the shelves. Books on nuclear physics, biology, mathematics were piled helter-skelter with handbooks on chiromancy, descriptions of telepathic experiments, and parchment rolls covered with script in unfamiliar languages. On the table a huge folio in a worn pigskin binding—*White and Black Magic*.

Oh, what's the difference! The more absurd the better! Slipping the book under his arm, Rong dragged himself back to his room.

Lying on the divan, he lazily turned the yellowed pages covered with cabbalist symbols.

Interesting. Some of the figures were reminiscent of logical symbols.

Who knows, perhaps all this abracadabra was only a coded expression of certain logical concepts?

The thought barely flashed through Rong's mind, when a loud chomping sound rose over the divan. A green signal flashed and went out. It looked as though the machine was pleased with the idea.

Gobbled it up? All right, then, think on. What about? It does not matter, but think!

Rong flung the book into the corner, poured himself a glass of dark aromatic liquid from the bottle on the table, and emptied it in a single gulp.

Think!

"Wondering how our cow digests its cud?"

Rong turned. Next to him stood a pudgy man in a crumpled suit, with a face covered with stiff, gray stubble. The acrid smell of wine came from his mouth with every hoarse, asthmatic breath.

"It does look like it, doesn't it?"

"Just think"—the man tapped his fist on the transparent wall—"just think that I gave fifteen years of my life to create this monster!"

"You designed it?" asked Rong.

"Oh, well, not I alone, but much of what you see here is the work of Jan Dorick."

Rong knew the name. A brilliant cybernetist, once upon a time one of the most popular men in Donomag. His work was always veiled by an air of mystery. During the war, Dorick headed the Brain Trust, which consisted of scientists of the most diverse disciplines. However, nothing had been heard of him for the last five years.

Rong looked at him with curiosity.

"Then you are the originator of the program?" he asked.

"The program!" Dorick's face broke out in purple patches. "The devil! I am only a guinea pig here, just like you. None of the people working here has the faintest idea of the Problem. They are much too cautious for that."

"They?"

"Those who hire us."

"Latiani?"

"Latiani is only a pawn, a front. Even he is probably ignorant of who our real employers are."

"But why all this secrecy?"

Dorick shrugged.

"Evidently their Problem demands it."

"And what are you doing here?" asked Rong.

"From this day on, nothing. I've been dismissed . . . for insufficient imagination. A dearth of ideas."

Dorick struck the partition again with his fist.

"See it? There it is, the parasite who feeds on the juices of our brains. Impassive, self-satisfied swine! Of course! What are ants like us, compared with this abomination behind its transparent armor? And, on top of everything, it is immortal!"

"Well, you know," said Rong, "every machine can . . ."

"Look!" Dorick pointed. "You see those turtles?"

Rong looked in the direction of the pointing finger. Among the tangle of bulbs, condensers and resistors, there crawled two small machines that resembled tanks.

"I see."

"All the schemes of the machine exist in duplicate. If any element breaks down, the spare turns on automatically. After that, the turtle nearest to the defective part removes it and replaces it with a new one. There are storage containers scattered throughout the machine. It's quite something, isn't it?"

"Interesting."

"That is my invention," Dorick said proudly. "I made the machine absolutely foolproof. Well, good-bye! Don't you know you must not speak to me? If Latiani finds out, you'll be in trouble. But you know what?" He lowered his voice to a whisper. "Take my advice. Get out of here as fast as you can. It won't lead to any good. Believe me, I've had enough experience."

Dorick pulled a checkered handkerchief from his pocket, loudly blew his nose, waved good-bye, and walked away toward the exit.

Don't think of Dorick, don't think of Kirby, don't think of Latiani, think only of scientific problems. The bolder the hypotheses, the better. Think, think, think. Don't think of Dorick . . .

Rong glanced at the clock. Thank God! The working day was over, he could go home.

He was already halfway to the exit when one of the doors was flung open and a young woman stumbled into the corridor.

"Noda!"

"Oh, Dan! So you are here too?"

"What are you doing here?" asked Rong. "What about your work at the university?"

"It's a long story. Noda Storn no longer exists. There's only that . . . what d'you call it . . . chrysanthemum. A mathematician in the service of a machine . . . the pride and glory of the Problem," she said with a twisted smile.

It was only now that Rong noticed the deathly pallor of her face and her unnaturally dilated pupils.

"What's the matter with you, Noda?"

"Nothing! It's the heroin. Too much heroin this past week. But the work I turned out today! Fantasmagoria in six-dimensional space. Wow, my head is spinning!" She swayed and caught at Rong's shoulder.

"Come," he said, taking her by the arm. "I'll see you home. You look sick."

"I don't want to go home. There is . . . Listen, Dan, do you ever have hallucinations?"

"Not yet."

"I get them. It must be the heroin."

"You must go to bed at once!"

"I don't want to go to bed. I want to eat. For three days I haven't . . . Take me somewhere where we can eat. Only there must be people around, and . . . what do you call it, now? Oh, I mean music."

Wrinkling her face, Noda swallowed several spoonfuls of soup and pushed away the plate.

"I can't eat any more. Listen, Dan, how did *you* get there?"

"Mostly by chance. And you? How long?"

"Long ago. More than six months."

"But why? After all, your position at the university . . ."

"Oh, well! It all started way back, when I was still a student. Do you remember our parties? The usual kid's bravado. And gradually I got into the habit. And they know everything, of course. They probably were watching. And so they offered me a job. Excellent pay, as much heroin as I want. At first I didn't realize what was going on there, but now, when I've begun to guess . . ."

"Do you mean the Problem? Do you know anything about it?"

"Very little, but you know that I'm an analyst. When I developed certain suspicions, I worked out a system of indices. I began to systematize everything the machine was interested in, and then . . ."

She hid her face in her hands.

"Oh, Dan, it's all so frightening! The most terrible thing is that we're so helpless. Nobody knows the program of the machine, and half the addicts and alcoholics working there are former military men. Can you imagine what they could do?"

"You think," asked Rong, "that the Problem has some connection with a possible new weapon? But then, why did they invite me? I'm a biochemist."

Noda broke into hysterical laughter.

"You're a child, Dan! They're looking for new ideas, chiefly on the borderline of various sciences. They're going over everything mankind has ever known from the dawn of time. They juxtapose and analyze it all." She lowered her voice. "You know, in geometry there are imaginary values. No one has ever thought of their physical meaning. But when you are . . . well, under heroin . . . you never know what can come into your head. And every idea I had on the subject was gobbled up by the machine. Haven't you noticed that the bulb over your head often flashes at the most improbable theories?"

Rong thought it over.

"Yes, I suppose you're right. One day—it was close to the end of working hours—I was tired and didn't feel well. And I had the wild idea that if blood contained chlorophyll in addition to hemoglobin, then, given a transparent skin, metabolism within the organism could take place in a closed cycle."

"And then?" Noda leaned toward Rong. "How did she react to it?"

"Chomped like a pig devouring slops."

"You see! I was certain there must be something of the kind . . ."

"I don't know," Rong said reflectively. "All this is very strange, but I doubt if any weapons can be constructed on the basis of such . . ."

Noda interrupted him. "It may not be a matter of weapons. But if my suspicions are correct, this group of maniacs will get into their hands such means for enslaving everyone that even the darkest pages of our history will seem pale in comparison. It's not for nothing that they spare no money and stop at nothing to get the scientists they need into their claws."

"But what can you and I do, Noda?"

"I need two more days to finish checking my hypothesis. If everything is confirmed, we must try to get it out into the open. Perhaps, the newspapers . . ."

"Who will believe us?"

"Then we shall have to destroy the machine," she said, getting up. "And now, Dan, please take me home. I must get some sleep before tomorrow's duel."

Two days went by. Rong did not succeed in his efforts to see Noda. The door of her study was locked from within. No one answered to his knocking.

Rong could not rid himself of anxiety. What had troubled him subconsciously from the very first had turned into certainty after his talk with Noda. Now he was convinced that if the mystery that surrounded the Problem had not been set up to conceal the ominous plans of their employers, there would have been no need for these isolated rooms, the flower codes for the names of their occupants, or the impenetrable wall to protect the machine against all contact from without.

Vainly he waited for Noda at the exit. Evidently, she did not emerge from her study. Or, perhaps, Latiani had suspected something and taken countermeasures.

It was about three o'clock in the afternoon when Rong heard a woman's shriek. He ran out into the corridor and saw two burly guards in white coats dragging Noda away. He rushed toward them.

"They're taking me away," cried Noda. "They must have . . ." Her last words were muffled by the huge paw that covered her mouth. Rong caught one of the guards by the collar.

"Give him a knock on the head, Mike," the guard roared to his companion. "They're all nuts here!"

Rong felt a dull pain in his temple. Varicolored circles flashed before his eyes.

"Where is Latiani?"

"He left about half an hour ago. He won't be back again today."

Rong pulled the door open. The room was empty.

"Where did they take Noda Storn?"

The secretary's face showed astonishment.

"Forgive me, Dr. Rong, but I don't understand . . ."

"Stop playing the fool! I ask you, where did they take Noda Storn?"

"Really, I don't know anything. Perhaps Mr. Latiani . . ."

Rong raised a threatening fist.

"Wait, I'll get back to you!"

He kicked away a chair and went downstairs.

He had to decide.

Unquestionably, Noda had been removed because she had come too close to the solution of the riddle that was the secret of this criminal gang. There would be nothing simpler than to declare the woman insane, with a nervous system unhinged by the constant use of narcotics. Whatever Noda might say, it could always be dismissed as the ravings of a lunatic. After all, she could prove nothing.

Flinging himself back against the cushions on the divan, Rong tried to bring some order into the thoughts rushing through his head, still dazed from the blow.

It would be very difficult to find Noda. They had probably taken her to a psychiatric hospital under a false name. Even if this were not so, medical institutions were reluctant to give information about their patients. And who was he to demand information? As far as he knew, Noda had no relatives. One could search throughout Donomag without discovering anything.

But what was to be done if Noda was not found?

After all, the machine continued to work, and every day brought the dreadful conclusion closer and closer. Damn it! If it were only possible to penetrate that transparent armor!

Rong recalled the two turtles Dorick had shown him. Even if the machine were somehow put out of order, they would immediately repair it. All they needed was the signal. . . . Wait! That seemed to be an idea!

Rong's forehead was covered with beads of perspiration.

The signal indicating the breakdown of any of the elements called the turtle to the trouble spot to replace the defective part with a new one. But what if the process were reversed? What if the absence of the signal made the turtle replace a functioning part with a broken one? But how could this be done? Evidently, somewhere in the scheme you had to switch input to output. Change the direction of the signal, and the self-preservation program in the machine would be transformed into suicidal mania.

There was a sudden click overhead, and the green signal flared up.

Ah! Well, then, let's go on! How penetrate the wall to switch the contacts? This must be done in both turtles. Hurrah! Good for you, Rong! Thank God there are two of them! Let each switch the contacts in the other.

The relays clicked continually over Rong's head. The signal blazed with a bright green light. The machine was obviously intrigued. It remained to be seen whether any practical conclusions would be drawn from the idea.

Rong stepped out into the corridor. The turtles stopped in mid-motion, staring at each other with red eyes. With his heart thumping violently, Rong leaned his head against the transparent wall.

Several moments passed, and then one of the turtles began to feel the other with thin, spiderlike arms. Then, with a motion so quick the eye could barely follow it, it threw back the other's lid . . .

All doubts vanished. The two turtles moved again over the machine, removing condensers and resistors. Judging by their speed, it would all be over in a few hours. Rong grinned. He had nothing more to do here.

Next morning Rong burst into Latiani's office.

"Ah, Dr. Rong!" Latiani greeted him with a mocking smile. "I must congratulate you. As of today, your salary will be raised by five hundred sole. Your idea concerning the turtles has given us a chance to improve the machine's reliability to a very considerable extent. It's simply amazing that we had not foreseen the possibility of such a diversion."

Rong seized him by the throat.

"What did you do with Noda Storn? Where is she?"

"Calm down, Rong!" Latiani flung him back into the chair with a sharp blow. "Nothing will happen to your Noda. She'll have a week's cure for hysteria, and then she will return to us. This has happened several times before. And we shall be delighted to take her back, although the preliminary research has now been completed. Today the machine will start production. It will turn out a thousand science-fiction stories a year. We have invested more than a hundred million sole in this business, and then an ass like you comes along and nearly wrecks the whole thing. Luckily, the automatic safety switch —one of Dorick's ideas—cut off the current in time. I must say, Kirby sent us just the right man! And he's one of the biggest shareholders in the business, too . . ."

HE WHO LEAVES NO TRACE

by

MIKHAIL YEMTSEV AND YEREMEY PARNOV

MIKHAIL YEMTSEV *was born in 1930. A chemical engineer, he has been engaged in scientific research since 1955. Author of numerous scientific works, he lectures, speaks on radio, and does a great deal to popularize the newest achievements in science. In 1961 he began to collaborate with Yeremey Parnov in science fiction and is coauthor with him of many stories and several collections.*

YEREMEY PARNOV, *born in 1935, is a chemical engineer who works in a laboratory of the Soviet Academy of Sciences on problems of the prognosis of oil deposits. He began to publish at the age of eighteen and is the author of more than thirty scientific works and popular science books.*

"There she is," said Nibon, pointing at the pale blue screen.

But Andrey had already distinguished the little planet known as Green Pass. Nibon was always impatient. The ship had not yet come out into orbit, but his mind was already on

Green Pass. He hated waiting; he was always in motion, as if hurrying to get everywhere ahead of anyone else.

"Korin signaled. We'll make a beam landing."

"That's good."

Andrey got up from the control panel, switched over to automatic, and lay down in the start couch. Nibon was already stretched out next to him. Under the transparent violet lid Andrey saw his dense cap of hair and his large black eyes with gleaming, bluish whites. His dark face was covered with a greenish pallor. Since the catastrophe on Black Titan, Nibon had difficulty during landing.

They had had a bad time on Black Titan. Andrey shut his eyes for a moment and recalled the immobile, oppressively heavy planet in the system of the Black Sun, without a single ray of light. Nothing but the faint glimmer of distant stars, which did not penetrate the gloomy clefts in the planet's surface. A planet of eternal night. Andrey shuddered remembering the months they had spent there. Well, it was over. They were going to take a well-deserved rest. The delightful Green Pass that he loved lay before them.

"I think I see George's place," said Nibon.

"We'll be home in a moment." Andrey smiled.

And, indeed, in twenty minutes the two cosmonauts were standing on the landing field on Green Pass.

They were dazzled by the bright light.

"Well, this isn't Black Titan." Andrey smiled, putting on his dark glasses.

"Almost as good as Earth," Nibon said dreamily. "What greenery!"

"Only the sky is a bit too violet. But who cares? The main thing is the air: you can breathe. Not from a cylinder, but like a proper human being—in space, in the sky. . . . Look at the distances around! Ho! Ho! Ho!"

Andrey shouted into the sky, and a faint echo rolled over the deserted green plain that surrounded the landing field.

"But where's George?" Nibon wondered. "Isn't he coming to meet us?"

"What for? He's got the robots to do everything for him
—meeting, sending, loading, checking. . . . We'll go to his
house now and have tea with him. Real, earthly tea. There's
the car."

A small open-topped car drove up. The cosmonauts
loaded their belongings in it and started.

"How good." Andrey smiled.

The narrow road curved in and out through thick grass.
Soft leaves wide as a man's hand brushed against the faces of
the travelers. The delicate aroma of huge mauve-colored flowers filled the air. Andrey plucked some foliage, greedily
smelled it, and licked off the drops of moisture appearing at
the stems.

"What is George's field?" asked Nibon.

"Biophysics. Radio waves and life. We may find him inventing a radio beam that will outstrip the expanding universe, or . . . Ah, but here is Korin's tower!"

The thickets gave way to a clearing, and the cosmonauts
emerged into a small green valley. In the middle of it stood a
clean white little house and next to it a massive tower, bristling with antennas of fantastic shapes and sizes.

No one was at the house. The cosmonauts passed
through all the rooms, from foyer to bedroom. George was
not in.

"Can he be in the tower?"

"No, not likely. He would come out when he saw us.
Let's listen to his secretary."

Andrey turned the knob on a black box in George's
study. At first they heard a child's song performed in a hoarse
basso. Then the same voice said, "I am going to the biozone
for a week. Will return on the seventeenth."

"What is today?" asked Nibon.

"We'll find out in a moment. Here is a local calendar."
Andrey turned a complicated chart in his hands and muttered,

"I can't make head or tail of it. There seem to be five Thursdays and seven Fridays in a week."

"The planet turns pretty fast!"

"Yes, before you have time to look around. George worked out this little calendar for himself in relation to terrestrial time: Monday, a dash, Monday, two dashes, Saturday —Z . . . I don't understand. Wait . . ."

Andrey thought a few moments and exclaimed, "Oh, I see! George will be here the day after tomorrow! Here is a number circled in blue—the day he left—and here is one circled in red—that's today, the fifteenth. There's even a note that we are coming. That means he'll be back in two days."

"Well, then, let's take a rest."

"The best place for that is the roof."

On the roof it was very pleasant. The awnings over the soft chairs kept the air cool. Five-fingered palm leaves swayed gently. From the fields came the faint rustling of grass. The air streaming down from the dark sky was cool and as potent as rum. Andrey felt pleasantly drowsy.

"How good," he said softly, as if to himself, and added, more loudly, "Just like home, in our own garden."

A beautiful, melancholy sound came from the distance, like the twang of a breaking string.

"What's that?" asked Nibon.

"A bird, perhaps, although I didn't see any last time," said Andrey.

"Yes," said Nibon, "if you try hard, you can even forget that there are other . . . terrible worlds."

The distant sound faded slowly, together with the day. Night came quickly on this planet, the sky turned dark at once, and stars began to appear.

"It must be hard for George, being alone here," said Nibon, looking at the tower with the antennas some fifty meters from the house. "I couldn't do it."

The green plain became a deep purple and gradually turned black. The air pouring down from the dark violet sky was now cold and moist. The night seemed to have covered everything with a huge black paw. Nibon looked with regret at the narrow bright strip of light on the horizon.

"It somehow happened this way," said Andrey. "In the beginning there was a large brigade working here—builders, geologists, biologists. When the studies were finished, the brigade was transferred, and George and Mary stayed on. They helped the astronauts who stopped over, and carried on their own research. Whatever there is of the Earth on this planet, is their work. All this greenery, the plantation, the trees . . ."

"Will you show me the place where Mary died?"

Andrey glanced at Nibon with sympathy. All these feelings were familiar to him. It was Nibon's second year in space. Andrey had been flying seven years. Seven terrestrial years—that was a very long time. Until just recently, he used to feel as stricken as Nibon at the news that another human being had perished in space. Now it was different. What he felt now was not so much grief as sadness and sympathy for those who had lost a loved one.

But why yield to such sad thoughts now? They had managed to escape from the deadly grip of Black Titan. There were three of them on this marvelous, comfortable planet—two here, and one somewhere nearby. They must rest and gather strength, prepare themselves for new ordeals, new and difficult tasks.

"It's far from here. In the old mangrove wood. Mary and George were developing plantations of 'stone-eaters' there, and worked in space suits. 'Stone-eaters' are very capricious plants, but they did an important job: they transferred oxygen from oxides of elements into the atmosphere. And so George and Mary had to tend them from dawn to dark. They worked in different places on the planet, because it was important to create an atmosphere as quickly as possible. At that time small meteorites often struck the planet. Today the atmosphere impedes them, but at that time there was none. A fragment struck Mary's helmet when George was far away. She lay unconscious too long . . . George hardly ever leaves Green Pass since then. He visited the Earth several times, but he always returned. I think he is kept here by memories, and also by some research that he began together with Mary. He told me about it last time when I was here, but I didn't quite understand it and had no time to go into it."

Andrey was silent, staring at the black sky, and Nibon tried to imagine what it was like for George to live on this planet by himself. His work probably helped: it always does. It was important work, useful both to people back on Earth, and here, in the endless cosmic spaces.

"You know," Andrey said, so loudly that Nibon gave a start, "I'd call Green Pass a whispering planet. There are no loud sounds here, everything rustles, whispers, hums, purrs."

"And miaows." Nibon smiled faintly. "I wonder, why shouldn't George breed cats here?"

"He's planning to. He's looking for a suitable breed. Shall we go to bed now?"

Morning burst into the bedroom suddenly. Andrey awakened, as if someone had roughly pulled away his blanket.

Nibon was already in the dining room, drinking tea and scanning the pages of the visitors' album, which were filled with sketches, photographs, and inscriptions. Whoever came to Green Pass left an entry in the album as a memento of his stay.

"Here is John the Syrian," Nibon said calmly, pointing at a photograph of a man with an aquiline nose and curly hair. "He never returned from Gor."

"They are gone, Nibon, there's no need to trouble them. Better pour me some tea."

Nibon looked up attentively at Andrey and silently returned to the album.

"This album is a precious record," he said. "I'll ask George to make a copy of it for me. I'll talk to him today."

"You mean tomorrow?"

Nibon did not answer.

Andrey drank his tea with pleasure. Nibon, he thought, was clever, no one would question that. But there was something of an ancient Egyptian in him, a kind of secretive craftiness.

"You saw him?"

"I did."

"When?"

"Just now."

"Then why isn't he here? He isn't hiding from us?"

Nibon silently shrugged his shoulders.

"I saw a man from the window. He was walking across the yard, and I called him. He turned, and I recognized George. He waved his hand and said he'd be right in."

"Where is he?"

"In the tower."

"You're wrong, I'm here!" said a loud voice, and George's smiling, sunburned face appeared in the window.

"Greetings, friends!"

A slender hand with pink nails was laid on the window sill, then another, and George vaulted into the room. He was tall, broad-chested, with slender legs. Dressed in a flowered shirt and shorts, he was more like a carefree vacationer than the master of a planet, burdened with large and complex responsibilities.

"Since when have you taken a dislike to doors?" Andrey grinned. "Meet my partner, Nibon. We were together on Black Titan."

George raised his hand in greeting and, not noticing the hand held out by Nibon, walked over to an armchair. He sat down, crossed his legs, and rested his hands on his knees.

"Well, my friends," he began in solemn tones. "I must tell you right off that our visitors are expected to feel at home on this planet, just as they would on Earth."

"Thanks. If somebody would only bring over the few billion who populate the old lady," remarked Nibon.

"They'd have to sleep standing up," George quipped.

Nibon was right, as always. The thing that was disturbing on this charming planet was its emptiness. People, dear people, with their laughter and tears, their love of beauty, their obstinacy, and even their quarrels! How far away they were!

Something seemed to cross George's mind, and a light grimace ran across his face.

"It's amazing," he said. "Amazing. Not only our ideas coincide but even the formulations of our innermost feelings. How alike we all are! I've been thinking about it. The universe must be colonized with people. Cosmonauts alone are not enough. We need people, lots of them. On the right and left, before us and behind us, on all planets, all asteroids, on large meteorites and even stars."

Nibon glanced at him with interest. Andrey opened and closed his mouth, saying nothing.

They were silent awhile. Suddenly George got up and leaped out of the window. Andrey saw his slightly stooped back float off toward the tower. Nibon went to the window and, following George with his eyes, said:

"Five years alone is, after all, a long time, don't you think?"

"Well, he's not entirely alone. He is always having visitors, like us."

Suddenly Nibon cried out, pointing at something at the end of the yard. Andrey ran over to him.

"What happened?"

Nibon passed his hand over his face, as though to drive away a persistent fly.

"Nothing. It seemed to me . . ."

George's clear, calm voice was heard in the room: "My friends, I am in the tower. Drop in to see me, now, or anytime. I have some new gadgets here to show you."

The interior of Korin's tower was like a large radio laboratory. Andrey remarked to himself on the impeccable order and tidiness in the room. Blue signal lights flashed; the generators hidden behind dazzling white enclosures hummed diligently.

George himself was upstairs. Andrey saw his shoes through the grillwork pattern of the ceiling.

"Come up here!" he shouted. "The elevator is working."

The upper level was a round platform with a window that circled the tower like a glass ring. Under the window, hundreds of control buttons were ranged in fantastic zigzags.

Besides George, they found on the platform an odd-looking mobile construction resembling an octopus. A great many arms, thick and thin, branched out of the spindle-like body resting on casters. The mechanical octopus rolled around the control panel, pressing buttons here and there.

"My robot," George smiled. "Jimmy, meet our guests."

Jim rolled up to Nibon and held out a forest of arms.

"You'll have to shake them all, or he will feel offended," said George.

Andrey touched with repugnance the cold hooks and hammers of Jim's arms.

"Too bad he's blind."

"He had eyes. Red. But the bulbs burnt out, and I've had no time to replace them."

Nibon took out a pack of cigarettes and suddenly threw one to George.

"Catch, have a smoke."

With lightning speed Jim's hand intercepted it.

"Thanks. I've given up smoking," George said, smiling.

Nibon nodded understandingly.

"And what are your new scientific wonders?" asked Andrey.

"Well, of course, they wouldn't be new to you. Soon after your first visit to Green Pass the Office of Reserves sent me a computer. There it is." George pointed down, where the metal partitions of the installations gleamed faintly.

"An old piece of junk, I suppose?" Andrey asked carelessly.

"Why, no! It works very well," said George, and it seemed to Nibon that there was a note of resentment in his voice. "This machine is my only friend—more than a friend, in fact. It's my brain and my soul."

"Now, now," Andrey muttered, puzzled.

"But of course it's a great acquisition for Green Pass," said Nibon.

"It certainly is. You know how many biological problems I've inherited from Mary. It's not only a matter of making the planet resemble the Earth. Green Pass must become better than the Earth. It's important to create here the optimum conditions for the life of the human organism. I have to do a tremendous amount of work in the selection of plants. And in connection with that"—George pondered for a moment— "and with many other things, I have several questions I'd like to clear up with your help."

"Of course, we'll do anything we can."

"You see," George began, somewhat uncertainly. He seemed embarrassed. "Sometimes it seems to me that I've forgotten, or simply do not know, the most elementary things in biology. Take biological immortality . . . All the plants that Mary and I developed will perish, but their offspring will give life to new generations, and so on. But such immortality requires two plants, or two flowers, male and female, but always two, you see. Two kinds, two sexes. In short, two opposites whose combination produces new existence. But what if there is only one side, one sex? How then can it assure its immortality?"

Nibon was silently studying George, and Andrey raised his eyebrows with astonishment.

"Well, after all, there is vegetative reproduction, when every part of the organism can serve as the germ of a new plant," he said. "Stick a cutting into the soil, and it will grow into a new plant as like its parent as two drops of water. Of course vegetative reproduction cannot go on to infinity. At some point degeneration sets in. But take, for example, the asexual reproduction of microorganisms. A simple division of the cell results in the practical immortality of the simplest organisms."

George started, soundlessly clapped his forehead, and burst out laughing. Andrey thought that his laughter seemed forced. Nibon stood motionless, watching the master of the Green Planet.

"Yes, that's true. Of course, division, simple division leads to immortality. I don't know what's wrong with me, how could I have gotten so confused! True, I had other ideas, but still . . ."

He fell silent, as though he were completely muddled. And suddenly he said with utmost calm, "It's time for breakfast. You'll find everything you need in the dining room."

I think he's trying to get rid of us, Andrey thought with surprise.

"Are you coming with us?"

"No, I'm on a diet today. And, generally, my friends, pay no attention to me. I am up to my ears in urgent work, and you need rest. Make yourselves at home."

"Listen, Korin," said Nibon, approaching George. "If we disturb you, tell us directly."

He raised his hand to put it on George's shoulder. But George quickly evaded his touch and withdrew to the window.

"Frankly speaking, my friends, I shan't be able to give you much attention."

"What is it, George?"

"I am preparing for an experiment I want to try, a brilliant, unprecedented experiment. If it succeeds, George Korin's name will be celebrated on all the planets. I cannot talk about it now. It's still a secret. Even to me, it was a secret until today. But you have just spoken the word, Andrey, that

I've needed for a long time. Now I know what to do. I know
the direction I must take!"

"Perhaps five years of solitude is really too much. Even
on Green Pass," Andrey said gloomily, sipping his coffee.
"What do you see out there?"

Nibon stood at the window, watching Korin's tower.

"Half an hour ago Korin and his autospider drove off to
the rocket field. They left the door of the tower open, and I
went down and shut it."

"What for?"

"I don't know."

Nibon knew or sensed something. But then he was always like that. Even when he knew nothing, he had the air of
a well-informed man. When he knew one hundredth of the
facts, you'd think he knew them all. And when he knew half,
he was as arrogant as an encyclopedia.

"Come here," called Nibon, and Andrey saw George skip
lightly out of the car. Jim clambered out behind him, clutching at the doors with his feelers. The robot was loaded with
boxes.

George stopped motionless before the closed door. Jim
put down the boxes and stretched a thin, long arm to the
doorknob. The door flew open, and the robot rolled, growling,
into the dark rectangular opening. George went in after him.

"Well?"

"Nothing." Nibon shrugged. "Shall we take a walk in the
field?"

"With pleasure!"

The field on Green Pass resembled the neatly mowed
lawns of a city park. Andrey walked briskly over the bright
green grass, as resilient as rubber.

"The first symptom of psychic disturbance is fear of society, the wish to withdraw from any human contact," Nibon
said indifferently, walking ahead.

"I can't believe it."

"The second symptom is megalomania. A constant expectation of a mantle of greatness dropping from heaven to encourage the man of genius."

"I can't believe it."

And suddenly they saw George.

Korin appeared so unexpectedly that Andrey almost cried out. How could they have failed to see him in this absolutely flat field?

George stood, swaying slightly and turning his head this way and that. Then his eyes halted on the cosmonauts approaching him. Something akin to confusion and dismay flitted across his face. He turned and rapidly walked away from them.

"George!"

Korin silently increased his pace.

"George, wait!"

Korin sped toward the tower.

"Wait, Andrey," Nibon said calmly. "Look at him running."

"Why?"

"He doesn't crush the grass. He leaves no tracks. He is running in the air."

"You're mad!"

"Too many madmen for such a small planet."

Korin was gliding over the grass. Not a single blade swayed under his steps.

Andrey rubbed his eyes, "I have no fondness for unscheduled miracles."

"Nor I. We must have a talk with George. All those superhumans, walking on the waters, leaving no tracks, outrunning time . . ."

"Look here, Nib, sometimes it seems to me that you know more about George than I do. Or, to put it more precisely, that you suspect him of something. I have no claim on total frankness from you, but still . . ."

"I assure you I know nothing. I have all kinds of suspicions, but I'm afraid to give them free rein."

"What are they?"

"You see, at first I simply decided that he was unhinged. Jumps into windows, does not remember elementary biology, fears people, fears action, and so on. But now I don't understand anything. Madmen don't run like angels. Look, he's disappeared in his tower."

"How did he get in?" exclaimed Andrey. "It seemed to me that he entered without opening the door."

"I had the same impression this morning," Nibon said reflectively.

When they came to the tower, they found the door closed. Nibon knocked several times, and a muffled reverberation rose through the building.

"George!"

Silence.

"George! Korin!"

No one.

They returned to the little house, exasperated and disappointed. Sitting in Andrey's bedroom, they tried to analyze the situation. Many angry and violent words were said, but everything remained as puzzling as before. Nibon divided George's peculiarities into two groups—physical, or visible, and logical, or mental. The former seemed unquestionable; the latter he doubted. Andrey, on the other hand, did not find many of George's actions especially strange, but felt alarmed over his ideas. And, most important of all, this George seemed in some indefinable way different from the George he had known.

"In what way?" Nibon persisted.

"I don't know, I don't know," Andrey repeated, "but it is not the George I knew."

A movement in the room interrupted them. They saw George in the doorway. He walked across the room with soft, silent steps and sat down opposite Nibon. Such a familiar, characteristic pose! Legs crossed, hands on the knees. Andrey avidly studied his face. Nibon drew in the air through his flaring nostrils with a furious snort.

"George, we must have a talk," said Andrey.

George silently stared at them, then, with a pained frown, he said, "Yes, I know. I have to explain many things, but I won't be able to make it all clear to you. Therefore, I don't want you to ask me too many questions. I'll tell you all I can, but no more. Andrey, you are not looking at the George you knew. I am George, and I am not George. I preserve his physical likeness, but I exist in a higher state of matter, qualitatively higher. George is on a lower level. I am more perfect, more ideal, and therefore much higher. The correlation between me and George is the same as the correlation between the brains of a man and an ape."

"What do you mean by that?"

Andrey jumped up from his chair.

A lightning-fast movement, and George slipped out of the bedroom. When Andrey ran into the dining room, it was empty.

"He must indeed be much more perfect than the former George," said Nibon, following him in. "He is able to disappear from a room where all the doors and windows are locked."

"It's some sort of delusion," Andrey cried excitedly. "I could understand monsters on an alien planet, but this is one of us, an earthly man."

"Less earthly, perhaps, than heavenly at this point. There is so little of the material in him . . ."

"What do you mean?"

"It simply seems to me that a man of flesh and bones could not move so fast."

"You think . . ."

"Nothing so far, nothing at all. It only seems to me that you shouldn't have scared him off."

Andrey smoked cigarette after cigarette. He was extremely nervous and irritated.

"The whole trouble is in the tower," he said. "You know what I'll do? I'll go there, knock out the door, grab George by the throat, and make him tell us everything."

"If you can grab him by the throat," Nibon said reflectively, "which I doubt. And another thing: George's tone does not inspire me with confidence. Who knows what danger awaits us when we see him again! We must be careful."

"No, let's go right now. We can't delay. I think that something must have happened on this planet. . . . We must get to the root of it. Something is wrong. We must act."

When they left the house it was dark. Dense black shadows glided along the horizon. Korin's tower, lit from within, seemed ominously mysterious. Andrey's throat contracted with anxiety. They slowly walked toward the tower. To their astonishment, they found the doors open. Nibon boldly moved into the bright strip of light and entered the building. Andrey followed. The hallway was brightly lit, the elevator empty.

As before, the tireless voices of the generator came from behind the steel partitions: George's "brain" was working at full speed. Andrey looked up. Nothing was seen through the latticed ceiling.

"Go up there," he said to Nibon. "I'll look around here."

Nibon entered the elevator, pressed the button, and rose to the upper level of Korin's domain. No one. Jim, looking like a big spider, dozed in the corner, his many arms and antennas drooping.

"Andrey, there's no one here!" shouted Nibon, bending over. At the same moment, he felt someone clasp him tightly from behind.

From below, Andrey saw Nibon's face twist in a frightful grimace, something dark flitted across the semitransparent floor, and everything was silent.

Seconds later he was standing in Nibon's place. The

upper level was empty. The buttons of the control panel stared at him like meaningless rows of dots. Breathless with rage, Andrey kicked the white and black dots. The monotonous hum of the cybernetic machine changed to an angry roar —like the howling of a stricken plane.

A part of the panel dropped off, and Jim appeared in the opening, stretching all his arms toward Andrey.

The encounter with the angry robot boded no good. Andrey rushed to the elevator, but the cabin was not there. Without a moment's thought, he slid down the steel cable. Jim's metal arms clicked greedily behind him.

Blind with fury, Andrey rushed out into the dark night and ran to the rocket.

For several hours he made preparations to fight all the tricks Korin might try. He put on a space work-suit and armed himself with a "sun ray" plasma gun and a special radio device to be used against Jim. The little black apparatus suspended from his neck emitted radio waves of enormous power and could put out of commission any receiving or transmitting apparatus. He was certain that Jim was equipped with such an apparatus. That damned metal octopus would go into a fine dance under a radio-wave barrage.

The "sun ray" was a cosmonaut's best weapon. The gun could throw out a blinding, flashing beam over distances of up to fifty meters. This beam could cut through any rock, any substance, leaving a gap with molten edges. The beam was strong enough to slice into the surface of planets.

When Andrey approached George's domain, there was no one in the yard. He decided to investigate the house first. Stepping heavily with his metal-shod soles, he went through all the rooms. Nothing had changed there since the previous evening. A pack of cigarettes lay on the table; the jacket thrown down carelessly by Nibon was on the chair. Andrey sat down by the window, aiming the radio-gun and the "sun ray" at the door of the tower.

He had to wait for a long time. No one appeared, and he was on the point of going to the tower himself. But the moment he left the house, Jim rolled out of the tower door and crept toward Andrey with a low growl. George appeared in the doorway behind Jim and stopped, leaning against the door.

"Listen, George," Andrey said hurriedly, one eye on the approaching robot. "I don't understand what's going on here. There are many things I can't understand. And, damn it, for the sake of our old friendship you might tell me what it's all about. What is the matter with you, George? Why did you attack Nibon? Where is he? Is he alive? Oh, take away that blasted spider!"

Jim stopped obediently.

"I'll try to explain it to you." George spoke in an even voice. "I am fulfilling my life program. Just as you have to eat, breathe, and sleep, so I have to perform a number of operations in order to live. And I shall eliminate everything that stands in my way."

Andrey looked into his eyes, and all the absurd hypotheses and vague feelings that had stirred in him turned into certainties. George's eyes were more terrible than a madman's. There was nothing human in them. The bottomless vacuum in those eyes filled Andrey with heavy, oppressive fear. There was no doubt that this George was a mortal danger to everything alive on the planet.

The horror that chilled his heart sent his hand in an unconscious movement to the handle of the "sun ray" pistol.

At the same instant Jim, his arms spread out like a fan, rushed at Andrey. Another second and the robot would have wrapped him in his steel embrace. But Andrey pressed a button, and Jim grunted and came to a standstill.

George, who was standing near the door, made a strange, hurried movement. This movement was astounding, fantastic. A part of his body entered the wall, as though it had been sliced off, and the other half stood out like a carved relief. Andrey saw everything in detail. He was stunned with surprise, which seemed to amuse the master of Green Pass.

Andrey felt the sweat on his gloved palms. His throat went dry. George grinned silently. The cosmonaut saw the wrinkles on his face, the gleaming of saliva on his white teeth, the depth of his transparent, light gray eyes, but he could not believe that this was a man before him. An ordinary man of flesh, blood, skin, and muscles.

Some sort of delirium. Diabolic mystification. Forgetting everything, Andrey cried out and rushed toward George. He clutched him but felt his hands sink deeper and deeper, until they met somewhere inside George's body. George was there, he stood before Andrey, but it was impossible to grasp him. He was impalpable.

When Andrey's head struck George's chest, it entered it easily, as though sucked in. At that moment Andrey ceased to distinguish anything around him. It was as if he had been caught inside a milky sphere. Rainbow-colored fans scattered before his eyes, and a strange heaviness pressed against his temples. With a violent effort he leaped back, pulling his head out of George's body, which was viscous like molasses. Everything returned to its place. He could see the yard again, and the tower with its antennas, Jim's remains in the grass, the bright violet sky, and the still-smiling George.

"Calm down," said George.

And suddenly Andrey noticed for the first time what it was that distinguished this George from the one he had known. The sound of his voice did not come from his mouth but somehow from elsewhere. Now his voice came from the tower, as though a prompter were hidden there. That's what it was: George's voice was somewhere outside his . . . no, not body, one could not call this apparition a body. It was, rather, an image of a body.

Oddly enough, Andrey felt calm. When there are too many wonders, they cease being wonders, they no longer amaze you. After all, Andrey decided to himself, this unnatural claptrap had to have some explanation. The most important thing at the moment was Nibon.

"Well," said George, "now you've had an opportunity to convince yourself that I am far superior to the George who was your friend. However, through force of habit, his habit, I still feel friendly toward you, although the instinct of self-preservation tells me that I will probably have to revise this feeling. And the same instinct prompted the need to isolate your companion. You need not worry, Nibon is safe. But neither can he harm me. As for me, I am not a man. Or rather I am a man but in a purer, more refined state. I am purged of everything low and carnal.

"I am an extract of man's whole spiritual and intellectual content. To paraphrase a well-known adage, I can say: I am a man, but everything human is alien to me, if by 'human' we mean the usual range of petty weaknesses common to men of flesh and blood. I am not material in the generally accepted sense of the word. As you have seen, I am not subject to the barriers and limitations that exist for humans. I don't need air, I don't need food, I am not afraid of high temperatures, I can move at any speed I choose, even at the speed of light. I might say that I am divine, but until now there has been one thing I lacked, which limited my powers. I am speaking of immortality."

Andrey listened to George's tirade with mixed feelings of revulsion and astonishment. This was not an insane George but an insane phantom, which in some miraculous way had assumed George's likeness. Hence he must listen and try to understand what gave this phantom its vital energies. George, in the meantime, continued to expatiate:

"Last night's talk with you gave me an opportunity to establish a fact which had not previously been programed into my memory. I knew that immortality consists of continuous reproduction and the appropriation of more and more space. I have decided to utilize this biological principle, but purged of your earthly vileness. Today you will see George's immortal, impalpable, and invincible images start out from here to all ends of the universe. The great civilization of the impalpables will take its first steps from the little planet called Green Pass. In our conquest of the universe we shall go much further than men, for we are not afraid of any material barriers. Try to be calm, or I shall have to isolate you too."

George turned and withdrew into the tower. Andrey went back into the house, removed the clumsy work suit, and sat down near the window opening on the yard. He studied the tower, heavy and gloomy like the statue of an antique idol against the clear sky, and thought of how he could fight this George. What could an impalpable being feel? What were its vulnerable spots?

Andrey tried to think logically, but the recent events defied logic.

So George was not George but an apparition. Yet he possessed powers over material bodies: he commanded Jim, he attacked Nibon. It was impossible to seize him or to kill him. But he himself was also incapable of seizing or killing. He was incorporeal; this was both his strength and his weakness. Formerly, George had Jim at his disposal, an obedient robot —servant, laboratory assistant, aide, and friend. Now Jim was paralyzed for a long time. Hence, George had no material arms. Hence, too, he was defenseless against a material entity like Andrey. But perhaps George still had Jim's brothers? Hundred-armed monsters, automatic henchmen of that newly manifested, incorporeal dictator?

It was necessary to reevaluate everything, to weigh all factors carefully again.

Meantime, George reappeared by the window. He no longer had to be afraid of being seen. He no longer took any account of Andrey, since his secret was out.

George had come directly through the wall of the tower

and hung suspended several meters above ground. He waved to Andrey, who bent over the windowsill. Brightly lit by the daylight, he resembled a rope walker over a circus arena. Suddenly George began to expand like a toy balloon. Gradually he lost all human shape and turned into a huge, gleaming sphere. George disappeared. In his place there hung a quivering, vari-colored globe. On the surface of this globe, there was constant movement. White, black, and colored dots were sliding right and left, up and down in complicated combinations.

Then the globe flattened, stretched, and became spindle-shaped. The spindle split in the middle, and two new spheres were formed. Their formation was accompanied by a loud re-port, and huge blue sparks, as big as a fist, flew from the an-tennas on the tower. The two spheres quivered and spread, changing their outlines. Another report, and two new Georges hung in the air. They seemed to be very happy over their "birth." The apparitions shook hands, clapped one another on the shoulders, and smiled. Then they began to blow them-selves up and turned into iridescent, colorful spheres. A few seconds later these spheres produced four new Georges.

I see, thought Andrey. The ghosts are carrying out a pro-gram for the conquest of space. The Georges are multiplying. This was the beginning of the great offensive of the impalpa-ble, incorporeal Georges.

Look at them! Just like people! They smile to one an-other, stroll around. But they are not speaking, I hear no sounds.

Oh, you damned soap bubbles! Do you really intend to take possession of the planet, the universe, space? Will our beautiful world be overrun by these mock-Georges, these shad-ows of humanity?

Look, they seem to be engaging in sports. What would apparitions want with sports? Does Satan need calisthenics? Perhaps they have feelings too? Perhaps they can cry, or fall in love with one another? Or with their idea—pan-Georgism?

But they are not all equal. Some are so inert that one begins to doubt their intellectual capacity as well. But others are as self-satisfied as masters of ceremonies. Oh, we're in a bad way, they multiply like infusoria.

In the meantime, the Georges were constantly growing in numbers. They shut out the view of the tower, and Andrey could guess only from the flashes that the multiplication went on at a furious rate. The backs, faces, stomachs, and legs of the Georges floated before Andrey. He saw groups of three fly up to great heights and seem to dissolve there.

Going into the cosmos! Andrey said to himself. And what if they should meet a space craft? What then? What are the people to do? Stop? Or try to catch them?

Andrey imagined the endless confusion and complications that the appearance of the Georges in space would bring about.

No! These soap-bubble conquistadores must be fought! They must be destroyed.

Andrey's thoughts rushed faster than light. Where was the solution? What was the weakest spot of those impalpables? Where was their Achilles' heel?

And if this was not George before him, but an apparition in his shape, then . . . where was George himself? Where was that material body which moved, breathed, and worked on Green Pass?

It was possible, of course, that George's experiments had led to some disaster that destroyed him and produced those unholy permeable puffballs. Or . . . But anything was possible, and only experiment and investigation could provide an answer.

One of the Georges detached himself from a group of ghosts, floated over to Andrey, and putting his head in through the open window, asked, "Well, what do you think of it, eh?"

And all the specters in the air and on the ground cried out in chorus, "Well, what do you think of it, eh?"

There was something preposterous in this unanimity.

"It's depressing," Andrey said with an angry snort.

"Just wait and see what comes next." George winked significantly and disappeared.

Was it a threat or a boast? Andrey was suddenly struck with the whole absurd unreality of the moment. All familiar ideas and norms were blurring and dissolving. Even to an experienced cosmonaut, who had long learned that earthly concepts and limitations had only relative validity, what was now taking place before his eyes was excessively, irritatingly unreal. The air seemed to be heavy with tension, with the threat of something even more absurd to come.

Yet, at the same time . . . Andrey could not quite define it, but there seemed to be an almost ludicrous artificiality in the situation. These spectral Georges looked much too unnatural in the bright light of day, against the violet sky, especially to one who knew their true insubstantiality.

"A stupid comedy," he muttered.

He wanted to rub his eyes and walk out of this dream, but one could not walk out and leave Nibon behind. And George . . . What had become of him? Everything was much too confused.

He must go up into the tower. Jim's mechanical brothers could, if they existed, be put out of commission in a single moment. And there was no one else he feared.

In the doorway he encountered two Georges and boldly plunged through them. But this turned out to be more difficult than it seemed. It was easy enough to walk into an apparition, it sucked one in like a bog, but, also like a bog, it would not let its victim go. The left half of his body was caught in a ghost, and Andrey could not pull himself out until he made a sharp effort. He got through the second ghost by taking a running start. This was a good method: there was almost no resistance, only a sudden vivid flash of light.

When he ran out into the yard, Andrey stopped in astonishment. The entire space between the house and the tower was filled with Georges. The phantom host swarmed all the way to the horizon. Some Georges floated in small groups over the heads of others, who were sitting below, on the grass. And although they were all the same Georges, in the same jackets and trousers, and Andrey was by now thoroughly sick of them, he sensed that they were becoming different now.

He noticed their fidgety, seemingly nervous movements. The ghosts were excited and upset by something. Some were hurriedly moving away, others hung helplessly, with outspread hands, their heads turning around rapidly, like tops. A child had appeared among them, or, rather, a "micro-George." It was a ghost exactly like the big George—a miniature model, faultlessly true in every detail. Andrey also noticed several giant Georges in the crowd.

So that was it! The ghosts began to stratify. Among them there appeared both titans and midgets, and it seemed that they were not on the best of terms. Andrey saw a huge George bump, as though accidentally, into a normal-sized one, and the latter stuck to him, wriggling desperately, as if trying to free himself. Andrey watched with amazement as the smaller ghost shrank and withered to the size of a year-old child. And finally, the big George, grown still larger, shook off the midget George from the palm of his hand and, swaying with a great sense of importance on his huge pillar-like legs, approached the next George, who darted away in panic.

They are sucking each other in! Andrey exclaimed to himself. So much for pan-Georgia! What will become of it now?

The giant ghosts wandered among their brothers like mammoths in the grass. For some reason, the strongest of them gathered around the tower, as though held to it by invisible chains.

The larger a ghost became, the more easily he absorbed the others. He did not even have to touch them anymore; they seemed drawn to him as to a magnet. The midget ghosts were swept up into the air like autumn leaves driven by a storm. They clung to the giant's back, head, feet, and disappeared . . . And the titans grew and grew. Some of them were as much as thirty meters tall. The chain reaction of mutual absorption swept all the Georges. A storm broke in the air. A violent blast of wind knocked Andrey off his feet. The battle was now between the giant ghosts. But it could scarcely be termed a battle. Andrey could not distinguish between attackers and attacked. All of them seemed to be puzzled and confused. In an accidental movement one brushed against another, they clung together, there was a loud report, and one disappeared, while the other grew bigger. The face of the enlarged George bore the same expression of consternation as that of his recently swallowed brother.

There was no fire during this fusion of the giants, but the air wave threw Andrey back several times as he sought to return to the house. The ceaseless flickering, the dull thumps, as though bags of sand were tossed down from a great height, the howling of the wind and the booming of the fusing Georges, reminded Andrey of the eruption on Black Titan.

"A fine planet for a rest cure!" the cosmonaut said to himself wryly. He raised himself on his elbows, trying to crawl, but at that moment the "sun ray" plasma gun slipped off his neck and rolled toward the tower. And by the tower stood the last George. Indeed, it would be more exact to say that Korin's tower stood next to this George, since it did not reach much higher than his knees.

"A jinn! The thief of Baghdad! Nassredin in Bokhara! Old Man Khottabych!" whispered Andrey, his eyes glued to the gun.

At first it moved slowly, catching against bumps in the ground, then it somersaulted and entered George's shoe as easily as had the midget Georges. It was followed by a large rock which had been lying near the entrance to the courtyard.

Andrey saw all the relatively small objects in George's vi-

cinity swallowed up within him. Everything that was not
fixed, nailed, or tied was drawn toward the giant phantom.
Stones and paper flew toward him, bits of grass and leaves
were swept through the air in his direction, a cloud of gray
dust surrounded his giant shoes. He seemed to work like an
enormous vacuum cleaner, sucking into himself rubbish, dust,
sand, and stones.

"He'll get me next," flashed in Andrey's mind. His appre-
hensions were borne out. George stepped forward, and at that
moment Andrey felt as if a dense cloud had dropped upon
him from the sky. There was a chomping sound; red, blue,
and yellow sparks flashed before his eyes; and a powerful jolt
lifted Andrey from the ground, at which he was clutching
with his hands. Then he was turned upside down and carried
upward along an invisible spiral. He floated, feet up, through a
rainbow-colored mist. A heavy weight seemed to be crushing
his body. The blood pulsed feverishly in his temples. It was
very hot.

Reaching an invisible apex, he dropped smoothly to the
bottom and began a new ascent along the spiral. Gradually,
Andrey became accustomed to his extraordinary situation. He
realized that he was revolving inside the ghost. Around him
whirled all the objects swallowed up by George. Andrey was
repeatedly struck by them. The vast quantity of dust that
filled George made it difficult to breathe. Andrey sneezed and
cursed, but no matter how he tried, he could not alter his position. A stubborn, powerful force turned him around and
around inside George as simply as it swirled all the trash collected by the giant.

The most irritating thing was the stone. It revolved somewhere next to Andrey, and at the sharp turns of the spiral it
moved faster than he did, hitting him painfully in the shoulder or chest. The situation was rotten. Andrey was suffocating
with heat and dust. His body, which seemed compressed with
invisible elastic bands, was burning. His nose, ears, eyes, were

filled with dust. Andrey could not see anything in the milky jelly surrounding him. The approach of an object was marked by a flash, a sheaf of dazzling sparks.

The stone kept hammering at Andrey with dull, methodical persistence. In a rage, he grabbed it with his hands and suddenly felt that his ascent was broken. At first he spun rapidly, then he began to slide down a gently sloping spiral. Andrey dropped the stone and fell upon the ground. Sweet, pure air filled his lungs.

He rubbed his tearing eyes and found that he was lying, covered with dust, scraps of paper, and other trash, on a pile of rubbish before the tower. The George ghost was gone. The yard was empty.

Andrey clambered out from under the trash, picked up the "sun ray" and walked to the tower. It took a minute to cut away the door. Andrey entered.

Inside the tower, he heard a muted, almost soundless buzz, like the hissing of a squashed snake. The cybernetic brain was working. There was an acrid smell in the air. The insulation must have burned out somewhere.

Andrey entered the elevator with the gun in his hand. He pressed the button, but the cabin would not start.

I'll have to pull myself up, thought Andrey, examining the cable over the elevator. He jumped up and seized the metal cable with his hands. The thin wires stung his palms like needles. With his feet braced against the wall of the shaft, Andrey inched up slowly, step by step. It was not very difficult, but the ominous silence took away his breath.

At last he found himself upstairs, on the platform before the main control panel. The chute from which Jim used to appear was open, and light coils of smoke rose from it. Andrey looked in but could see nothing through the smoke.

Going down was risky. Nevertheless, Andrey climbed into the chute and began to crawl down, pressing his back and his feet against the opposite walls of the passage.

At the bottom his hands found a small door, like a hatch. His bruised fingers were barely able to feel the rough heads of the rivets. He pressed with his shoulder, but the hatch did not open. With the "sun ray" Andrey neatly cut an opening the height of a man. The metal plate fell back with a deafening crash, and a bright sheaf of light dazzled him for a moment.

He realized that he had come to the heart of Korin's laboratory. The large room was crowded with elaborate apparatus. The numerous extinguished screens stared at Andrey in mute reproach. In the middle of the room stood a contraption enveloped in flames: it was reminiscent either of a throne or an electric chair, enclosed in a transparent egg-shaped bubble. The smoke and fire made it impossible to distinguish the details of the device.

Suddenly a human cry made Andrey start.

"Here! Here! Here, Andrey!"

He recognized Nibon's voice. Nibon stood in the corner of the room, behind a grating. Andrey rushed to him. A few moments later, the friends embraced.

"I thought we were done for!" Nibon said, smiling. Then he turned toward his prison and cried, "Come on out!"

George appeared on the threshold. With an angry, mocking glance, Andrey rushed at the ghost, head foremost, and gasped with pain. It seemed to him that he had wrenched his neck.

The ghost, heavy and hard as a sack of shot, lay on its back, kicking its legs, moaning and cursing.

"George! George!" cried Andrey. Before him was the old Korin. A palpable, lean, and jolly earthman.

The cosmonaut's eyes filled with unexpected, stupid tears.

"All right," he said in a choked voice. "You'll explain everything later, let's get out of here before we're roasted."

And now the three friends were on the roof of Korin's house. Andrey kept feeling George.

"I hope you won't reincarnate yourself again?" he asked mockingly but with persisting anxiety.

"Oh, no, my friend, no! I'm not the right material for a god. And all the higher posts in paradise are taken. I wouldn't want to work as a supernumerary angel."

"I'd say the impalpable George was more interested in the role of a devil," remarked Nibon.

"I guess so," George agreed. "But I must tell you how it all happened."

George glanced dreamily at the darkening sky. Green Pass was turning its face toward night.

"We're such fools," he said reflectively. "We're still so stupid. We don't foresee the most immediate consequences of our actions. There is still so much we don't know, so much that is beyond our grasp. What do you think started this whole business of the impalpable George, whom you've both had the pleasure of meeting?"

"We've not only met him, we've been his victims," said Nibon.

"Well, this is what started it. At first I had only an idea, and it was a simple one. I defined it with a single word, *stereo-television*.

"Ordinary television requires a screen made of certain materials. On such a screen the electronic beam produces an image. So I thought: Why not use space as the screen? If we can project the image in space, we shall have a three-dimensional representation of the object. But I got nowhere with ordinary space. All my efforts ended in failure.

"Then I concluded that some kind of screen was necessary, after all. But a very special one.

"And here a certain phenomenon came to my aid. You've heard, I am sure, of spherical space and of the deformation of space under the pressure of large masses.

"Well, I succeeded in building a generator of curved space. The powerful gravitational field obtained in a vacuum accelerator possesses entirely new, remarkable properties. The more powerful the gravitation, the greater the curvature of space. When the curvature attains its maximum, space closes up, as it were, forming a spherical gravitational field which does not manifest itself in any way. But if you are within it, you feel a considerable increase in weight. It was this increase in gravitation that seemed to compress your head, Andrey, when it was inside the impalpable George. It was that, too, which whirled you inside the giant George.

"Besides, this gauss-space (I call it GS) is entirely opaque. Light rays are caught in it as in a prison. They are unable to break out, and revolve in circular orbits.

"But light striking the surface of such a sphere is well reflected and can be seen by any outside observer. Once it originates, the GS will persist as long as energy is fed into it. It can move in ordinary space at virtually any speed, up to the speed of light. By altering the field of force, the GS can be expanded or compressed, like a football bladder.

"When I succeeded in obtaining the spherical gauss-space, I had a great sense of triumph. The huge white sphere —the potential screen of the future three-dimensional television—hung suspended in the air before my tower. Every morning, as I passed by, I greeted it. How could I have imagined where the tortuous road of the inventor would lead me?

"For a long time I tried to impart to the gauss-space the form of the object whose image I wanted to transmit. I finally succeeded after I developed a special telebroadcast camera. You saw the egg-shaped bubble in my laboratory? That was the camera. It is badly damaged now, but it can be repaired.

"The man or the object was enclosed in the camera. The electronic beams directed from every side at the object found every curve, every fold of its surface. Information about the size and shape of the object was transmitted in the form of definite impulses to the gauss-generator, and it deformed space in accordance with this information.

"And so, one fine day, I obtained a replica of myself in

space. Suspended before the tower was no longer a sphere but a figure of George, which looked as if it were carved in marble."

"But wait," cried Nibon. "What about colors? You had perfectly real, natural coloring! I remember your cheeks and your eyes."

"Right. But that came considerably later. At first the phantom George was milky white. Manipulating it with the aid of the gauss-generator, I made my image grimace and move in any way I wished. I must confess, that clown brought me a good deal of amusement. Infinitesimal changes in the radiation force made the image go into the wildest contortions. It was controlled with the utmost ease. I could, without any effort, make it fold its legs behind its head and send it galloping across the field on its hands. Then I got tired of controlling the ghost's movements and turned the task over to the electronic brain I received from the Office of Reserves. I must say that it's an extremely powerful machine. I set up all of it in my tower and adapted it for my purposes. And in less than three weeks the Big Cyber, as I named this electronic brain, mastered the work of the gauss-generator and began to guide the ghost's movements better than I myself. Of course I first had to program it with all sorts of information on human movements. But then it became very easy to control the stereo-image. I would command it to waltz, and the ghost diligently performed a waltz; I'd command St. Vitus' dance, and the image went into spasms. To make it short, I attained a high degree of perfection. When I was not in the cabin, the Big Cyber itself thought up 'commands' and directed the 'ghost.'

"Everything was going well. The only thing that troubled me was the question of color. The whiteness of the image began to irritate me. For a long time I could not think of a solution, until I began to study the structure of the gauss-space. I found that the density of gravitation on the surface of the sphere could be altered by altering the power supply. At times electromagnetic waves could penetrate inside the gauss-space. This meant that some of the light rays could penetrate and be absorbed by the gauss-space, and hence, that the rest of them, reflected from it, would give it color. The trouble was that the absorption and reflection of light rays occurred only with a low intensity gravitational field, when the gauss-space was not closed up into a sphere. Then I tried to apply space over space. Two gauss-spaces, of different intensities, were brought into the same spot. I covered a high-energy grav-itational field with a weaker one, which served as a kind of sheath. And it was this surface layer that absorbed and re-flected light-rays. The degree of absorption changed in accord-ance with the density of this layer. I began to produce three-dimensional colored images of various objects. It was a com-plete triumph, and I was just about to report it to Earth when something happened that made me forget everything else in the world for a long time.

"The colored images of a chair, a hat, apparatus, a gas burner satisfied me completely. They hung in the air before the tower. I studied them in detail and found no fault. Every-thing was right. Perfect objects."

"Except that you could not use them," remarked Nibon.

"Of course. But after repeated experiments, I decided to try an image of myself. My cabin became even more complex. It was surrounded by a solid electronic measuring field, which fixed the spatial position of my body, its form, dimensions, the color of my face, clothing, and hands.

"And one fine day I climbed into my transmitting appa-ratus, switched it on, and began to wait. Before me was an or-dinary television screen, on which I could see the yard, the tower, and the milky sphere of the gauss-space. I observed the changes in the white sphere as it acquired the shape and color of my clothes. I could already distinguish my own hands and feet, then my head, when suddenly . . . something happened. I no longer saw the television screen, the Big Cyber, the gauss-generators. It was as if I had been flung out of the tower, although I had not felt any jolt. The only thing I felt was that my eyes hurt.

"I found myself out in the yard, where the gauss-space was. I saw my house, the tower, the grass, several meters beneath my feet, and the sky overhead. At the same time I was in my transmitter, although I did not see it at all. When I raised my hands, they touched the smooth plastic walls. I took a step, and my forehead struck an obstacle. With great difficulty, knocking myself black and blue, I managed to find the switch with my hands and turned off the current. And then I was back in the cabin where I had been all the time, or, rather, I saw it again.

"And so I discovered the feedback effect. I had seen inside my cabin what my incorporeal eyes saw outside the tower. Then I realized that this was another important discovery. I decided to check it once more. Experiments confirmed the existence of feedback.

"Remaining in the cabin, without moving from the spot, I flew all around the planet, looking into every nook and cranny. I was delighted. It was better than any television."

"I can imagine," Nibon snorted disapprovingly.

"I even managed to rise above the atmosphere of Green Pass. But I could not rise still higher, into outer space. The big gauss-generator was not strong enough for that. But in principle it should not be impossible.

"I don't know how to describe my state of mind during those first days. I worked almost without sleeping. I was elated and full of hope.

"And one day . . ."

George paused to reflect, shook his head, and went on: "You see, while I was studying the feedback, I was all the time inside the telecenter. This was necessary in order to see with my own eyes everything outside the tower.

"Later I decided to leave the telecabin. Instead of myself, I installed a device along the feedback line that would receive the light signals, and connected it with the Big Cyber, which was to interpret the visual information received. By doing this I provided the Big Cyber with eyes, as it were, and lent the stereo-image a cybernetic brain. Now this machine could lead an independent existence. I was superfluous. The machine had the eyes of the impalpable George, the brain of the Big Cyber, and a heart in the shape of the gauss-generator. As long as there was current in the lines, the heart beat efficiently. Oh, yes, I've forgotten to say that it also had hands—the robot Jim. Of course, the robot obeyed me, but the machine had a separate powerful transmitter and often controlled the robot as it wished. And this was how the pseudo-George came into the world as an independent individual.

"I began to teach the 'ghost.' At first I made extensive use of the imitation principle. The ghost traveled about with me on the planet, observed, looked, and learned.

"I taught 'George' to read, but, unfortunately, he could speak only inside the building or near it. Out in the field he was mute. This was because I had provided for microphone-telephone communication with the Big Cyber only within the limits of my courtyard. When you conversed with the impalpable George, you were actually conversing with the Big Cyber.

"You might ask what I needed the pseudo-George for. What, indeed, did I want with it? Well, feedback and the creation of a stereo-image are important in themselves. Besides, George was the logical next step in my experiment. And secondly . . . Secondly, all of us students of the cosmos can use such an assistant. Not a robot like Jim but a real assistant, with a mind, experience, knowledge. Can you imagine how marvelous it would be to have such an invulnerable companion on our dangerous journeys to other planets? He would enter noxious atmospheres, go into fire and smoke, have no fear of the cold of space . . . But why elaborate? You are well acquainted with the virtues of my double.

"And this is why it seemed particularly important to me to educate him, to bring him to an advanced level of technical and intellectual development. He was to become a walking encyclopedia, an adviser and consultant.

"And then I realized that pseudo-George could also be used for gathering information without man's presence. For example, you leave the Big Cyber on an unknown planet and go on to take care of your other cosmic business. By the time you return, pseudo-George will have investigated the entire planet and studied everything he could. If you provide him with a Jim, capable of lifting weights, moving rocks, collecting samples, and analyzing them, pseudo-George will become an indispensable explorer, whom you can send even to such grim places as Black Titan. The geologists and builders who come to these places later will owe many thanks to such all-round electronic explorers.

"And if, for any reason, it is impossible to set up the Big Cyber on the planet itself, it can be installed anywhere else— on an artificial satellite, a neighboring planet, anywhere within reasonable distance of the exploration site. I can even envisage pseudo-Georges speeding ahead of our interplanetary rockets. The cosmonauts will be able to see approaching danger from vast distances 'with their own eyes.' And, incidentally, they will be able to visit planets as they fly past, without landing on them.

"Pseudo-George has one special characteristic. Because of his nature (for he is only a bit of curved space), he is very sensitive to increased gravitation. When he gets into a strong gravitational field, he is deformed, flattened, and disappears. There you have an excellent gravilocator for cosmonauts: the approach of a strong gravitational field will be signaled by the clouding of the ghost's field of vision."

"Oh, well, you couldn't respond soon enough with such a gravilocator," said Nibon.

"Why not? Pseudo-George can fly at a sufficient distance

from the rocket. If there is a powerful generator, of course. And then, just think of the new forms of communication between planets populated by humans. A man will be able to visit Mars, Venus, all the planets of the solar system without leaving his apartment on Kutuzov Street."

"Incredible," Andrey said quietly.

"Of course, for the time being pseudo-George is not for individual use. But I've digressed. . . . There was still another aspect to all the things that happened here . . ."

George paused. He rubbed his forehead with evident confusion, spread his fingers, and slowly went on, without looking at his listeners: "There is a great deal that I still don't understand and cannot explain. I have a nagging feeling that a mistake was made somewhere along the way. Or, perhaps, not a mistake, but simply failure to foresee everything—hence the unexpected results. But it is still unclear to me what exactly went wrong. Let me tell you how this whole thing happened.

"It was a great pleasure to work with my double. During the early stages of his development he was like a child with an extremely curious mind. But the infantile period ended quickly; it lasted only several weeks.

"I programed the Big Cyber with the basic principles of self-teaching machines and so gave my ghost an opportunity to develop and perfect himself. For a time he was so damnably like me that it began to irritate me. It's not that pleasant, after all, to have a mirror before you all the time! To hear your own thoughts, spoken in your own voice, to see your own smile of the day before yesterday. Who wouldn't be annoyed? At times it seemed to me that I was watching a strange film about myself and at the same time participating in it. But very soon everything changed.

"The self-improvement program given to the machine began to bear fruit. Not bitter fruit at first, not by any means. But there was an element of surprise in its progress that occasionally staggered me. My impalpable double was changing radically. He became more independent, and no longer simply imitated me. He acquired something distinctly his own, which quickly replaced my little habits and eliminated much of his resemblance to me.

"He was a nice enough fellow on the whole. Disciplined, well-informed, able. He was responsive and observant. When I was sick, the ghost himself diagnosed the illness, prescribed medication, and looked after me better than any doctor or nurse.

"Noticing that I was taking flowers every week to Mary's grave, the ghost began to do this every day. His bouquets were much more tastefully arranged than mine. But his most important characteristics were his extraordinary diligence and talents. We carried out a great number of most interesting experiments in evolutionary genetics. And he was always ahead of me. Original insights seemed to spring up spontaneously in his mind. At times I had difficulty in keeping up with him.

"I realized that pseudo-George had developed into a powerful intellectual machine. His thinking was sharp and fresh, and his work was carefully thought out and efficient. And yet there was something machinelike in him, qualities that belonged precisely to a thinking machine, not to a human being.

"I remember the time when an unusual weed appeared on the experimental plot where we were growing a new type of perennial grain. The weed was highly resistant to chemical and biological weed killers. Then suddenly it burst into bloom.

"I had never seen such beautiful flowers. Huge white chalices with bright red centers covered the plant from top to bottom. There was a multitude of them, and their fragrance was extraordinarily fresh, as if a brief shower had just fallen over them.

"I wanted to preserve the flower, but my double, without consulting me, enlisted Jim's help and destroyed all the plants. When I reproached him, he merely shrugged. Weeds were weeds and had to be destroyed, and that was all. They only interfered with the work on the problem at hand.

"But some time later he came to apologize. He realized, he said, that he lacked the associative link between our work and esthetic responses. Therefore he considered himself at fault. A machine of considerable delicacy of feeling, you see, though somewhat dogmatic.

"Generally, his self-assurance was phenomenal. His categorical arguments and pronouncements often infuriated me. And although he did everything with extreme good will, his arrogance irritated me so much that I finally decided to do something about it. I inserted a new block into the Big Cyber —programed for doubt. I wanted the machine to ask itself, 'What for?' and 'Why?' The moment my ghost became too confident, the doubt block signaled that the results achieved were but a small step toward knowledge and urged further investigation. We might say that the doubt block invested the machine with the restless human spirit of eternal dissatisfaction.

"And now my double really blossomed out! Those were the best days of our friendship. We worked, argued, and dreamed like two brothers. And he was the elder brother at that!

"To be frank, I was secretly very proud of my creation. I had created a perfect model of intellect, which was in many respects superior to man's. And it was true! His logic far outdistanced mine. As for his capacity for work, that goes without saying. His inventiveness and resourcefulness were way ahead of man's. He was kind, attentive, and . . . yes, humane. Don't laugh, he was humane! And, carried away by a scientific idea, he was ready to work on it around the clock.

"In order to save the sick scientists on Zvezda, he went through so much information within seconds that half his batteries burned out. The necessary synthesis was found, and the people were saved. And then the impalpable George turned